Published by: Cinnabar Moth Publishing LLC
Santa Fe, New Mexico

Cover Design by: Ira Geneve

ISBN-13: 978-1-953971-54-8
Library of Congress Control Number: 2022941576

Fixed Moon

KATIE GROOM

For Anyone
who has felt as if they needed to escape
but had nowhere to go except
into a world that only their mind knew

Mid-1880s
Small Village near
London, England

He watched from the shadows as the young girl skipped down the alleyway between the tavern and the blacksmith with a basket full of herbs in her arms and a head free of fear and corruption. It was nearing sunset, and he had followed her from the shop when she had departed with the herbs, blending in with the surroundings at every turn.

She was just about to turn left, to where no one would see them nor hear her screams through his hand, which he planned to use to firmly cover her mouth. Her blue dress bounced with every skip, and unlike the young women that he usually followed, her shoes did not click on the stones that made up the street.

He extended his arm to grab a handful of her golden blond curls but was yanked out of reach with a sudden jolt. His back and head slammed against the exterior wall of the tavern. He reached back and touched his head where it had collided with the wood. His vision was blurred, but he still knew that the dark red on his fingertips was blood. His blood.

Trying to focus his eyes, he turned his attention to who had attacked him. Paralyzed with fear, he couldn't even scream. Before him stood an enormous beast — towering over his own 6-foot frame. It had to be nearly 7 feet tall, if not more. Maybe fear had made him irrational, but he couldn't determine whether this was a man or a very large wolf in front of him.

A low growl and then a snarl came from the beast. He looked into its yellow eyes, then closed his own tightly. *Lord, please, forgive me of my sins*, he thought.

————————

With a gasp, Hugh sat straight up, sweating. His torn, bloody shirt was sticking to his skin. Checking his surroundings, he realized that he had fallen asleep on some dirt and dead leaves. Some branches created a roof over his makeshift bed, shielding him from the sun. He could smell the moss on the trees and hear the water cascade off of the rocks in a stream or creek nearby.

He had no idea how far he had run — when he was in wolf form, he could run exponentially faster than his normal, human pace for an inhuman amount of time. He had scaled entire countries in a single night before.

But it also made him sleep for at least twice as long, so in addition to not knowing where he was, he didn't know *when* either. He had no idea how long he had been lyingin this cave. What he did know was that it was daylight, and he was back in human form, so he could make his way to the nearest village and find his bearings.

After rinsing off a bit in the river (not a stream or creek, as he had initially thought), he decided to follow his tracks back the way that he had come from. The lonely walk gave him time to think. Time to figure out a solid reason as to why his clothes had seen better days and were covered in blood, or, even better, time to find new garments altogether. He likely had a few options for that. He could pretend to be a lonely traveler who had been assaulted on the road and ask for assistance from a family in a remote cabin or cottage in the woods, or he could just steal them right off of the wash line.

The walk also afforded him the opportunity to think about what he had done. Hugh didn't particularly like the idea of killing people, so he had to make peace with actions of the previous night — or however many nights ago it was that he had ripped apart that man — an evil man that was going to assault a little girl.

That's how Hugh excused his behavior. He only targeted evildoers. Who made him judge, jury, and executioner? He did. The men that had violently killed him, awakening the mutation in his genes — they gave him the power to decide the fate of evil men. They gave him the power to decide the fate of anyone, really, if he felt so inclined. He preferred to behave as a vigilante.

It didn't come easy to Hugh, though. He had been practicing his ability to control himself — both leading up to shifting into a wolf, but also his time as a wolf — for nearly two decades. Before his violent death, certain things would trigger his temper, too. Those things, though, lined up with his vigilante mindset. The night that he'd died, Hugh had been standing up for a barmaid.

He spent the first few years after discovering his shifting abilities learning about the supernatural part of the world. Before, he hadn't known they existed. He honed his fighting and shifting skills through his mentor Alvin, a centuries old werewolf — the oldest wolf known. Alvin's mate, a Hearth Witch named Edie, taught him about the other creatures from the fireside stories that children would tell to give each other nightmares.

Eventually Hugh set out on his own, only to find himself in the Austrian Empire, where he befriended a monk that had been studying the breeding of pea plants. The monk was a mathematician and scientist. He had determined that the ability of Hugh — and others like him —to shift into a large wolf-like creature at will was likely inherited.

In fact, Hugh was, or had been, on his way back to a village outside of London to meet with someone the monk had connected him with for further research. This scientist studied genetics, but that plan was shot to shit now that he ripped someone apart.

He had to remain unseen. He realized that he couldn't go back to the town that he had come from, just in case there had been a witness to his night playing executioner.

Listening intently for the sounds of nature to guide him, he heard some water flowing. He ran towards the sound, avoiding fallen twigs and low hanging branches to not cause too much noise. Wolves could be stealthy when they wanted to be.

As he suspected, it was a stream, a tributary of the river. Closing his eyes, he let the water speak to him. All water in nature had a little bit of magic to it, and he needed the water to guide him. He took in a deep breath and started to walk opposite of the current.

After a few hours, he found himself at the entrance to a cave, and after taking a few steps inside, he noticed that the source of the water was *nothing*. There was no true source to the water; it just started flowing *there*. In the middle of the floor of the cave. No pool. No dripping from the ceiling. Just water.

Hugh's eyes allowed him to see better in the dark than the average human, and he looked further into the cave. He saw a faint blue-green glow from a spot on the wall. Moving closer to it, he noticed that it was in the shape of a bear paw print — the mark of the Bear Shifters. He smiled to himself.

He placed his palm over the paw print, causing the glow to become more vibrant. The floor of the cave near the start of the flow of water fell away, as if they were only held together by pressure, and the slightest wobble of the ground would have knocked them loose.

Proud and relieved, Hugh walked down the stairs in that giant hole in the ground. He knew that a new beginning was on the horizon. From the city he was about to visit, he could go to hundreds, if not thousands, of places all across the planet. He could start over as many times as he wanted, and that's what he would continue to do for the rest of his existence. He was a nomad — he had to be. It was easy for him. Anyone he had known in his human time was gone, so he had no one to anchor him to any place.

He walked down the stairs and back to a familiar place that went by many, many names. Much like how in English speaking countries a place could be called Spain, for example, but in its own language it was España, and in France it was Espagne, etc., this place — a city — was called many things.

The familiar feel of the cool breeze — and the magic that created it — kept everything around 23 degrees Celsius — or for those who used the old measure: 75 degrees Fahrenheit, and for the Alchemists and Witches: a little less than 300 degrees Kelvin.

Hugh knew the city as Baldonia, or at least that's what it was introduced to him as when he first visited. Thousands of paths all lead to the same point — a lost city protected by magic that somehow always had enough food, ale, clothing, and lodging to support any amount of visitors.

Baldonia — or Nightbrooke or Saluthir or Qademiemahrit or whatever it was called to the visitor — was established long before

5

any of the current magical creatures that now used it existed. But the main hub of the city did appear as if it could have existed in the Scottish Highlands due to the stone buildings and moss growing from just about everywhere. It was that damp smell that drew Hugh in and made it feel like home.

But few actually considered the city their home, as it never fully became dark there. Magic kept it from having a time zone, so to speak; time stood still in Baldonia. If Hugh would spend an hour in the city and go back through the portal that brought him there, no time would have passed. But that didn't mean that he wouldn't be tired.

He needed to find a tavern to secure himself a room. Making his way into the center of town, he reoriented himself to where he was. His favorite tavern was actually near the Department of Supernatural Registration. It was a large building, built from the smoothest and coldest-looking grey stones. A line of people waiting to register themselves for legal access to this world.

Hugh noticed that many of the people in the line looked tired and miserable — so nothing had changed in the many years since he had waited in that line for hours, with Alvin and Edie by his side, for a five-minute appointment. They took an eye scan and a photo for their database. He wondered now, just like he had then, what took so long. Since the appointments took less than five minutes, and there was always more than one person working, as per safety protocols and laws in the Realm, why didn't the line advance more than one person in fifteen minutes?

He approached the line — which was far too long to try to go around — and tried to slip through.

"Oi! Line jumper!"

Hugh shook his head. "I'm just trying to get through to head to

6

that tavern right there."

"A likely story." The man rolled his eyes, but let Hugh come through by moving back the tiniest bit, which wasn't truly enough to let someone of Hugh's size get through comfortably.

Hugh snuck through the line, apologizing repeatedly to the woman who was in front of the man that had accused him of line jumping for requesting that she move a little out of the way. She was much more polite than Mr. Line-Jumper. She even smiled at Hugh as she let him through.

Hugh finally was able to rent himself a room for a bit. Upon shutting the door and locking it, the doorframe lit up with some symbols — a paw, a wave, and a tree. He placed his palm over the paw, and the room darkened and the sounds of crickets and other nocturnal creatures whispered in the room. Hugh took two large steps and crashed onto the bed.

———

Not sure how long he had been out, Hugh stretched, got ready for the day, and then emerged from the room, ready to move on to his next great adventure. He could choose any number of paths, and each time he came to this place, he chose a different one to start over from.

He headed out to the center of town — a large roundabout with a wooden platform in the center. The platform was more of a stage, really. In the many decades that Hugh had been traveling here, the stage had been mostly used for the representatives of the Realm of the Supernatural to make examples out of members of this secret world who didn't follow their laws.

And, on this day, the platform was fulfilling its planned destiny.

A large crowd had gathered, and in the center of the platform stood one of those representatives. Behind them to the left stood a man and a woman in restraints made of vines and leaves, and a shifter dressed completely in black with large black wings and a black mask covering much of his face — including his eyes — holding the end of those restraints like a leash. Representatives of the other parts of the Realm were standing off to the side of the platform.

Hugh found someone who looked friendly enough. "What's going on?"

Not making eye contact, but rather looking over the crowd at the stage, they replied. "Bounty hunter brought in that vampire and the mortal they were searching for." They added, "This is the execution."

Hugh sighed. "No one would believe the mortal; I don't know why they do this."

"They're just traditionalists. They don't think we could live in harmony if the mortals knew about us." They turned to Hugh and reached out their hand. "Cayden."

"Hugh." He shook their hand.

"…and you must all bear witness…" the representative continued with a ridiculously dramatic speech about how the mortals, even though they didn't have supernatural abilities, were a danger to the Supernatural Realm's way of life.

Suddenly, flames shot out of the hands of one of the witches, and a large bonfire erupted on the stone ground in front of the platform. Hugh stood on his toes and noticed a pile of logs there; those in the front had already known that today's justice would be served extra crispy.

The woman in chains started to sob and scream. It sounded like she was begging for her life — promising that she would never tell anyone about the secrets she was about to die for.

The representative held up a stone tablet towards the crowd. On it was a set of glowing symbols like the ones that in the room Hugh had stayed in. This was the trial for the mortal. If they saw the symbols, they and the one who'd brought them into this world would be innocent of their alleged crime. If they didn't, it was certain that they possessed no magic powers or supernatural skills, and they would receive their punishment.

Turning the tablet towards the mortal, the representative acting as judge asked, "What do you see?"

Shakily, the mortal answered, "A... a small paw, a tree, and... and a w-w-wave."

Not convinced, the judge continued. "What color are they?"

The woman turned to her partner for a clue. It was obvious at this point that the man had given her the answers in advance, likely having seen one of these executions in the past.

The judge smirked and then turned to the crowd. "Do you see how far these mortals push us? The level of control that they could have?" Handing the tablet off to someone at the side of the stage, they continued their show for the crowd. "This cannot stand! We *must* protect our world and way of life!"

"Stop! Stop!" The man in the chains was somehow maintaining some semblance of composure. "Let her go. I'll take the punishment, but let her go. She didn't know what she was getting into."

The Representative motioned for the girl to come closer, and she shook her head and cried. He chuckled, "No?" Laughing again, he turned to the audience. "This mortal — a nobody in their world — thinks that she is in the position to decline my request." With a serious tone, he used it to drive home the need for the law and that this punishment fit the indiscretion. "Imagine if she was in a position of power — a world leader. *This* is why we need to protect our secret." There were murmurs of agreement from the crowd. Turning back to the woman, he said, "I was going to get you out of those chains, as requested by your... whatever."

The bounty hunter loosened his grip on the chain for the woman and she made her way over, cautiously, toward the man who felt he was judge, jury, and executioner.

The Representative put his hand on her bicep. With his free hand, he commanded one of the witches to the platform. Hugh recognized her as Jade, whose specialty was Earth magic. She waved her hand over the collar restraint, followed quickly by the wrist and ankle restraints. The branch retracted quickly to the bounty hunter.

Even from the back of the crowd, Hugh could see the relief on the woman's face. But it didn't last long, as the Representative that had been leading the presentation tossed her in the fire as if throwing a ball of paper into the trash.

Half of the crowd gasped and the other cheered. The flames crackled and smoke shot up in the air. It almost instantly started to smell like a barbecue.

The man tried to pull out of the restraints, but of course the magic that was within them kept him held tightly. The bounty hunter yanked on the leash, causing the prisoner to choke. The man fell to his knees and cried, and it was obvious that it was about more than just the physical pain.

Hugh knew that it was the bounty hunter's job, but he couldn't fathom how someone could be so cold about this. He noticed that the man hadn't flinched during this demonstration whatsoever.

The Representative started speaking again while motioning for two of his lackeys to approach the prisoner. One put a hand on the man's shoulder to stabilize him, while the other took the chains from the bounty hunter.

One of the witches stepped up on the stage and waved her hands. A thick cyclone of dirt, grass, and other earthy debris surrounded the prisoner. As quickly as it came, it dissolved, leaving the prisoner as a stone statue — a gargoyle. He was crouched down, arms outstretched as if he had been pushing the debris away from himself, and his mouth was open as if he had been crying out. His teeth were now pointed and appeared sharp, and he had horns.

Being turned into a gargoyle was a common punishment for those from the Supernatural Realm. It was rumored that the transformation was painful, but being caught within gargoyle form was worse. The stories stated that the mind of a gargoyle is still active but the being held within is alone and cannot communicate. They are left with their thoughts for eternity to think about their crimes.

The lackeys lifted the gargoyle — which had to be extremely heavy, it was solid stone — on to a sort of uncovered palanquin. They would parade the gargoyle through the town while others threw trash at him or spit or even cursed him.

While many spectators stayed around for the rest of the show, Hugh turned to leave the City, without even acknowledging the acquaintance that he had made. He decided to head to Spain, where he could attend the University of Deusto and work on his language skills —including how to perfectly blend his voice in with everyone else's. Covering his thick Scottish accent could prove difficult, but it had to be done. It was essential for success as he travelled the world and made a life in a new place. So far, he had been successful at German and a few other languages., so he had confidence that he could expand on his basic Spanish skills.

Each portal had its own magic, but travel was usually straightforward from this end of things. It was the non-magical side that was more difficult because the supernatural realm wanted to keep their secret safe.

To get into the magical city, first the visitor had to find the entryway to the portal — they were usually marked by a glowing symbol — and then they had to use their magic to activate it. Those able to do that would have access to the city and all the magic within.

To exit, one just had to reach for the door and the magic would activate. As Hugh approached the door, he could smell food — specifically, a warm pork stew that was popular in Madrid and that he had remembered from a trip he had taken there before. Closing his eyes and smiling, he reached his hand toward the door, and the fruit on the tree that was etched into it started to drop off of the branches. As he stepped through the door, he decided instantly that he would stop for that stew before the long trek to Bilbao.

Present Day
Birmingham, Alabama,
United States of America

—Hugh—

Hugh bit into an ambrosia apple as he walked down the hallway, his nose shoved in a book, towards his office in the University Hall building. He had been working in the English department at the University of Alabama at Birmingham for three years.

He was absolutely engrossed in *Paradise Lost* and had been creating some course materials to lead a deep dive into the work at the graduate level. At this point, he had only taught at the undergraduate level, and he wanted tenure, so this was a major opportunity for him. He figured that he had a good five to ten years more that he could stay in Birmingham before he needed to start over some place new.

Suddenly he crashed into someone, dropping his book and his apple. Quietly, he said, "I ought to have been watching where I was going." His Scottish accent, while still present in his voice, had become much more intelligible to the non-native ear as he had learned to adapt over the years. Part of that, especially in the Deep

South of the USA, was slowing down his speech. It was essential to be able to change his voice enough to fit in or he would never last long anywhere outside of the United Kingdom.

He bent down to pick up the book, gently smiling at the person he had collided with.

The victim of his inattentiveness? Someone who had obviously never been to UAB before. Likely, she was a new student. Or, perhaps, she was a new adjunct professor. It didn't matter, though; Hugh found her endearing. Wavy dark red hair, freckles, emerald-green eyes hidden behind glasses — the kind a stereotypical librarian would wear with thick black frames. She was obviously embarrassed, as her cheeks were flushed.

She picked up his apple. "Not sure if you're going to want to eat that now that it's been on the floor." Northern American accent. Then she looked down at her feet and suggested aloud to herself, "I should really walk in the direction that my eyes are looking." She pushed her glasses up closer to her eyes, as they had slid down her nose in the collision.

As she handed him the apple, their hands touched, and it felt as if a jolt of electricity went straight through Hugh's body. It started at his fingertips and quickly radiated up his arm and then travelled to his feet and head. He almost heard it crack in his eardrums. He gasped, fixating his eyes on their hands. It was then that he noticed a small, blue cluster of dots on her wrist just below her thumb.

She quickly jerked her hand back and put her right hand over her wrist. "Sorry, I shocked you. It's pretty dry out. I don't know why that happens to me. I actually saw the spark when I touched my car door today…" She trailed off and looked down at her feet again. Hugh took the opportunity to bolt.

He quietly and quickly made his way into his office, shutting the door immediately. With his back to the door, he placed his apple onto the small table nearby. With his other hand, he slammed the book shut quickly, his heart pounding.

—Zoie—

As soon as she moved her gaze up from the floor, it was as if she had imagined the encounter. The man she had bumped into was gone — without a trace or a sound.

Zoie's anxiety bubbled up in her. Had she created the entire encounter in her head? Was it a ghost? Was she in some Harry Potter type world where Moaning Myrtle-like beings showed up to taunt students? Was she going to get a *Howler*?

Worried that the stress of returning to school had caused her to fabricate the situation, she decided to head back towards home. Her new home.

She quickly walked to the door, the click of her heels echoing throughout the hallway with each hurried step. She was short — less than five feet tall — so her little legs had to take twice as many steps as some people. To ensure that the door didn't slam, she turned and shut it lightly, peering through the window to try to determine if she needed an additional appointment with her therapist or just to call a trusted friend. Perhaps, she could simply write about it in her journal or add it to a list of short stories she was compiling.

She couldn't shake how she didn't hear any footsteps when he walked away, and she had even less of an idea as to where he had gone off to. Also, she questioned if she needed to slow down her latest binge of romance novels, as her imaginary collision was with someone that could have replaced Fabio on the covers for the books she had confiscated from her mother's bookshelf. She, of course, would need to get a better look at him without his plaid button-down on to know for sure, but from what she had seen in their brief encounter, she was pretty certain.

—Hugh—

Two beer steins and a glass of wine clinked together, slammed on the bar before making their way to the lips that lead to their contents' destiny.

"Tell me what's going on with you today." Cayden put their mug down and looked at Hugh. "You seem off." Cayden and Hugh had known each other for decades at this point, and they suffered from the same affliction. They had a kinship that was more than the usual simple compatible interests in pop culture, for example.

"You're going to think I'm overreacting." He had to basically scream it over the loud music. Some band was playing mediocre covers of 80s pop hits and trying to reinvent them into music with a banjo, wooden framed washboard, and flexible handsaw.

"What's going on?" Stevie had quickly downed her wine and hadn't even swallowed when she'd run off to greet one of her many friends that frequented the Lunar Brewery, but she came right back into the conversation with her partner and Hugh at the sound of the word "overreacting," as if she had never left. She was always one to hear the latest gossip, but never spread it.

"Today, I ran into a woman and…"

"You've met a girl?" Stevie's face lit up, and she clapped with excitement. Despite Hugh's past denial, Stevie had believed that he could be aromantic or asexual; in the time that they had known each other, he had never shown romantic or sexual interest in anyone at all. Hugh had insisted that he just was picky.

Hugh rolled his eyes a little. "Not exactly."

Cayden motioned for him to continue. "Spit it out."

"I literally ran into her. But the thing is… when we touched…" He wiggled his fingers, trying to signal electric shock, but it came out more like Jazz Hands.

"You broke into song as if it were *High School Musical*?" Cayden teased.

Hugh nearly choked on his beer. "No." Wiping the evidence of his near death by hops from his beard, he explained. "The shock. The electric spark thing."

Stevie interjected, "Wait. Was it like when there's no humidity and you shock yourself because it's dry out? Or was it…"

"It was overpowering." Hugh smiled as he let out a sigh. He had never believed in love at first sight; in fact, he thought it was completely impossible. His experience earlier in the day was beginning to change that.

Cayden clapped and loudly called out, "Well, hot damn! You've finally found your mate." They called out to the bartender, "Another round!"

Stevie interjected, "Change mine to a Captain and Coke, please."

"Do you think she knows?"

Hugh shook his head. "No." His jaw clenched. "I don't think she's… one of us." He took a drink. "And, that's why it's complicated. I don't know if I want to actively pursue this, especially if it makes her feel like she doesn't have a choice."

"She has a choice, Hugh." Stevie adjusted one of her bouncy black curls that had a death grip around her large, pink hoop earring. "Just because you have the connection…"

Cayden shook their head. "Why wouldn't she choose him? He can protect her…"

"Who says she needs protecting?" Stevie rolled her eyes. "Honestly…"

Hugh rubbed his forehead. He really wasn't concerned with the supernatural connection that he had with her merely because he was a shapeshifter and she was somehow fated to be his soul mate. He was worried about something that he felt was much riskier. "I think she's a student."

Cayden and Stevie's heads nearly snapped off their necks when they turned to him. "One of your students?" Stevie asked.

"I don't know." He took another drink. "She appears older than a traditional student, so maybe she's a new professor. But I met her in the Humanities building, in the English department. You'd think I would know…"

"Maybe she's graduate level? Or was a new professor just looking around?" Cayden suggested.

"Wait, wait, wait…" Stevie put her hand up. "I have a really important question." Hugh nodded for her to continue. "Did she swoon over your accent?"

Hugh chuckled. "No. I just used my American one that I've been using for the five years that I've lived in Alabama." He shook his head. He had worked hard to not make his accent too southern since he was from "out of the area." The story he had told everyone that he'd met in Birmingham was that he had moved around a lot as a child, so he never got used to one accent. Every once in a while, though, he couldn't help but slip a Scots word or phrase into the convo or a hard R into the middle of some words.

"How is that a relevant question, *Stephanie?*" Cayden laughed.

"Women like that sort of thing," she laughed, nudging her partner in the ribs.

"You telling me that you want me to throwaway my *Mo-beel, Alabamy* accent for a posh, refined, quite-frankly-snobbish London accent?"

"I'm not from Lon— wait, I sound snobbish?" Hugh was taken aback.

"Bless your heart, no!" Stevie replied, with a laugh. "You're one of the most approachable people I've ever met."

"Ehhh… Stevie. He's a 6'4" beast of a man — literally. He could lift anyone in this bar over his head with one hand and throw them without breaking a sweat. In fact, I think he could do it with just one hand, while the other is lifting a Guinness to his mouth. I don't know that he's the most *approachable* person right off the bat…"

Hugh let out an annoyed sigh. Steering the conversation back in the right direction, he asked, "How do I get to know *her?*"

"Your mate." Stevie smiled. "She's your mate. This is a big deal, Hugh. Not every wolf meets their mate." She took Cayden's hand in hers. "Not even Cade and I are true mates."

"Just romance her," Cayden suggested. "How do you posh Englishmen say… *woo* her," they attempted — poorly — a British accent.

"First of all, I'm actually Scottish, but more importantly…" he paused. "I just don't know…"

"You still consider yourself Scottish?" Cayden's question was ignored entirely.

Stevie didn't even entertain it with an eye roll. Instead, she probed further into Hugh's insecurities. "What's holding you back?"

Hugh took another drink, and closed his eyes for a second. Then, opening his eyes and pulling his long, wavy brown hair back, securing it in the mauve scrunchie that was on his wrist, he replied, "Consent."

Cayden shrugged. "Then let her decide. Just romance her. I'm sure it will come naturally."

Hugh slammed his hand on the bar. "You're missing the point, Cayden."

"No, I don't think I am, but, please, enlighten me." They motioned for Hugh to continue.

"Cade, I have to tell her the whole truth. Beyond us having this supernatural connection, I'm able to shift into the form of a wolf, and who — please, name one sane person — who would believe that?"

"Don't tell her."

Hugh's jaw dropped. "I can't do that."

"No, hear me out," they said. "You don't have to tell her right away. You don't tell everything to her on the first date."

Hugh asked, sarcastically, "Is this a third date revelation? Tenth? Night before the wedding?"

Cayden chuckled. "I don't know. Maybe deathbed. You'll know when it is, but it's definitely not a first conversation sorta thing."

Cayden went to request another round, but Hugh declined. He drank the rest of his beer, put the mug down hard, and wiped his mouth. "I had best not go too far with this, since class starts tomorrow. I don't want to be hungover for the first day of the semester."

"The students wouldn't know what to think," laughed Cayden. They ran their hand through their hair and then put their arm around Stevie, pulling her close to them, placing a kiss on her cheek.

"Well, I don't want them to think I'm an angry, grumpy old man

23

on the first day of class."

"You are an angry, grumpy old man," Stevie replied.

"Pfft." Hugh didn't have a comeback.

Cayden put their hand on his shoulder. "She's really got you pinned there, my dude." They chuckled.

"Oi, I can be angry and grumpy, but old? I don't know. Jack over there is ancient compared to me." He nodded towards a patron at the corner of the bar.

Jack turned slowly towards Hugh. After a loud hiccup, he slurred, "Keep my mouth out of your name." He then drew his gaze back towards the bartender and simply pointed at his glass.

The bartender took his glass and, as she was filling it from the tap, she said to both Hugh and Jack, "Now, we're not going to be having any trouble, are we?"

Hugh stood up and put his coat on. "None from me. I'm actually on my way out." He glanced at has friends. "Cayden. Stevie. See you this weekend?" They smiled and nodded, and Hugh made his way to the door.

The spring semester had been mostly monotonous. It was leading into finals week, and Hugh had spent most days grading papers, preparing lessons, holding meetings, and thinking about *the girl*. He hadn't seen her since the collision. In fact, he was beginning to wonder if he had imagined her.

Cayden and Stevie asked about her each time they met for dinner or drinks, and Hugh never had an update. Cayden even asked once, "Are you even trying to find her again?" Hugh explained that he was hoping that it would be serendipitous. Cayden flat out called him a coward in that instance but was met with a light smack on the shoulder from Stevie.

Hugh leaned back in his office chair and stretched. Looking at his watch, he decided that he was at a good stopping point from grading papers and could take the rest home for the weekend and grade from there.

He opened the door and quickly shut it most of the way, because he saw the young woman he had collided with earlier in the semester in the hallway, mid-conversation with another student.

"...you wanted to go with me to see a movie this weekend?" Hugh recognized this student as Miles Gardner, who he had in class a few times when he was in undergrad.

"Oh, um... I have a lot of work to do this weekend. Two major papers due, and..." He watched her red hair move as she nervously ran her hands through it.

"I see..." Miles put his hands in his pockets. "Well, I'll see you around, Zoie." He turned and walked away.

Zoie. Hugh smiled a bit to himself as he said her name in his head. He also chuckled a little that she turned down Miles, and found it a good sign that she didn't mention a boyfriend or partner in the reasoning.

Closing his eyes and gathering his courage, he decided that he was going to approach her. He opened the door to step out, but she was already gone.

—Zoie—

Confused, Zoie's shoulders slumped as she walked towards the exit. She didn't understand men. She truly was busy and had plans for the weekend. Truthfully, she was going to invite him to join her, but his reaction made her glad that she didn't have the opportunity.

"Why do they only want to hang out when it's on their terms?" She asked herself as she looked in the rearview mirror of her car.

The drive home was only four songs long, as traffic was light —
and one of those songs was Bohemian Rhapsody.

She immediately put her bag and purse at the foot of the stairs
upon entering her townhouse and went directly to where she kept
her hobby witchcraft supplies. Pulling out a jar of sand — which
she realized she needed to replenish soon, she also grabbed a white
pillar candle, a clear quartz tower, her notebook, and a pen.

She used a match to light the candle that she had placed in a bit
of the sand and once she blew out the match, she used the smoke
to cleanse the quartz. She held the stone close to her heart for a
moment before putting it down.

"All of my intentions are light and peaceful." She looked at the
flame as it danced on the candle's wick. "Please help me to clear
my mind." She began writing down the things that were bothering
her or creating stress in her life, focusing on the flame between
each thought.

My interaction with Miles. Why didn't he believe me?

Will I pass my finals?

Is going to the show this weekend a good idea?

Will I ever trust again?

—Hugh—

Hugh felt his phone buzz in his pocket. *Not going to be able to make it; Cayden had a rough night last night.* He sighed and, while he wanted to respond with a singular letter "k" to show how annoyed he was with the late notice, he opted for a much friendlier, *Oh that really sucks. I hope C recovers quickly.*

Shoving his phone back in his pocket, he rolled his eyes and contemplated leaving. Both of the opening acts had already played, so it was pretty obvious that Stevie and Cayden weren't going to show long before the time she had texted. So much for helping him celebrate the end of another semester.

Just has he was getting ready to leave, he noticed a bit of a situation brewing. A man, quite large in the middle, wearing a shirt that was too small in the middle, was obviously attempting to intimidate a younger, and much smaller, woman.

"Look, girl, I want to stand there." He and his two buddies, relatively of the same size, stood over the woman, essentially surrounding her. Hugh then heard one of the men say, slurring his words, "And I'm going to stand there." He then let out a loud hiccup, followed by spitting on the floor next to the woman.

Unbelievable. Hugh thought to himself as these three grown ass men bothered the young woman. His jaw clenched, and he looked at the woman again, and his breath was nearly stolen from his lungs. It was Zoie, the student from the hallway at University Hall that he had run into just before the start of the semester. The girl who he had just seen in the hallway the other day. His *mate*.

Hugh stepped up next to her, making himself look as big as he could — essentially puffing out his chest. "Gentlemen, the lady was standing here first."

Hugh took another large step forward towards these hooligans, who were well past their prime and should have definitely known better. He let out a low grumble. They backed off.

She said what Hugh believed was "Thank you," but he couldn't really hear her over the noise of the crowd.

"Don't mention it." He smiled softly at her, his eyes taking in every inch of her. He couldn't deny that he found her attractive — mating bond or not, and she could probably tell from the way he was looking at her. "My name is Hugh."

"I'm Zoie," She smiled back, pushing her glasses up on her nose. She then took a sip of her drink, looking away.

Hugh wondered if he was making her nervous or uncomfortable. "Well, Zoie, how are you enjoying the concert so far?"

"Well, I am here for the headliner, so..."

"...yeah, those first two bands left a little bit to be desired." He chuckled.

"A little? You're being generous."

The lights went low, and the first kick of the music hit. The crowd screamed in unison — both Zoie and Hugh laughed. It was a cover band, so no need to be overly excited. Hugh's eyes left the stage, though, and focused in on Zoie. She was singing along —

pretty poorly — and dancing, very freely.

Zoie suddenly stopped dancing.

"Why'd you stop?" He asked, flashing a smile her way. "I was going to ask if I could join you with the dancing." He offered his hand to her.

She placed her hand cautiously in his, and the moment that their skin touched: electricity. He pushed the feelings aside as he twirled her and sang along with her.

At a pause in the music — the part where the band pretends that they're done playing but it's just very obviously an intermission — Zoie mentioned that she was planning to leave around 9 to beat the traffic and avoid intoxicated drivers. Hugh nodded and agreed that it was a good idea, but in his heart he wondered if maybe she just wasn't having fun and was looking for an excuse to leave.

9 PM was quickly approaching, so Hugh leaned down to Zoie's ear and asked, "Wanna get out of here?"

He noticed the flush of pink in her cheeks as she nodded. He walked with her to the door, placing his hand on her back. Hugh smiled as she blushed again.

Once the door shut behind them, Zoie laughed, "That was fun!" It was more of a very loud exclamation, since the music had been so loud and hearing damage was imminent.

Pausing for a moment, Hugh asked, "May I walk you to your car?" He knew that he was probably screaming as well, since he also likely had fallen victim to hearing damage. It would heal for him, though, and quickly. One of the perks of being able to shape shift into a wolf.

Blushing again, Zoie replied, "Yeah, I'm towards the back of the third row."

"So, do we need to end this night when I get you to your car?"

Zoie stopped walking, in shock. Turning to him, she looked down at her feet and holding her purse strap with both hands "...I don't have any plans for tomorrow morning, so..."

"Want to go to my place for a cup of tea?" He opened her car door and helped her in.

The electricity that Hugh had gotten a break from while they walked returned as he touched her to guide her.

Since his house wasn't actually more than a few blocks from her townhouse, they parked Zoie's car and walked to his place. Hugh explained to her that he was sincere about the tea and also wanted the opportunity to be able to walk her home, as silly as it seemed.

—Zoie—

Hugh led Zoie into his red brick bungalow. She was incredibly nervous and unsure of how to behave. She had never done something like this before — going back to a stranger's place at night. Well, he wasn't entirely a stranger, but they weren't exactly friends either.

He started filling the kettle. "You still want some tea?"

She turned away from the bookcases that she was admiring to reply. "Sure, if it isn't too much trouble." She slid a copy of Hamlet out and flipped through the pages. "It must have taken you forever to collect all of these books." She looked perplexed. "This looks handwritten."

He smiled and she noticed that when the smile went to his eyes, it also wrinkled the scar that adorned his cheek. "I love literature. Especially older editions." He turned and opened a cabinet, revealing several dozens of types of teas — flavors, bags, loose leaf — to choose from. "What kind of tea do you want?"

Zoie's eyes lit up. "There's so many options!" She reached in and grabbed Dandelion and Peach by Steep. "My favorite."

"Interesting choice." He smiled and nodded a little. "So you are a fan of tea?"

"Well, it looks like you have me beat, but I do enjoy tea. I try to have a cup each day." He poured the water into their cups, as Zoie set a timer on her phone for four minutes. "I do prefer a black tea over green, and sometimes I enjoy — dare I say it — herbal." She said it without the 'h', the way Americans pronounce it.

He produced an exaggerated shudder. "I only have *herbal* so I can judge those who ask for it." He chuckled a little, exaggerating the 'h' sound.

A moment of awkward silence fell between them. Zoie broke it. "...So about all these books. Which is your favorite?"

He didn't hesitate. "*The Neverending Story* by Michael Ende." He continued, "I have read it hundreds of times."

"I used to love the movie when I was a child, but I've never read the book."

He quickly walked over to the bookcase and retrieved the book. Handing it to her, he suggested firmly, "You have to read it. I hate to be that cliche jerk, but the book is far superior to the film." Their hands touched as they made the exchange and her heart fluttered right along with the butterflies in her stomach.

He brought over her tea and sat down across from her. "I'll drink mine first so that you know it isn't poison." He winked and then took a big gulp.

Zoie replied, raising an eyebrow, "What if you've worked up a tolerance to the poison?"

"That's the risk you're going to have to take."

She looked over his shoulder to avoid eye contact and noticed what appeared to be a Loch Ness monster figurine on the table near the front door. "Is that Nessie?"

31

Hugh smiled. "Aye, my grandparents were Scottish, and I spent a lot of time there in the summers as a boy." He got up and brought it to her.

She admitted, "I love Scotland, but I've never been."

He smiled and jumped up. "You're going to love this." He took her hand and lead her to another room.

She stopped at the doorway, letting go of his hand. She took a nervous breath in.

When he turned to see what was wrong, he chuckled. "I'm not trying to take you to bed, I promise. I'm going to be a perfect gentleman. I just want to show you something that you may think is interesting."

She took three steps into the room while he opened the chest at the foot of his huge, neatly made bed. "Are those... kilts?

He nodded. "There's a casual one, one for special occasions, and one for battle." He then added, "I have all the accessories to match, too."

"This is actually very cool. Are they authentic? Or modern recreations?"

He pulled one out from the very bottom. "This one has been passed down since the mid-1700s. I am not sure how it's survived, especially since the loss of the Rebellion, but I do try to keep it good." He then added, "The others are modern."

She asked a few more questions and then neatly placed the items back in the chest before turning towards the door.

Once she was on one side of the threshold and he was on the other, Hugh asked, "Do you want to see the rest of the house?" She nodded. "Well, you've seen the dining room and the living room." He walked down a hall and pointed in a door. "I should have told you that there's a bathroom right here."

She glanced in to see what kind of decorating style he had. Zoie believed you could tell a lot about a person based on their bathroom decor. For example, some people had a sense of humor about it. Not Hugh. His was wood and big tile. Very plain. Plenty of reading material.

The room next to it was the laundry, and it was ridiculously clean and organized. Like, no lint dust or anything. Shocked, Zoie blurted out, "Do you watch those organization TikToks?"

Hugh looked confused. "What's a *tick tock*? I mean, besides the sound a clock makes?"

She laughed and shook her head. "Never mind."

He shrugged and opened the last door. "...and this is my office-slash-guest room."

Zoie's mouth dropped. "More books?" She did a twirl in the middle of the room. "You have a library!" Three of the walls had floor-to-ceiling shelves. The desk was situated at the window, and the bed had shelves on either side of it. "Wow!"

"I told you that I really love literature." He offered, "You can borrow from it any time that you want."

She ran over and gave him a hug. "Really?!" The moment she realized what she'd done, she wanted to let go, but his arms were around her, and she felt safe and warm. She let herself melt into him.

"Yes, really."

She felt his voice vibrate in his chest and heard his heartbeat. Then she realized that she was being awkward, so she let go. His arms slowly released her.

The grandfather clock in the living room bellowed at them — ten times — breaking the moment, causing them both to jump. "It's late. I'd best be getting you home. Wouldn't want you to turn into a pumpkin."

She let him take her hand and lead her back to the entryway. He grabbed her sweater and helped her put it on before handing her the book he had offered her. She made a mental note that his chivalry skills were top notch.

As he locked the door behind them, Hugh glanced over at the book. "That story is really sad, as you know from the film. But it's, well, it's...very — no, extremely — sad when you read it."

"I've always felt like the film, while sad at some parts, was more about courage, imagination, friendship, and knowing your self-worth." Zoie pulled the book close to her chest, as if she was protecting it.

As they made their way towards Zoie's townhouse, she realized that Hugh — the professor? *You had best clarify that, Zoie,* she told herself. She realized that *he* moved to walk more closely to her than previously.

He must have sensed that she was curious about his behavior because he put his arm around her and explained, "Zoie, I don't mean to alarm you, but someone has been following us." Zoie nodded slowly, and Hugh pulled her closer. "Stay close to me."

It was only a few blocks to get to Zoie's townhouse. When they arrived at the front door, Zoie, with the book held tightly to her chest, said, "Um…"

Hugh smiled. "Y'know, maybe I should check…"

"Please." She welcomed him in, taking any excuse to get a few more minutes with him.

He shut the door behind them. "This is very cozy."

"I hope that's a good thing. I've always wanted to live in a Hobbit Hole." She walked through the living room and up the stairs to her bedroom. He followed but kept himself just before the threshold of the bedroom doorway.

"It is." He then added, "Hobbit Holes mean comfort."

Zoie turned after placing the book on her bedside table. He moved from the doorway to let her through, and she led him back down the stairs and to the kitchen. "Would you like a drink? Or how do you Scots say — a wee dram?"

He smiled, with a light chuckle, and reached for her hand. "As much as I want to, I think that I probably should go. Your place is safe. Just lock the door, okay?"

Zoie put her hand in his, but instead of just holding her hand, he opted to pull her into a warm hug. Not like an Olaf-style warm hug — meaning, loving hug. It was literally warm.

"Umm…" She looked up at him and placed her hand on his chest. Boldly, she asked, "…can I see you again?"

His smile reached his eyes. "Yes." Nervously, he asked, "Are you available tomorrow evening?"

Zoie's smile grew. "Yes, but I won't be done with the book by then…"

He put his hand gently on her chin, tilting her face up a little towards his. "That's okay. Take your time with it. I'll use it as a repeated excuse to come see you again and again." He put his arms around her more tightly. "I'll pick you up at 4." Releasing her from his arms, he opened the door and stepped out. "Lock this behind me," he reminded her.

She did as told, immediately followed by putting her back to the door and smiling wider than she had all night. "Wow, wow, wow!"

—Hugh—

"…Stevie, she's incredible. So vivacious — full of life! But she's so shy the moment she realizes someone's watching," Hugh said as he checked on the breakfast in the oven.

Stevie smiled as she drank her cold brew coffee. "So you finally made a move?"

"Kind of…"

She rose an eyebrow. "How does one *kind of* make a move?"

"We have a date this evening."

The front door opened, and Cayden walked in, rubbing their eyes, still full of sleep. "When did you leave this morning?" they asked Stevie, with a hint of annoyance in their voice.

"Eh, I started getting ready maybe 30 minutes ago and walked over here. I just got here maybe 15 minutes ago, so you weren't alone long." She patted on the bar stool next to her. "Come sit down, Sweetheart."

Cayden looked at Hugh, "I'm so sorry about last night. I shifted and was just exhausted when I came out of it."

Hugh nodded. "Totally understand." He looked over at Stevie. "What'd you do to piss them off?"

37

"Nothing! Honestly!" She laughed.

Cayden smiled and rubbed her back. "It wasn't her. I had a rough day at work and felt like I was going to lose my job over something."

"I found them over by Regions Field."

"The clothing she chose to give me," they laughed, "was pink sweatpants with a hole in the crotch and an orange camouflage tank top. Mismatched Vans. One green sock. No underpants." They shook their head. "I had to walk home in that."

"Hey, it worked! The remedy for shifting is any item of clothing, not elegant ballroom wear," Stevie laughed, taking another drink of coffee. "You turned back, and that's all that matters."

"You're lucky no one saw you." Then he clarified, "in wolf form or in that outfit."

Changing the subject, Cayden asked, "So, how was the concert?"

Stevie very quickly interjected, "He finally had the opportunity to *actually* meet his mate!"

Cayden nearly jumped across the breakfast bar. "Tell me everything!"

"Zoie." Hugh felt the rush of blood to his cheeks. "Her name is Zoie, and she's a graduate student in the English department — creative writing." He added, "I think she's into witchcraft, Stevie."

"That's awesome!" She made excited fists and shook them a little.

Cayden looked back and forth between the two of them. "...So?"

She looked over at Cayden. "She has an open mind, Cade. She's into the occult. So she may be willing to be understanding of Hugh's *condition.*"

Cayden pressed their lips together. "I hate to be the downer, but witchcraft can just be the way she practices her spirituality or a hobby. That doesn't mean that she believes in our folklore."

38

Hugh added, "The first time we met, I thought I saw the mark on her wrist. She was wearing long sleeves last night, so I couldn't get a better look. Stevie, you're the subject matter expert. Do you think you could help me? Maybe if we all got together, you could get a chance to look?"

"It's probably just a random tattoo," Cayden dismissed. After an awkward silence, Cayden said, "Sorry. I'm being really negative. I think I'm just still tired."

The oven timer beeped, so Hugh pulled out the breakfast croissants he had baking in there. When a werewolf shifts, they were typically exhausted and in major need of nutrition the next day, so he prepared extra to accommodate Cayden. "No, it's fine. Thank you for being a voice of reason."

"When are you seeing her again?" Stevie asked, picking up one of the egg, cheese, and turkey sausage croissants without even letting them cool.

"This evening." Hugh flashed the biggest smile.

—Zoie—

Zoie woke up with the biggest smile on her face, but it faded quickly when she started to convince herself that Hugh wasn't genuine in his desire to spend time with her again. Why would he be?

She brought the image of him to the front of her mind. Tall, handsome, rugged, and smart. She was able to effortlessly list off all of his best qualities. She looked at her stuffed Maltese, Judy, and continued to list Hugh's best qualities. "He's warm, inviting. He's brave."

She frowned, thinking about her qualities, as she looked in the mirror. Short. Awkward. Ginger. Overweight. Anxious. Unable to let go of past traumas.

She went back and forth all day, wrestling with her self-confidence. She decided to finally do something about it. After having a bit of lunch, she decided that she would start getting ready — but first, she wanted to clear her mind of negativity.

She went over to her little corner for her magic supplies and grabbed a couple things: a pink pillar candle and a rose quartz crystal. Then she ran to the closet across from the bathroom and snatched her bag of Epsom salt and her essential oils set —

particularly wanting the jasmine and rose.

This combination was meant to help her relax and focus on her positive qualities.

And, for the most part, it worked. She soaked for about 20 minutes in the bath and reminded herself that she was worthy of positive relationships — and that her past trauma did not predict her future.

She was ready for her date with Hugh by 3:30, and the downtime let her mind wander back into the negative thoughts from earlier. Taking a few deep, cleansing breaths, she reminded herself that Hugh was not anyone who had broken her trust before. "Don't punish him for things that other men did."

—Hugh—

Hugh approached Zoie's door and looked at his watch. 3:57. Should he knock? Wait until 4? He hadn't dated in a very, very long time, and he wasn't sure of the etiquette.

Taking a deep breath, he knocked. Then he heard her footsteps approach the door. When she opened it, he smiled and handed her a bouquet of tulips. "For your table."

She giggle-squeaked, and took them in her hands. "Come in, come in!" She smelled them and walked towards the kitchen. "They are so beautiful, Professor —"

"Hugh," he said. "You can call me Hugh."

She put the flowers in a vase, and explained, "I just wasn't sure. After last night, I didn't know if you were going to rethink things…" She looked at her feet.

"Absolutely not." He touched her chin, still feeling the electricity of the mating bond travel through his entire body. "I'm here, aren't I?"

Her hand traveled to his and she looked up into his eyes. With a smile, she simply said, "Good. I want to see where this goes."

He kissed her hand. "Well, first *this* is going to go to English

Village for a stroll and supper, and then *this* is going to go to the Vulcan for fireworks. You'll meet a couple of my friends there, if that's all right with you."

"English Village?"

"You've been in Birmingham since January, and you've never been to the English Village part of Mountain Brook?" She shook her head, and, shocked, he asked, "Have you been to the Zoo or the Botanical Gardens?" When she confirmed that she hadn't done either, he smiled. "Well, then I know that there's two more dates right there."

She smiled widely and grabbed her purse.

Hugh took her hand, and as they walked out the door, she asked, confused, "Am I driving?"

"We're taking my bike." He pointed towards his Harley. As soon as he said it, he turned to her, realizing he never asked her feelings on motorcycles. "Is that okay?"

"I've just never been on one before."

He paused for a moment. "I'll tell you what. If it's all right with you, I'll take you for a quick ride around the city — maybe just a few blocks — and if you don't like it, I'll go get my car." She nodded, and he handed her a helmet. "You can put your pocketbook in the saddlebag."

"How do I hold on?" Zoie asked, innocently.

Hugh chuckled. "You hold onto me. Put your arms around my waist." He fired up the ignition. "Don't fight the turns, okay?"

He felt her pull herself as tightly to his body as she could. He took in a deep breath, fighting the explosion of electricity that overtook his entire body.

They took about a five-minute ride to his house, and he pulled over.

Zoie didn't wait for him to ask. "You can keep going. I feel safe with you."

Hugh's heart nearly exploded with joy at the sound of those words, and he took off towards English Village.

The loud rumble of the engine echoed off of the buildings, and the upper crust of Birmingham society turned their nose up at the sight of them when they rode past. He pulled into a parking spot, turned off the bike.

"Are you ready for me to get off the bike?" Zoie asked, instinctively knowing to communicate with Hugh before making any sudden moves.

"Yes. Steady yourself with one leg and swing the other over." He then dismounted, locked the bike, and pretended to lock the imaginary doors of the bike by saying, "Beep beep" and pressing the nonexistent buttons on the bow of the key.

Zoie giggled and then took his hand. She looked up at him and their eyes met. Hugh, unsure of what the flow of a new courtship should be, wanted to stop and kiss her, but he also felt that it was too soon. He didn't want to scare her or come on too strong.

"I hope you like Mediterranean food." He indicated that they would be going to a restaurant called Vino.

She put her free hand on his forearm, moving closer to him. "I do." She then admitted, "There's really not a lot of *genres* — is that the right word? — of food that I don't like."

Hugh shook his head and smiled. *She's so cute.* "Ha! I don't know. Types? Cuisines?"

When they got seated, Zoie opened the menu and her eyes grew wide. "Hugh, I can't let you —"

He cut her off, instinctively knowing that she was concerned about the pricing. "Yes, you can. I want to." He watched her

45

nervously glance at the menu. "If you order the side salad, I swear that I will never take you on a date again."

She teased, "What if that's what I want? Hmm?"

"It's not," Hugh replied, with confidence.

She blushed and pushed her glasses up. "Fine."

————

After dinner, they walked over to a small shop that was both a bakery and an ice cream shop. As he opened the door, the smell of the baked goods hit them so hard that they almost couldn't hear the bell on the door.

The cashier asked for their orders: Mint Chocolate Chip for Hugh; Cookie Dough for Zoie — after she discovered that her favorite flavor of all time (Chocolate Marshmallow) was not an option.

"What are you two celebrating?" the cashier asked.

"Hmm?" Hugh replied, not sure that he heard her correctly.

She handed them their cones. "You two look very happy and in love. What are you celebrating?"

Hugh looked over at Zoie, who was blushing so hard that she was essentially red from head to toe. "It's actually our first date," he admitted.

The cashier told them that they made a really cute couple and wished them luck before they left.

The pair of them took a walk around English Village while holding hands and enjoying ice cream cones. Much of the walk was silent because the ice cream was so good — and because even though it was the evening, it was already warm enough in Birmingham to melt it quickly.

Throwing his napkin in a nearby bin, Hugh asked, "You ready to head to the Vulcan?"

"Oh…"

He saw that she was anxious. "I can tell them not to come, if you aren't ready for that…"

"No, it's not that. It's…" she paused. "Are you not having fun with me?"

Hugh stopped walking and turned to her. "I *am* having fun. I just wanted to introduce you to my closest friends." She blushed and looked down, hiding a little smile. He let out a little chuckle. "Why do you do that? Why do you hide when you're happy like that?"

She finished the last bite of her ice cream cone and softly said, "Well, to be honest…"

"Please."

"Well, I've had quite the crush on you since we bumped into each other at the start of the semester, and I sometimes have trouble believing that you return the sentiment." Hugh felt her hand start to loosen its grip; she was going to retreat again.

"Why?"

She laughed. "What do you mean?"

"Why would you think I wouldn't want you?"

She let out a laugh and then admitted, "Have you *seen* you?" She motioned as if it should be obvious.

Hugh's reply came with ease. "Have you seen *you*?" She blushed and smiled, and Hugh brought her hand to his lips, gently grazing the back of her hand with a kiss. "From this moment forward, I want you to never, ever doubt how alluring I find you."

She basically giggled into herself. "I've never been called alluring before."

"I'm a Professor of Literature, Zoie. I have loads of words that are more descriptive than *beautiful*." He continued, "I'm not sure that beautiful is good enough for you." He acted as if he was deep in thought. "Enchanting. Irresistible. *Bewitching.* A total knockout." He pulled her close and touched her chin gently. "I like you. A lot. A lot more than I should after one cup of tea and the first half of a date."

—Zoie—

Then kiss me, Zoie thought so loudly that she worried Hugh could hear her. She chickened out. "I enjoy your company as well."

She felt him release the hold he had on her. "Then let's continue our date." He led her over to the bike. "I packed one of my plaid shirts in the right saddlebag. It's for you to put on if you're cold. You might want to put that on when we ride for the rest of the evening."

Zoie was worried it would be too small — which wouldn't make sense to any other person in the world that saw them together. Hugh was a big guy: tall, muscular, definitely romance-book-cover build. But Zoie had always battled body image issues, and after losing a lot of weight, when she looked in the mirror, she still saw that person at her heaviest.

When she put the shirt on, she smiled because it was Hugh's but also because it was big enough to wrap around her a little bit. He walked over and pushed a bit of Zoie's hair behind her ear and then rolled up the cuffs of the sleeves. "Hot." He got on the bike, stabilized it, and ordered, "Get on, Goddess."

She bit her lip and blushed as she got on the bike and sat as close to him as she could. She tapped him twice to let him know she was ready to go.

———————

"Do you enjoy fireworks?" Hugh asked, as he switched off the ignition to the bike.

"Yes and no. They are beautiful, but sometimes loud sounds

scare me." The *sometimes* was a little bit of a downplay.

Hugh's eyes grew wide. "Zoie, why didn't you say something? The Harley is really loud."

"That's different. It's continuous and I expect it."

"Promise?"

"I promise."

He took her hand and led her towards the Vulcan statue. At its feet was a beautiful overlook of the city of Birmingham, which was the reason that Zoie had fallen in love with Birmingham when she came to visit the University before confirming that she would attend.

Zoie put her hands on the railing and looked over the city as the sun sunk lower in the sky. "It's beautiful. It looks like a smaller scale version of my city, Pittsburgh." She wiped a stray tear from her cheek.

"Why did you leave?"

"Well, I got accepted into grad school —"

"No, I get that, but why?"

"It's possibly too heavy for a first date." There was just so much to unpack, and, if she felt earlier that he may bail, she knew he would if she unloaded everything on him.

"Let's talk about it on a fourth date." He put his arm around her.

"There's going to be a fourth date?"

He nodded and smiled. "Hopefully. We have the Zoo and the Botanical Gardens. I'm sure we can come up with another."

Just as they turned towards each other, Zoie was starting to think he was going to move towards giving her a kiss. However, an excited, albeit extremely southern, voice — and the most colorful person Zoie had ever seen — interrupted them.

"Aaahh! Is this Zoie?" The woman's curls bounced as she practically skipped over to them, giving a welcoming hug that Zoie happily accepted. Enveloped in what felt like every color imaginable, Zoie felt as if this woman already knew her and loved her.

Hugh let out an annoyed sigh. "Zoie, this is Stevie."

"I've heard so much about you!" Stevie took Zoie's hands in hers, smiling excitedly. Her long nails were bright pink, with gem accents on some of them.

"Honestly, Stevie," Cayden interrupted. "Give her room to breathe." They shook their head, annoyed on behalf of Hugh and Zoie.

"Zoie, this is Cayden. We've been friends for, oh gosh, years."

"Lots of years," they laughed, patting Hugh on the shoulder.

Zoie nodded. "It's wonderful to meet both of you."

"Don't be nervous, Sugar," Stevie encouraged. She turned to Hugh and Cayden. "Can you go get us some drinks? Leave us girls to get to know each other."

Hugh mouthed *water*? Zoie nodded and smiled.

—Hugh—

Hugh and Cayden headed towards the bar.

"Did you tell her yet?" Cayden asked, once certain the ladies were out of earshot.

Hugh shook his head. "I feel like I'm between a rock and a hard place. I have to tell her, but if I do she's going to run." He continued, "If I were her, I would." Chewing on his lower lip, he then added, "Telling her the truth is the right thing to do. I just don't know how to do it."

"I'm sure you can find a way."

He chuckled and then jokingly practiced as if he was speaking to Zoie. "Hey, Love, just wanted to let you know that I'm actually over 160 years old, and I change into a giant, hideous wolf-like creature when I get pissed off. Oh, and, as if that wasn't enough,

50

Zoie, you're fated to be my mate and have no choice in the matter."

It was that moment when Hugh realized they had gotten to the front of the line, and the person working the register was just staring at them, obviously having heard, at the very least, the last part of what Hugh had said. As they walked away with their orders, both Cayden and Hugh burst out laughing.

"...So Hugh said that you're a bit witchy?" Stevie asked, as she and Zoie sat on a blanket in the grass, waiting for the fireworks to start.

Taking a bottled water from Hugh, Zoie responded with excitement. "Yes! I just dabble a bit. Tarot, Moonology, the sea... It's just to bring positive energy into my life."

"So you don't cast spells?"

Zoie shook her head, confused. "I mean, very rarely. What good would that do? I mean, is magic even real?" She explained, "It's more like... well, does anyone really believe that 'thoughts and prayers' does anything? Spells would be the same." She added, "I just use it to center myself and as a cleanse from my own personal negative energy."

Before the conversation could continue, the fireworks took over the sky above Birmingham.

Zoie moved closer to Hugh and leaned her head on his shoulder. She let out a long, comfortable sigh. "You smell really comforting."

"Hmm?"

"Like... warm tea and old books." She paused, with a soft smile. "...and something else that I just can't place." She closed her eyes and cuddled closer to him.

He put his arm around her. He contemplated kissing her, but he didn't want to take away from the beautiful fireworks display.

He then felt her move even closer — if possible — and put her hand on his leg.

Nervously, he swallowed hard. Hugh wasn't sure to react because the fireworks entered their grand finale section. Not only was the sky lit up like the Vegas Strip, but the entire crowd was also loudly ooh-ing and aah-ing. Would he want to take this moment from her?

Quickly changing his mind, Hugh felt that this might be the perfect time to make an *actual* move. As he placed his hand to Zoie's cheek, his heart started to pound. He slowly moved to kiss her…

…but was interrupted by the feeling of some sort of liquid being poured on him.

At first, Hugh thought that it was sudden rain, but he heard commotion. He stood up, and realized that it had, in fact, been intentional and that he had been hit by what was actually beer.

"What the actual f—" Hugh stopped and, his mouth dropped. "Alvin?"

Stepping closer, the man replied, shoving his fingers in Hugh's chest. "First of all, Chief, I go by Vin nowadays." He shoved Hugh's shoulder. "And you will pay. You will pay dearly for what you cost me."

Hugh stepped back, trying to avoid a fight. "It was an accident, A— Vin. I never intended…"

Vin closed the gap between them again. "What's coming to you is no accident. I promise you that. I fully intend to make you pay." Some security guards grabbed Vin by the arms, and he pulled himself free. "I'll leave of my own volition." As he made his way passed Hugh, Vin turned back and made eye contact with Zoie. "You be careful, now."

Hugh was more concerned about Zoie than anything else. "I'm so sorry about that."

Zoie wiped the beer that had splashed onto her purse with a tissue she found in one of the inside compartments. "Some people are so dramatic."

"What crawled up his ass?" Stevie asked, absolutely disgusted.

Cayden couldn't find any other place to slip this joke in, so they shoved an "insert here" joke into this space. "Insert joke about Chipmunks?" they said with a complete lack of confidence, almost asking for permission. "You get it? Alvin? Alvin and the…"

Ignoring Cayden's poorly timed joke, Hugh replied, "I don't want to talk about it here." He shot Stevie and Cayden a look that Zoie missed while she was looking for a place to throw away the beer-soaked tissue.

Realizing that Hugh really was indicating that he just didn't want Zoie to know — meaning it was a "wolf thing," Stevie suggested, "Zoie, how about we make sure we get all of that beer off that beautiful purse. I bet there's better paper towels in the ladies room." She ushered Zoie away. "Is that a Kate Spade…?"

—Zoie—

"Yes," Zoie said, "but I got it on clearance during a major sale; it's not like it's irreplaceable." Everyone had already gone back to watching the fireworks, so Zoie no longer felt the anxiety of having the attention of strangers.

"Still, we need to clean it off as best as we can," Steve said. Then she added, "and your shirt may be a little stained."

"Oh, that's all right. I have a stain stick at home that has never failed me yet." The truth was, Zoie was actually disappointed. The shirt was one of her favorites and it was no longer in stock at the store that carried it. She just wouldn't want anyone to feel inadvertently sorry or sad for her.

In the restroom, Stevie was able to quickly find a roll of paper towels despite both dispensers actually being empty. "I'm going to get a couple of these wet to get the stickiness."

"Thanks." Zoie looked around to make sure that no one else was in the restroom with them, and asked, "What was that all about?"

Stevie shook her head. "I don't really know, but it seems like they knew each other before. I've never seen that Vin guy before."

Zoie threw the paper towels away and grabbed a few more, just to be sure that the stickiness was gone.

"That's an interesting tattoo," Stevie said, pointing to her wrist.

Zoie quickly covered her wrist. "Oh, that's not a tattoo. It's a weird birthmark." She blushed and looked away.

"Oh, I'm so sorry. I didn't mean to offend you."

"You didn't. I'm just really self-conscious about it. It's kind of odd and ugly." Zoie shrugged. "I never thought to claim it was a tattoo if someone saw it."

"You could say it's…" Stevie pondered for a moment.

"It's the Earth, like Phoebe says in Friends when she and Rachel get tattoos."

"What's Friends? Is that a book?" Stevie grabbed some dry paper towels. "Here, it should be good now. Just dry it to be sure and so it doesn't get ruined."

"You don't know what Friends is?" Zoie no longer cared about the purse. "It's the greatest television series ever of all time ever!"

Stevie shook her head. "Never heard of it."

Zoie's jaw dropped. This was more surprising than getting beer poured all over her. "Stevie, that's appalling. We're going to have to change that." She threw the dry paper towels away. "Let's discuss on our way back to the…" She trailed off.

"Were you going to say 'the guys'?" When Zoie shyly nodded,

Stevie replied, "It's OK. Cayden's understanding about people adjusting at first. They'll help you." She suggested, kindly, "Let's get back to our partners."

—Hugh—

Hugh looked around quickly and saw that they were no longer the center of attention. When he realized that it was safe to, he said to Cayden, "I lost control and shifted one night, and his mate got in the way…"

"So? Did ya scar her face or something?"

Hugh shook his head slowly.

"Take a limb off?"

Hugh shook his head again. "Worse."

"You didn't!" Cayden realized they had gotten a tad loud, so they stepped closer to Hugh and whispered, "You killed her?"

"It was an accident. I was furious…"

"What wolf doesn't get the Hell outta the way when another one is shifting?"

"She wasn't a wolf. She was a healer. A witch. A Green Witch. Y'know, a Hearth Witch." He pulled his hair back. "And it wasn't her fault at all. She just got caught in the crossfire."

"Damn." There was an awkward silence. "But I mean, I've known you for 100 years. So you're telling me this mother fucker has held a grudge against you longer than that?"

Hugh glared at Cayden. "You wouldn't kill for Stevie?"

They shrugged. "I love her, Hugh, but I'm sure I'd meet someone else after a few decades…"

Hugh's jaw about hit the ground. "I can't believe you would say that. I mean, I'm about ready to hunt him down for…" As Hugh figured out what Vin's plan likely was, he couldn't even finish his sentence.

"Hugh… you look like you're trying to divide 78,579 by 148. What's going on?"

"Get the girls. We need to go."

Before Cayden could even make a move towards the restrooms, Zoie was approaching Hugh, visibly concerned. "What happened?"

"We need to go. Now."

Zoie's facial expression quickly changed into confused. She looked at Stevie. "I'll give you a call tomorrow, okay? We'll do lunch this week?"

"No need," Hugh stated. He looked at Cayden. "Let's meet at the Gulf. We'll figure out what's next from there."

"What? You're leaving?" Zoie's shoulders slumped and tears filled her eyes.

Hugh put his hand on her cheek. "You're coming with me. I'll explain when we stop off at your place to get your stuff."

"Excuse me?" She took a couple steps back.

"Vin threatened you. I'm not going to let him hurt you."

"So you think the answer is taking me away for the weekend? While that sounds lovely, we just met, and I don't understand what the big deal is…" She grabbed her phone out of her purse and started walking towards the parking lot, as she pulled up the Lyft app.

"You have to tell her," Cayden suggested.

Hugh caught up with her and grabbed her wrist. "Let me take you home."

She yanked her wrist away. "Let go of me." She looked back at her phone and continued to search for a ride, now on another ride share app.

Hugh put his hands up in defeat. "I'm sorry. I didn't mean to hurt you or scare you."

She looked up from her phone. "Thank you."

"Can I take you home?"

She took a deep breath in, obviously thinking about her options. "Please."

—Zoie—

"Are you going to come in?"

The right corner of Hugh's mouth curled into a smile. "I wasn't sure if you were going to want me to."

With her back to Hugh, walking into the house, Zoie rolled her eyes a little. *If he thinks that my allowing him in my home means all is forgiven, he's got another thing coming...*

Zoie started to empty the contents of her purse onto the table, methodically, and then she put it next to the kitchen sink. "So, are you going to explain why you went completely over the top over that guy telling me to 'be careful'? A completely common southern turn of phrase?" She turned on her kettle.

"I want to, but I need to know that you're going to be open minded."

"I'll do my very best." She grabbed two mugs and two teabags out of the cupboard.

"That guy... we used to be very close, but we had a falling out." He paused for a moment. "I accidentally..."

She turned towards him with pure annoyance. "If you say you *accidentally* slept with his wife... I'll just...Ugh."

"No, it's not that."

Without a word, Zoie's face ordered Hugh, "Well, go on" — with a dash of *I can't wait to hear what bullshit this is* on the side.

Her hope that she would be able to understand had been steadily retreating since he grabbed her wrist at the Vulcan. It backed up even further as he stated, "She's dead because of me."

Zoie looked him up and down for a moment, and then it became obvious that she felt his pain. Her tough girl facade melted away, and she walked over to him, putting her arms around him. "I'm sure it's not truly entirely your fault, Hugh."

He kissed the top of her head. "Aye, it is."

"Whatever happened," she said, looking up at him, "I'm sure that he may view it that way and that you blame yourself, but it can't be entirely true."

Hugh took a deep breath in. He knew that she was going to want details so that she could prove him wrong, but those details meant he was going to have to reveal things that she wasn't going to believe.

The timer went off for the tea, and she released her arms from Hugh's waist. As she poured the hot water over the tea bags. "Why do you think that it was your fault?"

He took his tea from her, and they sat next to each other on the couch. "Remember when I asked you to have an open mind? This is that part."

She shifted her eyes. "Oh... I thought the..."

"You thought the 'I killed someone' part was the piece you needed to have an open mind about?"

She nodded.

—Hugh—

"I wish." Hugh thought about the best way to go about this.

60

"What could be more unbelievable than — what I'm sure was an accident — killing someone?" Zoie shifted a little closer to him.

He smiled and laughed a little. "Not that this is a funny situation, but you seem oddly okay with the fact that someone is dead because of me."

"You wonder why?"

He nodded and sipped his tea.

"Well, there's something obviously off balance about what I'm about to say, but..." She took in a deep breath. "It's just nice to know that you might not be completely perfect." The flush in her cheeks returned.

"I'm not even close to perfect."

"I know that," she admitted. "I just have this habit... maybe it's a problem. I just refuse to the see the flaws in someone that I only want to see the good in." She shrugged. "It gets me into trouble a lot."

He searched her face to try and figure out what she meant. "Well, I know you've not gotten into major trouble with the law..."

She about choked on her tea. "Did you Google me?"

"No, no." He chuckled. "The admissions team wouldn't accept someone into the Graduate school if they had serious charges."

"Ooooh." She explained, quickly, "I make bad relationship choices." She shifted her weight again, closer to him. "Stop stalling. Tell me what this big secret is."

"Okay." He took a deep breath in and held it. Looking around, still searching for a way to tell her, his eyes fixed on her bookshelves and then her witchcraft altar. "What's the absolute craziest thing that you have been told all your life was a story, but you still believe it's real or just really, really wish was real."

She didn't hesitate. "Santa Claus!" Then she laughed. "There's so many things. But I guess with Santa, he kind of is real. In spirit."

"Tell me about those *so many things*."

"You're going to make fun of me."

He put his arm around her and pulled her closer. "I promise to not." He took a sip of his tea, while waiting for her answer. When it was clear she didn't believe his promise, he emphasized, "I *sincerely* promise."

"I always kind of hoped that the *Twilight* universe was kind of real. Even beyond the vampires and werewolves." She sat up with a bit of excitement. "And those werewolves were shape shifters, but I don't want to call the author out on that because she can call them whatever she wants…"

Hugh chuckled.

"You promised not to laugh."

"I'm not laughing at *you*. I'm laughing at the shape shifter comment." It was much too on the nose for him to not laugh about it.

She pressed her lips together, not believing him. "What's any of this have to do with what you have to tell me?"

Well, here goes nothing. "Alvin — Vin, whatever name he's going by nowadays — his wife… she's been… I… everything happened a long time ago."

She looked at Hugh as if he had lobsters crawling out of his ears. "…Then I'm sure you've paid your retribution for the accident that caused her death. I mean, if that man is vocally accusing you, I'm sure you've stood trial and been proven innocent…"

He took her hands. "No. I've not at all." He continued, "That's not what I'm trying to say anyways."

"What are you trying to tell me?" He felt her squeeze his hand.

Okay, this is really it. "What if I told you that all of it is real?"

"All of what?"

"The stuff in the books you like to read. The universes in those books. The monsters, the faeries, the magic." He looked in her eyes. "What if I told you that it's all real?"

She stared back into his eyes, intently, for a few moments. Then she burst out laughing. "C'mon."

He let her laugh for a few moments — maybe 45 seconds. "I'm not joking."

Her laughter stopped abruptly. "I mean, I've always believed that if something was in pop culture — if someone thought it up, there has to be some truth to it. But I meant that with science fiction, because it's based in some sort of science…"

"Whoever said that there isn't some science behind, I don't know, werewolves?"

"Find me someone who turns into a wolf each month on the full moon, and I'll believe that they exist." She scoffed and shook her head.

"It's not like that. The moon thing is a myth." He paused to take in her reaction — which was just squinting her eyes a little. "At least for me."

She stood up. "What the actual fuck, Hugh Davies?" Walking her mug — still full of tea — to the kitchen, she shook her head. "Of all the fucking excuses I've heard from men that don't want to see me anymore… I've got to say, don't waste your time, and just leave."

"That's not the case, Zoie." He stood up. "I'm telling you this because I want to *keep* seeing you."

She rolled her eyes. "So we're going this route?"

"Yes. Yes, I'm *going this route* because it's the truth." He stood up and walked over to her. He unbuttoned the top two buttons on his shirt, and then grabbed her hand.

Zoie attempted to jerk away, but he held on, firmly. "What are you doing?"

"Trust me." He placed her hand just below his left collarbone. "Do you feel this scar?" He moved her hand to his back. "And that one?"

She nodded. "So?"

"No one could survive that, right?"

"I mean, maybe..."

"I got those the same night I got this one. Sometime in Scotland in the 1860s." He pointed at the long scar from his eye to his chin.

"Again, so?" She blinked. It was obvious she wasn't buying into it.

He decided that she was either going to believe him or she wasn't. "I got into a pub fight, and got my ass severely kicked. They shoved a sword through my shoulder, and leaned on it, so it stuck in the ground. I died, and woke up later as a part of this supernatural world."

She crossed her arms. "Keep going with this fairy tale."

He felt the electricity between them start to fizzle. "Zoie, it's breaking my heart that you're not giving this any chance."

"Hugh." The look on her face was extremely serious and cold. "This is not logical."

Hugh reached towards her, and she stepped back. "Zoie Seaver, you're a writer. A creative writer. Logic isn't how you work." He pointed at her witch's altar. "You're a practicing witch, Zoie. Your spirituality is magic."

"Nothing you have said, Hugh Davies," she replied with fire, "has shown me that you died in the 1860s and came back as a werewolf."

"I don't know how to prove that to you."

"Change. Right now."

"Even if I could shift on command, Zoie, I wouldn't want to do that in front of you," he lied — for her safety. "You could get hurt, and that's how Edie — Alvin's mate — died." He explained, "Vin and I got into an argument; I shifted. I was a young werewolf and couldn't control myself the way I can now. She was too close and tried to cast a spell to stop me." He continued, "The spell did hurt me, but, more than that, it pissed me off — and I was already in wolf form — so I attacked her." He reached out and took her hand. "If I ever hurt you, it would kill me."

"You're already hurting me." Her lower lip started to shake, and a tear fell from her cheek. "Just go."

Hugh knew that he was defeated at the moment, so he agreed to leave. As he grabbed the doorknob, he turned to Zoie. "Lock your doors and windows."

"Hugh..."

He let go of the doorknob and went back to her, pulling her into a hug.

She squeezed him tightly in return, but then pushed herself free. "How do you expect me to believe this?"

"I don't, Zoie." He closed his eyes and then all but whispered, "I wouldn't if I were you."

He walked out and stood at his bike for a few moments before getting on. The ride home wasn't long enough for him to gather his thoughts. He didn't want to think at all, to be honest, so when he got in the door, he went straight to his bed and let his body fall face first onto the mattress.

————

A glutton for punishment, when Hugh woke up, he prepared to

go over to Zoie's, unsure of how he could even begin to convince her that he was telling the truth. Unsure if she would even want to see him.

He'd never had to prove it before; he had never had to tell someone that he was a werewolf who wasn't already involved in their underground world.

He rode his motorcycle over to her place and just as he was about to knock on the door, it flung open.

"I don't think this is the best time," Stevie said, with her hand on her hip.

"Why are you here?"

She sighed. "She invited me."

He glared at her. "Stevie."

"Look, Hugh…"

"Who is it, Stevie?" Zoie said, carrying a tray full of breakfast items from the kitchen, and, as soon as she made eye contact with Hugh, she simply and coldly said, "You."

"Zoie, can I come in?"

"No." She placed the tray on the table. "Stevie, please, don't wait for me to get started. I'm going to speak with Hugh on the porch for a moment."

He cleared the doorway so she could come out. "Thank you for speaking with me."

Her back was to him. "Hugh…" She turned around. "Most men just ghost or say it's not going to work out."

"Zoie, I know how this seems…"

"Shut. Up." She rolled her eyes. She paused to see if he actually would. "I was watching a movie last night after you left. It was a Christmas movie. One of those Hallmark-esque ones. *The Knight Before Christmas*."

It wasn't winter; it wasn't even Christmas in July time — he felt like this was an odd choice of movie, but didn't feel like it was a good idea to state that in this moment. "Okay…"

"No one believes that Cole is a time traveling knight, but he really is. And even if he wasn't, they decided to let him believe that he was." She added, "I don't know that I can do that."

He frowned. "Zoie…"

"But!" She spoke over him. "…but I can give you time to convince me."

"I will find a way." He took her hand in his, faking confidence to cover the uncertainty of finding a way to prove it to her without showing his wolf form.

"You have a week." She looked in his eyes. "I'm not going to let this charade go on forever. One week, okay? If you can't convince me, I'm done."

Reluctantly, he replied, "And, if it comes to that, I will let you go." He was lying, of course. He would never stop trying. He couldn't.

—Zoie—

"Thank you." Zoie reached for the door. "Text me later?"

Hugh nodded and slowly started towards the steps of the porch. "Yes. Of course."

She knew that he wanted her to invite him to stay, but, truthfully, she didn't feel like it. She turned the doorknob and didn't look back to see him leave, but instead towards the dining room table where Stevie was.

"Everything okay?" Stevie took a sip of her tea.

Letting out a deep sigh, Zoie took a seat. "It's just a weird situation, and you're his friend, so I don't want to…"

Stevie leaned forward. "What happened?"

"How long have you known him?"

"Years, why?"

She bit her lip. "In the time that you've been friends, has he dated a lot?"

Stevie laughed. "Not at all." She added, "You're the first."

Zoie wasn't sure that she could trust Stevie, as they had just met the night before. She pressed her lips together.

"What happened?" Stevie's concern seemed genuine, with only a hint of wanting the gossip.

She paused for a moment. "I... I am very trusting. I let people wrong me — multiple times — before I give up on them." She continued, cautiously. "I've had a history of picking the wrong guys, and I promised myself that I wouldn't do it again."

Stevie's eyes seemed to have a fire ignite behind them. "Did Hugh hurt you?"

"Oh no, no, no." Zoie waved her hand in protest. "He wouldn't do that... I don't think." She explained, "I just don't understand the game he's playing with me."

"Why do you think he's playing a game?"

"Wellllll..." Zoie wasn't sure whether the next step was a smart one. "He told me this ridiculous story — he obviously doesn't want to see me anymore. And then..." She motioned to the door.

"And then he shows up here?" Stevie sighed. "I can understand the confusion."

Zoie ran her finger along the rim of her teacup. "I just don't want to fall into the same patterns. I moved here to change my situation, not to repeat it."

Stevie looked at her watch. "What are your plans for today?"

Confused, Zoie replied, slowly. "After showing you my favorite episodes of *Friends*? Nothing."

"I want you to meet me somewhere later." She noticed Zoie's apprehension. "Hear me out." When Zoie nodded for her to continue, she explained, "Cayden and I have supper with Hugh every week at this hidden gem of a place —"

Zoie cut her off. "Is this a ploy to —"

It was Stevie's turn to cut her off. "Honestly, yes." She said it so matter-of-factly that Zoie was taken aback. "I'm not trying to force you together, by any means, but I think if you spend more time with Hugh, you'll see who he really is." She continued to try and convince her. "Look, I don't know your relationship history, and what you're trying to escape. But I do know Hugh Davies. He's not a liar." She waited for Zoie to respond.

Wait until you hear this whopper. Reluctantly, Zoie replied, "Fine."

"Good!" Zoie clapped a little. "Let's not talk about boys anymore. Let's convince you that *Friends* is worth spending the time watching 10 seasons."

Zoie smiled and grabbed the breakfast tray and lead Stevie to the living room. They watched five episodes, as planned, and Stevie headed out, leaving Zoie to argue with herself about whether she was being stupid for giving Hugh the chance to manipulate her.

—Hugh—

The knocking at the door was fast and loud — and accompanied by repeated text message notifications. 47 unread messages. All. From. Stevie.

The knocking at the door kept up. "Holy Hell, Stevie! I'll be there in a second." He let out a "for fuck's sake" under his breath.

Hugh got out of bed from a nap that wasn't long enough for him, but was obviously too long for Stevie's liking. He grabbed his jeans that he had thrown over the chair in the corner, and nearly tripped as he walked while pulling them up.

He put on the sweetest smile — like a mother who was yelling at her children and then had to answer the phone — and opened the door slowly. "Oh, I thought I heard someone knocking. Were you waiting long?"

Stevie pushed her way in. "I've been knocking for like five minutes."

"You don't say!" He chuckled. Then he looked out the window and back at her. "Okay, so the world isn't burning down. So what was so urgent?"

She walked right into his kitchen and poured herself a cold glass of sweet tea. "So, that mark on Zoie's wrist. That Alvin debacle at the Vulcan actually gave me an opportunity to look at it." Hugh motioned for her to continue. "When we were in the restroom wiping off that gorgeous purse — which you should get her a replacement of that's a little bigger. She has that thing stuffed full, and it's bursting at the seams..."

Hugh rolled his eyes. "Stevie, I appreciate the gift idea, but could you stay on task?"

She scoffed. "Well, I was getting there but you interrupted." She took a sip of her drink. "Where was I? Oh, so anyways, we were wiping off the bag, and I got the opportunity to ask her about the blue cluster on her wrist. I asked her if it was a tattoo." She decided that she wanted a straw for her tea, so she started opening drawers where the straws may be.

Hugh let out an annoyed sigh. "Stevie, what are you doing?"

She finally found one of the reusable straws and dropped it in her glass. "What? I needed a straw."

"Oh-kaaayyyyy." He found a stray hair tie on a nearby table and pulled his hair back into a manbun.

Stevie put her hands up. "Okay, okay! I'll continue. No need to get upset." She took another sip and then said, "It's not a tattoo. She said it was a birthmark."

"...so?" he asked cautiously.

She nodded and smiled. "She's got the magic within her."

Hugh put a fist in the air and shouted, "I knew it!" He ran up behind where Stevie was and wrapped his arms around her in a hug. "Thank you, thank you, thank you for helping me. Helping us."

She laughed. "Don't get too excited yet, Hugh." She reminded him, "You can't tell her that she's magical. You know this."

He pondered this. "What if we didn't tell her, but she discovered

72

it on her own?" Then he added slowly, "With our help?"

Stevie twirled one of her curls around her finger. "Witches are supposed to have a cataclysmic event that awakens their magic. It's dangerous to force it. Plus, the Shrews can sense this shit. They let little magical slips happen, like an Earth witch at home putting her emotions in her food or a Sun witch using her déjà vu to change the course of the next few seconds — these witches don't know that they actually have powers. The witches know that these little things are just coincidences, but they can sense when something bigger and more deliberate is happening."

"Can't we just test little things to see what kind of magic she has?"

"Hugh, I don't know." She grimaced slightly. "If we go too far with it, not only is she at risk, we are too." She added, "I don't know about you, but I am not looking forward to an eternity as a gargoyle." To lighten things, though, she said, "Not only have I heard it sucks, but they are ugly. I don't want to be ugly."

Hugh laughed. "Okay, I understand. I mean, I don't. I've lived over 150 years as someone that's ugly, so I don't know what's so bad about it." He then suggested, "What if we don't go *too* far with it?"

"Huh?"

"You said that there would be a problem if we went *too far*. But what if we just went far enough, and then created a big event that she would need to use her power for?"

She thought for a few moments and then admitted with a sly smile, "I asked her to join us tonight for drinks."

"Is she going to come? Does she know that I'll be there?"

Stevie nodded. "Yes to both." She suggested, "If we take her to Lunar, we can test if the magic within her is strong enough to even bother exploring."

Hugh thought about it for a moment. "But she'll be able to

come in, regardless, as long as one of us is touching her. The portal would consider her as nothing more than an article of clothing that I'm wearing."

"The symbols," Stevie pointed out. "If she can see the symbols, then we will discuss the next steps." She finished off her tea so completely that the straw became loud as it tried to reach for more tea. "My mother would have smacked me for that," she laughed. She stood up to leave. "Hugh, let's just take this step by step. Let's not get too ahead of ourselves. If she passes this first test, we'll talk about different ways to test the different types of witch powers."

Hugh walked her to the door and gave her a quick hug. "Thank you, again."

She smiled. "Of course." Stevie walked off the porch and turned around. "Wear something better than that tonight. Even though you two have the power of magic making you mates, it doesn't mean you can just stop trying."

He chuckled. "You woke me from a nap!"

"Is that what you wear to bed? Hugh! You can't wear a torn T-shirt and jeans to bed with her!" She teased, "No wonder you've not ever gotten a girl to sleep with you."

He laughed, "Get the fuck out of here!"

—Zoie—

Zoie felt her throat close and her lungs burn. She was in her grandmother's pool. But how? Her grandmother had died a decade ago and they'd sold the house. Her water wings were supposed to be holding Zoie afloat, but they were failing — again. Just like when she was eight.

That's when she realized that this was a dream. She tried to tell herself to wake up. She tried to push the water away.

She gasped.

She screamed.

Then she suddenly sat up, taking deep breaths. Sucking in the air that she had so desperately needed moments before.

But she was safe, back on the couch, clutching Judy in her arms. Her nap must have been deeper than she had planned.

Checking her phone for the time, she realized that she had slept longer than the 26 minutes she had anticipated and got ready to go out with Stevie.

As she walked over to grab her purse from her table, her eyes caught her book for New Witches that contained some basic spells. Something inside her told her she needed to open it.

She felt compelled to cast a protection spell.

This was strange to her for many reasons. First of all, she usually just practiced to keep herself positive or to relieve stress, much like others practiced religion or prayed; Witchcraft was her personal form of religion. Secondly, she wasn't a witch that really cast spells — because she didn't believe it did anything, really. She felt that it was all in the mind. She knew the theory and had an altar, but it wasn't something she did very often. There were many other small reasons that came to mind, but there was one big one: She didn't know what she felt that she needed protection from.

For whatever reason, she decided to follow her intuition. She opened the book to the Protection Amulet spell. She ran upstairs and grabbed her crescent moon necklace. Then she ran back downstairs and grabbed the cumin and a black votive candle.

She had a little mini broom — a tiny broom that would be best for a Barbie to use as a hand broom — that she used to sweep the negative energy from the altar. "Spirits, please, bring only positive energy to this space."

She then took a deep, cleansing breath, and sprinkled a pinch of cumin on the candle. She lit the wick and closed her eyes for a moment. Holding her hands over the altar as if there was an invisible ball in them, she allowed herself to feel the power — her personal power — travel back and forth between her fingertips.

She then picked up her necklace and moved it through the smoke. She then spoke the words of the spell:

Necklace, be my protection;

Be charged with my intention;

Cast a shield in my direction.

She allowed the necklace to charge with her power and then put it on and blew out the candle.

There was a knock at the door, and she heard Stevie's voice. "Hey Zoie. It's me!"

She quickly walked over, as she put the necklace on, and opened the door. "Hey. Sorry, I overslept."

"You're fine. I'm early."

"So where are we going?" Zoie checked her hair and makeup in the mirror one last time before grabbing her keys.

"There's this hidden pub in Birmingham — Lunar Brewery."

Zoie scanned her memories of places in the city, but she couldn't even place a single mention of the Lunar Brewery before. "Never heard of it."

"It's *hidden*."

"Oooohhhh… kaaaayyyy…" Zoie was starting to wonder if she had made the right decision.

It was a short ride to the Five Points South area of Birmingham, and, upon finding parking, a quick walk to the Storyteller water fountain, which was in honor of Cecil Johnson Roberts.

"I love this spot," Zoie said, admiring the different figures in the water. She was deeply focused on the tortoise with the hare on its back.

She heard a deep voice behind her. "It's unlike anything else in the city."

—Hugh—

Hugh's heart fluttered as Zoie turned to look at him. But before he could approach her, she had already turned to Stevie, who was already in Cayden's arms. "I thought we were going to a pub. Why are we at a fountain?"

Hugh took a quick look around and walked over to the side closest to the Highlands Methodist Church. He motioned for Zoie to join him. "Take my hand." Hugh smiled at the soft touch of her skin in his palm. "We're going to walk into the fountain —"

"No way." She yanked her hand free. "This is a monument. I don't want to get arrested."

"Sugar, no one's going to see you," Stevie stated with certainty.

Cayden suggested, "Maybe we should go first and show her."

Stevie stepped up first onto the side of the fountain. She waved her hand and the water separated and made a path leading to the ram figure — in a suit, reading a book, and holding a staff with an owl on the top.

As soon as she stepped off of the side, Stevie appeared right next to the outside of the fountain, rather than where she stepped in.

Hugh watched as Zoie tried to figure out what just happened. "Why did she…"

Hugh pulled her close and whispered, "Once she steps in, her body disappears, but the magic creates a double out here so that no one loses their mind as they watch someone disappear."

"What happens to the fake Stevie? What if someone touches her or talks to her?"

He explained, "Well, the magic is designed to keep humans away from it. If someone talks to her, she'll just appear to ignore them." He continued, "Once she crosses into the portal, her double will walk over into that scary looking alleyway, so I'm assuming that if she was touched, she would just yank away and move towards the alleyway."

"What if a human follows into the alley?"

"Magic. It deters the humans from even going near it."

Cayden said, "You'll understand even more, once you do it."

The water splashed down, but Stevie still was gone. "Where'd she go?"

"You'll see her in a few minutes." Taking Zoie's hand, Hugh stated, "Each type of monster has its own way in. Stevie is what you would call a mermaid, so she waves her hand and the water splits for her. She can control water like that."

Zoie started to step back, but Hugh pulled her close. "If you're going to do this, you're going to have to enter with me. Do not let go of my hand, Zoie."

Cayden stepped up on the side of the fountain and pressed their hand to the top of the wall, separating the water again. They jumped into the fountain and it became apparent that they had caught up with Stevie because his double actually jogged to catch up with her before going into the dark alley.

"Our turn, Zo."

—Zoie—

Taking deep breaths, Zoie's palms started to get clammy. Even her feet were sweating. "How do you get in?"

"Cayden and I are both werewolves — or shape shifters, whichever you want to call us. We place our hand on the top of the wall."

"Has a non-magical creature ever…?"

Hugh shrugged. "I don't know. But worst case, you'll drown." When her eyes grew wide, he laughed. "I'm kidding! You just won't be able to cross, worst case scenario."

"How do you know?"

"People play in the fountain all the time." He took her hand and placed his other on the wall, over top of the glowing paw symbol that had grown brighter as they approached it. "Ready?"

She watched the water separate, and then felt him pull her as close to him as possible. Unsure of whether to close her eyes or not, she held her breath as she stepped into the fountain. *Please stay separated, water. Please. Please. Please.* As she looked around, she noticed that everything looked as if she had opened her eyes underwater. "Everything sounds… muffled." She realized that, somehow, the water had become the walls that surrounded them. Zoie held her free hand up and moved to touch the water.

"No, Zoie. I don't know what will happen if you touch it." Hugh pulled her hand away from the wall of water. "Just keep walking towards the center of the fountain. There will be some stairs."

She turned around and looked over at the magic-created doubles of Hugh and her. Her double was standing with her back to him, wrapped in his arms and looking up at him. The joy in the double was as real as it could be, with the smile even creating little wrinkles at the corners of its eyes.

Zoie saw a child jump in the fountain. "What if they walk into us?"

"They won't. I actually hope that they do cross through. It will be interesting for you to see."

Just as he said that, the kid walked right over them. One leg was on the left side of the water wall— and the other was on the right! Zoie gasped as she looked up towards what would be the child's torso. It was blurry, but she could definitely see organs and veins. "Are they…?" The kid moved and both sides of their body were reunited with each other. "Oh thank goodness!"

"Let's keep going." He guided her further towards the center of the fountain.

The cobblestone stairs were damp, and the walls felt like they were holding in every ounce of cold air the world could muster up. It was dark — only lit by lanterns.

When they reached the end of a long passageway, there was a

wooden door with a heavy doorknob. Hugh opened it with a creak and as soon as it was shut behind them, he said, "You don't have to hold my hand anymore if you don't want to. Not until we try to leave."

She continued to hold his hand and actually reached over with her other and touched his arm. "Is it okay if I don't want to let go?"

He smiled, the emotion reaching his eyes. "Definitely."

"What is this place?"

"It goes by lots of names, and it depends on where you enter it from. Most of us that come from the portal in Birmingham call it Nightbrooke." He gently smiled at Zoie.

Stevie came skipping over towards them on the cobblestone street, not worried about rolling an ankle in her purple heels. "So, what do you think?"

"I don't know what to think." She looked around, in wonderment. "It looks like England from all the old books I read." Then she turned to Stevie and whispered, "You're a mermaid? But..."

"But I have legs?" She chuckled. "Well, I wouldn't walk too well with my fin."

Zoie laughed and then asked, sincerely, "What should I do to blend in?"

"Look," Hugh said, "Everyone is going to know that you don't belong here, so don't even worry about acting like you fit in." He took her hand and lifted it to his lips, placing a gentle kiss to the back of it. She felt his smile through the kiss.

"To Lunar?" Cayden suggested. Hugh replied with a nod.

The alleyway that they took off the main street was dark. The stones of the buildings were old and looked as if they had never been washed. The air was damp in Nightbrooke, and the cobblestone street had puddles in some of the potholes. There was a lantern hanging at and old wooden door that had moss growing on it.

Hugh opened the door gently, but it still creaked loudly. Everyone turned and stared for what felt like an eternity.

After a few seconds, Cayden called the group to follow them to a group of free chairs at the far end of the bar.

Hugh's hand moved to the small of Zoie's back to lead her over. She was starting to think that the electricity she felt when they touched was more than just a schoolyard crush.

As they took their seats an older, a disheveled man interjected with "What's she doing 'ere? This place is supposed to be a safe haven for us." He finished with a loud hiccup.

"Jack, she can be trusted," Hugh replied, shortly. He turned away and rolled his eyes. "Anyways…"

"Whatcha havin', Love?" The bartender had perfect blond hair and flawless skin. She pushed her hair out of her face, revealing a natural sparkle on her cheekbones and pointed ears.

"Coke." It was Zoie's default when out.

Once they all received their drinks, Zoie turned to them, and began to ask a question, but Hugh answered, "Faerie."

"How many different… types? Is types the right word?" Zoie bit on her thumbnail.

"Well, Stevie, you're the most educated on our world," Hugh pointed out, suggesting that Stevie take the reins.

"Oh, geez, there's the usual — vampires, were-beasts or shapeshifters, faeries, mermaids — of course. We're the best."

"Hey now!" Cayden laughed.

"But there's also trolls and dragons. Oh, and you're going to love this one — witches." She then explained, "There used to be things like immortals, elves, and dwarves. But they all died out —

and I know, it's ironic about the immortals."

Hugh put his arm around Zoie and pulled her close. He placed his lips near her ear and whispered, "Do you believe me yet?" He then placed a gentle kiss on her cheek.

She blushed as she nodded. "This is incredible." She then asked the group. "You said that there's different portals to this place?

"Aye, yes," Hugh replied. "There's entrances all over the world. It's how many of us get to start our lives over again and again." He continued, "If I've stayed too long in one place, for example, I'll just come here and leave to another place."

"So we can go anywhere?"

"Oh, Zoie, you can go places you've only imagined," Stevie explained.

Zoie was very obviously intrigued, and she was about to ask more questions when Jack approached them again, drink in hand. He stumbled between Hugh and Zoie and some foam from his beer splashed on Hugh's shirt. Hugh wiped it off with a flick and pushed Jack back a little. Jack didn't leave, though. "You risked us all, Davies. All o' us. Stupid girl is going to tell all her li'l friendssssssss, and then our secret's out." He hiccoughed loudly.

"Jack, back off." Hugh pushed him again, a little more forcefully than before.

Cayden stood up and got in between them. "Stop, guys. We can't —"

Jack growled and then suddenly howled. His muscles expanded, tearing his shirt and the thighs of his jeans ripped open; it was a shame because, despite being disheveled, the suit jacket he wore was well tailored. His nails grew and the hair on his face sprouted.

Stevie grabbed Zoie and moved her out of the way. "Jack just about shifted; we need to get you outta here!"

"But I wanna…"

As he pulled his hair back, Hugh turned quickly, not letting Zoie finish her sentence. "Take her. Go!" The first sentence was clearly for Stevie. The final order was directed at Zoie. No goodbye. No hug. Just "Go."

Stevie grabbed Zoie and dragged her out of the back of the pub — but not before Zoie noticed Hugh's muscles starting to twitch. If she didn't believe his claim of being a werewolf before, she surely did at this point.

Stevie wouldn't let go of Zoie's arm and dragged her in the opposite direction of where they entered NightBrooke. "Don't let go of my hand, Zoie."

"Why? Where are we going? How is Hugh going to find me?"

She looked Zoie directly in the eyes and said firmly, "Hugh will always find you."

Zoie yanked her arm out of Stevie's grip. "No. Answer my questions or I'm not going to take another step."

Stevie scoffed. "Are you joking right now? You're in danger. Like actual danger."

Folding her arms across her chest, Zoie asked. "Why can't I stay with Hugh and wait for this business to be over?"

"The shifters are unpredictable. If you stood too close to him he could scar you or even kill you. That scar will never, *ever* fully heal, Zoie. The power of a wolf's claw is something that even other forms of magic cannot fix. You would be disfigured for life. And if he accidentally killed you, Hugh would never forgive himself." She added, "if Jack or someone else hurt you, even then, Hugh wouldn't forgive himself for not being able to protect you better in that situation."

Zoie chewed on her lip a little. She wanted to believe that she could hold her own in a situation like this, but she was obviously out of her element. "Fine. But where are we going and how?"

Stevie rolled her eyes a little. "You see those palm trees up ahead?" Zoie nodded. "One of them has a door in it, and we're going to walk right through and go to a safe house on an island off the coast of Hawaii." She held her hand out. "You coming?" When Zoie hesitated, Stevie said, "There's not a lot of time. If you stay here, you could be in danger." She continued, "Like I said, Hugh will always find you."

Zoie wanted to know about this belief that Hugh would always be able to magically find her, but she didn't think that this was the time to ask. She cautiously took Stevie's hand. "Okay. Let's go."

They walked briskly towards the palm trees until they were in front of one that was abnormally large with a pool of water next to it. Zoie smiled as she could smell the salt and hear the water gently ebb and flow from the sandy shore at the pool's edge.

Zoie noticed a glowing tree symbol near the doorknob. Without even saying a word or asking Stevie what to do, Zoie hovered her hand over top of the symbol. "What do these symbols do?"

"Mark the doors to show the portals." Stevie waved her hand gently and a few drops of water lifted out of the pool of water.

Zoie stepped back from the door and watched in awe as the water floated through the air. Stevie somehow directed the drops to combine into one slightly larger droplet and then they entered the keyhole of the doorknob.

The door opened towards them, and Stevie motioned for Zoie to go through. Zoie turned around as Stevie was shutting the door, and the hinges and any evidence of a door vanished instantly. The exterior wall of a decorative tiki hut left no trace of their travel.

"Incredible, isn't it?" Stevie smiled.

Zoie nodded. "What was it like for you the first time that you experienced magic like this?"

Stevie shrugged. "Mermaids are born into it, so we grow up with it our entire lives. It's like... television for you. You grew up with that, right? It's not extraordinary to you, is it?"

"Ah, I see." She followed Stevie down the sidewalk towards a dock with several boats just waiting to hit the sea.

There was a man tending the dock, wearing cutoff jean shorts and a — what Zoie could only assume used to be white — A-line tank top. He had a patchy black beard and wore a baseball cap that seemed to be held from dropping further down over his eyes by his bushy black eyebrows — well, eyebrow, as they seemed to be fused together.

Stevie slipped some money into his hand slyly and made her way to a boat. "Come along, Zoie. We need to get to our destination before dark."

Zoie nodded and got on the boat. While the ride to the island wasn't overly lengthy, it was colder than she had anticipated, so by the time they dropped the anchor at the dock, she was shivering. The sun had just set, and the wind on the water was not as warm as people that have never been to Hawaii believe that it would be.

"Let's get you inside," Stevie said, pointing towards what appeared to be the only house on the island.

Zoie noticed that there was a light on, so she stopped walking. "Ummm..."

"There's some timers on, in case someone comes poking around where they shouldn't and we aren't here." She took the lead and when they got to the door, Stevie pressed in a code and the door unlocked. "Welcome home?" She laughed.

Zoie took her shoes off immediately upon entering and the

wood floors were cool on the soles of her feet. "So, this is a safe house? What makes it so safe?"

"It's remote. It's pretty much impossible to find unless you know where to find it." She added, "There's back-up generators. Weapons. The works."

Zoie made her way further into the house to the kitchen. "Where do we get food?"

"There's lots of canned stuff and non-perishables. But you all can fish." She shrugged. "I won't be participating in that, but when Hugh and Cayden get here, go for it."

"What about like... fresh fruit and veggies?"

Stevie chuckled. "Most of the time, we're not here very long when we have to hide out. So we're good with ramen noodles and stuff."

Zoie noticed a tea kettle on the counter, so she started opening cabinets. She found a few mismatched mugs. One was plain orange; another had RETIRED written in big letters. There was one that was actually the shape of a cat's face. But Zoie selected the one that had #1 Grandpa written on it.

She pulled down a box that was on the top shelf in the cabinet. "Jackpot." She started rummaging through the assorted bags until she found an Earl Grey, Decaf. She figured that she had enough excitement to keep her awake, and extra caffeine would have just made her more wired than she already was.

As she brewed the tea, she asked, "How do you keep this place clean?"

Stevie laughed. "You ask a lot of... interesting... questions." She explained, "We have someone from the main island who was born into a family that is like us, but she has no powers or immortality. She cleans for us. If we need something, like your fruits and veggies," she teased, "she'll bring it to us." She added, "I notified her we were on our way when we were still in Nightbrooke, so she got us some essentials."

When her tea was ready, Zoie sat down on the loveseat in the living room. "We can get TV here?"

Stevie shook her head. "Just movies. We don't even have cell service here." She then said, "But we have a lot of movies to choose from. Pick anything you want." When Zoie put in *Twilight*, Stevie scoffed and shook her head. "Really?!"

"Hey! I like it!" She grabbed a blanket from the back of the couch and put it on to take the chill off from the air conditioner. Zoie pulled one of the baskets out from under the coffee table; it was full of books. "Ooooh. *Warm Bodies*! I love these books!" She opened it up and started to read, while still maintaining the ability to watch the movie.

Stevie placed a bowl of popcorn on the coffee table in front of Zoie and then sat down on the oversized chair on the other side of the room. They both settled in to wait for Hugh and Cayden to arrive, as they had no idea how long they were going to have to wait for the others to figure out where they were.

—Hugh—

Flinging the door open with more force than what was even remotely necessary, Hugh walked into the villa, followed by Cayden. Both of their clothes were torn to bits. Some of the tears were from the actual fight, but most of them were from their bodies changing and shifting and growing into their wolf forms. Hugh's shoes had even split from his feet growing. Cayden's left eye was bruised to hell and back, already turning purple, and Hugh had some blood dripping from a cut above his eyebrow — another possible scar for his collection. Both were chuckling, as if they had just been out having a drink with the pack and watching the game.

Zoie immediately put her book on the coffee table and stood up. Then, she froze in place. Hugh could read on her face that she was worried and possibly a little scared, so his laughter stopped. He hesitated, not sure if he should get close to Zoie while looking like he had clawed his way out of Hell to get back to her.

Cayden's eyes, however, found Stevie and their laughter paused. They took three large, quick steps to her, scooping her up into a hug and smothering her with kisses. "I missed you."

She smiled back and kissed them twice. Touching their face

gently, she said, "Let's get you some ice for that. I know you heal at an accelerated rate, but we can still help the process."

Zoie walked directly towards Hugh, ignoring the placement of the furniture. He was concerned that she would collide with the couch between them. Instead, she stepped up on the cushions and then on the back and jumped into his arms. "I have been so worried about you!"

Hugh barely had Zoie in his arms — he wasn't even sure if she was secure and safe there — and her hands were in his hair, pulling their lips together. Hugh didn't expect this, so he froze.

In a very short amount of time, several thoughts went through Hugh's head. *What is this? When was the last time that someone touched me like this? Decades? No... over a century. Maybe never. You've wanted to cross this plane with her since the moment you first saw her. Why are you standing as still as a tree? Do something. Touch her. Or, even better, maybe kiss her back, you fool.*

Zoie backed off. "Oh." She loosened her grip on him and slowly slid down towards the floor, causing Hugh to release her gently. "I'm sorry." As soon as her feet hit the floor, she began backing away slowly. "I misread the situation," she said quietly.

Hugh grabbed her arm and pulled her back towards him. His free hand made his way to her hair, and he leaned over and kissed her. The electricity of their mating bond shot through his entire body, and he pulled her closer. She didn't fight him. In fact, she grabbed the belt loops in his jeans and pulled him impossibly closer.

He broke their kiss only to make sure she understood, without any uncertainty: "You didn't misinterpret anything." Pushing one of her salty-sea-air sculpted waves behind her ear, he told her, "I take my time with you because I don't want to hurt you. I want you to be a thousand percent sure that you are comfortable with any

90

step we take forward. Everything will always be your decision and on your terms." Then he added, making fun of himself, "Plus, I'm a little out of practice with this sort of thing."

"Doesn't feel like it." She tugged on his belt loops playfully.

He laughed. "Trust me, I am." He looked up for a moment to see Cayden and Stevie sitting on the oversized chair, just staring at them.

Stevie fanned herself and mouthed, *H-O-T.*

"Yeah, we're still in the room," Cayden chuckled. Then they wiggled their eyebrows at Hugh, mockingly.

Zoie shoved Hugh away out of embarrassment and looked down at the floor. Hugh pulled her into a hug to hide the flush in her cheeks that he could feel on his chest through his torn shirt. "Never stopped the two of you to have other people in the room. Perhaps I should remind you of Tokyo?"

Cayden shook their head. "Oh, I don't need reminding," They took Stevie's hand, smiled mischievously. Motioning towards their bedroom. "Wanna go relive Tokyo?"

Stevie shoved Cayden's shoulder playfully. "Not if you're going to act like this." She still followed, though.

—Zoie—

Not sure how to behave alone with Hugh after that kiss, Zoie asked, "Is that Jack guy okay?"

"Oh, yeah, he's fine." He took a step back and then turned to the kitchen. He poured himself a glass of water. "We got loud; fought for maybe 30 seconds; his ass landed on the floor; Cade and I got kicked out of the pub for a few weeks."

"I'm sorry."

"No big deal." He waved it off. "Jack doesn't like new people. He is afraid that someone who doesn't fully understand our world and what it means would tell our secrets." He continued, "There's some people in our world who believe that mortals should never know about our world."

"Oh."

He lifted her up — effortlessly — and sat her on the kitchen counter. "Don't worry. Some of us don't care. Some welcome them knowing about our world."

She changed gears quickly. "Do you sleep?" Zoie asked Hugh, wondering if any of the legends and lore were true.

"Yes. A lot sometimes." He was standing between her knees, and her hand was on his chest.

She felt his heart start to pound. "Are you okay, Hugh?"

"Never better." He smiled at her, looking into her eyes so deeply that she felt entirely exposed to him. He put his hands in her hair.

He pulled her closer, yet again, and lifted her off of the counter. She instinctively wrapped her legs around his waist, but it didn't matter. He lifted her with ease. Hugh was able to carry her — with one arm — over to another door, open it, walk through and close it, and place her on the bed. All as if he was merely carrying a magazine.

On his knees in front of where Zoie was sitting on the edge of the bed, he put his hands up the back of her shirt. She smiled, noticing that his hands were shaking ever so slightly.

He was trying his best to conceal that he was nervous. Needing to give him a signal that it was okay to proceed, Zoie reached up and unbuttoned the top button of his tattered shirt. Afraid that she was reading the situation wrong, she paused.

Hugh looked in her eyes and then his gaze momentarily moved to her lips. "May I?"

Zoie didn't answer him. She was so tired of waiting, so she put her hands in his hair and pulled them together into a kiss. His hands, still on her back, pulled them closer. Then, one of his hands left her back to undo her shirt in a quicker motion than Zoie knew was even possible.

She continued unbuttoning his shirt while his lips traveled to her jaw and then her neck. "I want you," his low voice whispered.

She was, finally, able to confirm that, yes, he could grace the cover of a romance novel. "I'm yours." Her hands nervously traveled to his belt. It was now her turn to be the one that was shaking.

He paused and looked into Zoie's eyes. "I haven't done this in a very long time."

"Me either."

He chuckled. "No. Like… if you've ever had sex, it's been more recently than I have."

She blushed. "It doesn't matter, Hugh."

He swallowed hard, as if he was literally trying to swallow his nerves. "What if I hurt you?" He looked her in the eyes and sincerely told her, "If I hurt you, you have to tell me. Promise me."

"I promise." She held her pinky out in front of him. "I pinky promise."

He touched the tip of her finger with his index finger. "OK."

Her mouth dropped. "You don't know what a pinky promise is?" She then realized that he had never been a nine-year-old girl. She fixed his hand so that it was in proper pinky promise position. "You do this." She linked their pinkies together. "And then you say 'pinky promise.' But be sure that when you make a pinky promise that you *really* mean it and intend to keep it. A pinky promise is… it's like the unbreakable vow in Harry Potter."

He laughed. "Okay. Do you pinky promise to tell me if I hurt you?"

"Only if you pinky promise to tell me if I hurt *you*." She bit her lip and blushed.

Pinky still linked with hers, he leaned forward and kissed her. Lips still touching, he said, "Oh, I pinky promise." He released her hand so he could move it to her waist and gently push her back onto the bed.

—Hugh—

Hugh's back hit the bed and he let out a deep sigh. He pulled Zoie close, and she placed her head on his chest. He ran his fingers through her hair. "Did I hurt you?"

She smiled and traced his chest. "Yes, but not in any way I didn't enjoy."

He smiled and raised an eyebrow. "You promised to tell the truth."

"I am." She touched the scar on his shoulder and quickly jerked her hand back. "When's your birthday?"

She was obviously dodging asking for more information on the scar. "I don't know."

She quickly pushed herself up to a seated position, grabbing the sheet to cover up. Her jaw dropped. "You don't know your birthday?"

He chuckled. "Well, as you age, you forget things, no?"

"But your birthday?!"

"Tell me about your second birthday party."

She glared at him. "Who remembers their second birthday?"

He shrugged. "Well, you're in your mid-twenties, right?" She nodded. "You've forgotten your second birthday in a little over 20 years. I'm between 190 and 200 years old."

"You look *really* good for your age," she said, tracing a finger on his chest.

Hugh laughed. "Thank you."

She went back to their birthday conversation. "I'm not asking for the year. Just month and day."

"Hmmm." He searched for some sort of memory. "I remember a birthday where we were able to have a garden party because it was perfect weather. That didn't happen a lot in the Scottish Highlands." He looked at the ceiling, as if maybe he could find the memory there. "I think it was late April or early May." Narrowing it down further he explained, "It had to be late April because Alexander — my childhood friend — had a birthday in early May, I believe, and mine was a week or so before that."

"So you're a Taurus." She nodded to herself. "Makes sense."

He chuckled. While Hugh wasn't a big believer of astrology and the zodiac, he respected that Zoie enjoyed it. "When's your birthday?"

"October 7th." She added, "I'm a Libra." She frowned a little. "We're not compatible."

Hugh tugged on the sheet a little. "Come here." She lay back down beside him. Pushing a bit of her hair behind her ear, Hugh smiled, "Then I guess it's a good thing that I don't believe that our compatibility is dependent on our birth charts."

She cuddled closer to him and fell silent.

"Whatever it is that you're thinking, go ahead and ask."

"Ummm…" She hesitated. "I've always been scared of dying. What's it like?"

He closed his eyes for a moment. "Dying is…" he paused. "I felt a lot of pain when the blade went through." He guided her hand to the exit part of the wound on his back. "I may have told you this, but he stabbed through me, and his friends helped him shove the blade into the ground so I couldn't get up and come after him." This is not where he thought their pillow talk would go, but, even though she asked one question, he felt as if she was probably asking a different one at the core.

"Hugh, if you aren't comfortable talking about it, you don't have to tell me."

"I want to. I want you to know everything." He continued, "You know how I said that I've had memories fade or even get lost? This is one that I don't think that I'll ever forget. It was around the 1860s or 1870s, if I recall correctly. I wish I could tell you that it was part of some epic battle in a war, but it was just me and some guy in a pub fight." He kissed her temple.

"Do you remember what caused the fight?" She teased, "was it over a lady?"

He ran his fingers through her hair. "Actually, it was."

"Oh." He felt Zoie's heart drop a little. "Were you interested in her?" She was jealous.

He shook his head. "No, not romantically." He shifted his body so that they were laying facing each other. "Zoie, I don't remember ever — and I mean in my entire life — feeling compelled to pursue a woman." He continued, "Did I ever think of dating someone so that I wasn't alone? Sure." He ran his fingertips up and down her arm. "The way I feel about you… it's as if it's some innate part of who I am."

She tried to hide the smile on her face but was unsuccessful. Hugh did not try to hide his. He had never known before what it was to care about someone and have her care back — even if she wouldn't admit it just yet.

He traced the gold chain around her neck until he found the crescent moon pendant, which reminded him of their original conversation. "That night… the night that I died…" He continued, "A gentleman — and I use the term loosely — whom I already had taken issue with in the past, was bothering the barmaid. I didn't know her too well, but I could tell that she was trying to ignore his repeated advances. He grabbed her and tried to lift her skirt right out in public, and I attempted to stop him. He broke a bottle over my face." He took her hand from his chest and ran her fingers over the scar below his eye.

"I thought you healed more quickly and better than humans, er, mortals?" She kissed his scar. "My kisses have magical healing powers."

He smiled. "My scars are beyond help. I'm shocked that this healed as well as it did, to be honest." He explained, "Not to be too grotesque, but that side of my face was split open, with my skin hanging loose. Blood was everywhere." Continuing, he said, "He and his buddies pushed me out the door, and he grabbed a sword from the decorative knight that was in the pub. I guess one of his friends grabbed another. I didn't know how to wield a sword, so as we started to fight, I was losing from the get-go. Plus, I obviously couldn't see, and I was losing a lot of blood." He let out an annoyed sigh.

"I'm sure you were able to hold your own for a bit."

He chuckled softly, "Not at all. I don't even think I was able to get one solid swing."

"Oh."

"He pushed me into the grass and stabbed me. One or two of his friends leaned on the sword with him and jammed it into the ground — which was sort of hard as it was still snowing sometimes — it was at least frosting over at night regularly."

"Did it hurt?" He could almost hear her scolding herself in her own head for asking such an obvious question.

He swallowed his emotions as he placed his hand on top of Zoie's, which was on his chest. "It was painful. I knew I was going to die because they left me there. I closed my eyes because it was making me sick to see everything. It was like drinking too much.

And I don't even mean well past your limit; I mean well beyond even *that*. And, as a Scot, I can hold my liquor, so when I say beyond your limit, I mean a Scot's limit. The world spun around me. I could make sense of nothing that I saw."

"Oh, Hugh, I'm so sorry."

He knew that she was apologizing for making him relive this. "It's okay. I told you that I want you to know everything about me." He took her hand to his mouth and kissed her fingertips and then her palm. "I closed my eyes and was ready to die. I felt my breathing start to shake and I started to choke. I tried to get up a couple times, but, like I said: the blade was meant to keep me in place so it did. My heart stopped and I rested."

"I shouldn't have asked…"

He put his finger to Zoie's lips. "Suddenly I was gasping for air and I had the strength to reach up and pull that blade out of the ground and, somehow, out of me." He paused for just a moment. "I was feverish; I later came to realize that it was just how it was going to be."

"Is that why you are always warm to the touch?"

He nodded. "Eventually, I found a place to hide, but when I looked in a piece of a mirror or something shiny I found, I wasn't me." He was so invested in the memory that he was feeling the confusion all over again. "I was a bigger, much scarier looking me. Longer nails, huge teeth, and either I had just really let my facial hair go or I had been lying there for months — no, it was the wolf in me. I didn't know it at the time, of course." He shook his head. "I was a monster, though. That, I was certain of."

"You're not a monster…"

"You don't have to say anything." He placed his hands on her back, and the contrast between her cool skin and his warm hands reminded him that her lying next to him was not just a dream or fantasy. "I just want you to know me." He kissed her nose and then yawned. "But, as much as I want to tell you more, it is about three in the morning — and a different time zone than we started the day in — and you, my Goddess, have exhausted me."

"Me?!" Zoie giggled. "I think it was your fight earlier."

"That, sure, contributed. And so did shifting. But mostly, it was you." He touched her nose playfully with his finger. "My ancient body needs to rest now so we can do this all again."

—Zoie—

Zoie woke up as the sun came through the floor to ceiling windows. She looked over at Hugh, who was still in a deep sleep. He was lying on his stomach with his hair covering his face. His left arm and leg were uncovered, hanging off the edge of the bed. Sliding out of bed and wrapping a loose sheet around her body, she decided to shut all of the blinds so that Hugh could sleep longer.

She then realized that she didn't have any essentials — at all. She put her clothes back on from the night before — besides underwear, because she couldn't find them. Even if she could, though, she wasn't someone to reuse the same underwear without washing it. Slowly and quietly, Zoie made her way to the kitchen, careful to make sure that she shut the door without even a click.

A pot of coffee was already brewing, so someone else was awake. She got herself a glass of water and then started brewing some tea. Then she made her way out to the patio. The water was the bluest she had ever seen. She even noticed something splashing around.

She took in the beautiful site, not sure of what it was playing out in the water. Zoie wiped off her glasses, hoping that it would give her a clearer view. It didn't help, and it didn't turn them into a magnifying glass either. Her focus was interrupted when she heard the tea kettle scream, so she ran back in, trying to not take her eyes off of the mysterious creature out in the sea for more than a second.

Teacup in hand, she stepped out to the sand and started walking towards the water. The sand was so fine that it squeaked under her feet. Even in the heat of the sun, the sand was cool to the touch. She looked down the beach to either side and noticed that the house they were staying at was the only one within her line of vision. The breeze was so light that the palm trees didn't move.

Zoie closed her eyes and then let the sun warm her skin. Then, she looked back at the water and realized that she had actually been watching Stevie swim the entire time.

It was then that Stevie must have realized she was being watched because she headed back to shore. As she got to the more shallow water, she started to walk out, and that's when Zoie noticed that she was wearing purple rash guard pants with a hint of glitter.

Zoie did a bit of a double take, as she realized that the pants were disappearing, starting at her ankles and moving up her legs, until they became a bathing suit — a sparkly purple bikini.

"The water's a perfect temperature! You should get in, Zoie!" Stevie called out as she closed the distance between them. She shook her head and, as if it were magic, her black curls were dry and back in perfect form.

"Were you...?" Zoie couldn't even form a complete sentence.

"I have to swim in the ocean every so often or my powers — and beauty — fade." She threw a coverup on over her bathing suit and started off towards the house. "I have to be near water to use my powers, but my beauty," she said, proudly, "is always with me. I use that more often than I would like to admit to get what I want in situations." She added with a big smile, "It works like magic."

Cayden and Hugh seemed to still be sleeping still when the girls made their way back inside. Stevie immediately started making breakfast. She noticed that Zoie kept glancing over at her bedroom door. "They will sleep a little bit extra because of the shifting last night."

"It tires them out? I think Hugh briefly mentioned that."

"Yes, I've noticed that, depending on how active they are, they can sleep 12 or even 15 hours." Stevie added, "I've studied other supernatural species a lot, but nothing compares to actually experiencing life alongside them. Learning about the different supernatural beings was a part of my education."

"Oh."

"I'm sure you have questions. Ask away."

While she was relieved that Stevie had offered to answer her plethora of questions about the supernatural world, Zoie chuckled and asked something unrelated. "Where can I score some toothpaste and a change of clothes?"

Stevie smiled and laughed lightly. "Essentials are in the cupboards outside of each bathroom. Clothes… you're quite short — the height difference makes it super adorable when you stand next to Hugh, by the way — so, anyways, we'll probably have to get you some clothes. Do you wear makeup?" She continued without even breathing. "Of course you wear makeup. I mean, I saw you before we got here. We can get you that, too. Get me a list of your products. I'll take care of getting everything for you, Love."

Zoie blushed. She didn't know the appropriate way to acknowledge the comment about her and him being adorable. "Where? This place seems pretty remote," Zoie added. "Where are we exactly?"

"A small island just off of the western coast of Maui, Hawaii.

I'll take a boat into Maui and get you some. Just give me your sizes. In the meantime, you can wear one of my sundresses. It will look like a maxi dress on you, but it will be adorable. You can wear those cute little white sneakers you have with it. That's very in right now." She handed Zoie a plate and then sat down in a chair next to her. "So what other questions do you have? About Hugh, I mean."

"Are werewolves immortal? Shapeshifters, I mean."

"The terms are interchangeable. All that BS about the full moon is just that — total BS, legends that have evolved over time. Mostly to keep the mortals scared and in their place." She explained, "Shifters can take several forms. There's wolves, bears, birds, and big cats. Some say there are others, too. Whichever suits their personality best." She continued, "They have to change about every month or so to keep from aging. They can age and then die if they stop shifting or phasing, but it doesn't have to be with the moon." She took a drink of her coffee and then added, "I realize I didn't answer fully answer. Nothing is immortal. There is a way to kill everything."

"How does one become... like all of you?"

"You're born into it. All of it. The stories of being bitten or whatever are all made up, again, to scare people."

Zoie's heart dropped. There was no way for her to be with Hugh long-term. He hadn't opted to age for over more than a century, so why would he start now? She would age, and he would move on when he tired of the wrinkles and grey hair.

"You okay?"

"I just thought... Never mind." She looked down at her plate.

"You thought that since you were mated that he could make you immortal, too?"

Zoie blushed and took a sip of her tea, to hide her face. "I

104

mean, I wouldn't call what we did last night as 'being mated,' but I guess if birth control fails…"

"Oh! That's not what I meant!" Stevie's jaw dropped to the floor. "I thought…"

—Hugh—

Hugh had planned on merely opening the door like a normal human being and going out to the kitchen for breakfast, but then his wolf hearing overheard what Stevie had just divulged to Zoie, so he flung the door open, nearly knocking it off of its hinges as it slammed against the wall. Overdramatic, sure. But it did the job.

His plan to glare at Stevie so hard that she would feel it in her soul fled his mind instantly when he saw Zoie. The entire world disappeared as he walked towards her.

He placed a kiss on her cheek and then took her in his arms. That was when he decided to glare at Stevie, since his face would be hidden from Zoie's.

Stevie mouthed, *I thought you told her.* He just squinted his eyes in response.

"How'd you sleep?" Zoie asked, with her bright green eyes peering into his.

"Best in over 150 years. Thank you for closing the curtains so I could sleep longer." He bent over and kissed her cheek, lingering for just a moment. He whispered in her ear, "Also, thank you for last night." He felt the heat in her cheek as she blushed, so he kissed her jaw and let out a quiet, low growl. She let out the tiniest giggle and bit her lip.

The other bedroom door flew open, and Cayden announced themself by making a joke at Hugh's expense. "It's amazing that a whopping five minutes of sex tired you out enough for you to get such sound sleep."

Zoie buried her blushing face in Hugh's chest, and Hugh shook his head at Cayden. "Please, don't."

"She'll get used to it." Cayden shrugged while pouring themself a cup of coffee and grabbing a donut.

Stevie quickly spat back on Zoie's behalf, "She shouldn't have to get used to that." She rolled her eyes, took a bite of watermelon from her fork, and then looked at Zoie. "Honestly, sex jokes are so junior high. Don't you agree, Zoie?"

Zoie was still blushing and looking down at her feet. "I mean, it's not my kind of humor..."

"Zoie, you don't have to be so... polite. You can tell me that I'm being an asshole," Cayden laughed. "We're all friends here." They poked the fire a little more. "Well, I guess not exactly friends for you two. Fuck, you are loud, you know? I think they heard you back in Birmingham."

Eager to take the attention off of them, Hugh asked, "Soooooooo... what are we doing today?"

"Well, I need clothes..."

Hugh quickly replied, "Stevie can take care of that..."

"I... I want to pick out my own clothes..."

He cupped her cheek with his hand and looked her in the eyes. "I *need* to keep you safe."

Confused, she asked, "Why wouldn't I be safe?"

Stepping in, Cayden explained, "The world you live in today is not the same one that you lived in yesterday, Zoie."

"Now that you know what exists out there," Stevie added, "that world knows that you exist too."

"Oh." Zoie's mouth slowly closed as she realized that she had encountered the likely causes of many unsolved mysteries the night before. Then she added, "But they knew I — in a manner of speaking — existed before. It's them — your world — that has been blending in with mine. There has to be more to this."

Hugh quickly explained, "I didn't follow protocol when I took you into NightBrooke."

"Protocol?"

"You remember that building next to the pub with the ridiculously long line that wrapped around it?" Once she nodded, he continued. "That's where newcomers register to come in and out freely. I didn't do that with you. That's part of the reason that Jack flipped out."

She appeared to be deep in thought for a moment, and then she asked, "How would he know whether I registered or not?"

Hugh motioned for Stevie and Cayden come over. Instinctively, they both presented their forearms, and Hugh did the same. Hugh waved his hand over Cayden and Stevie's arms, and Stevie waved her hand over Hugh's. Glowing green symbols appeared in the center of their forearms: a wolf paw for Hugh and Cayden, and a wave for Stevie. "We can bring out the symbols any time they are available. They are just like the ones on the fountain…"

"…or the door to get here." Zoie added slowly. "So, since I didn't register, I don't have one." Then she asked, "What kind of symbol would I get?"

Stevie interjected, "Not sure. It's very rare that a mortal enters lawfully."

Hugh silently thanked Stevie. He, Cayden, and Stevie had been traveling together for so long that they could simply shift their eyes or touch their face in an otherwise unnoticeable way and communicate securely with each other.

Zoie didn't push, but Hugh noticed her eyes squint ever so slightly. It was out of character that she wouldn't question further about the symbol; Stevie had given away earlier that she had extensive education into this sort of thing. It was obvious that she had more questions, but perhaps she couldn't formulate them just yet. Maybe she was going to pull them out with questions later. Either way, Hugh knew she was going to interrogate him later if she didn't get all the answers that she wanted.

"You said that the violation in protocol was *part* of the reason that Jack was not happy." Ah, here came the next line of questioning. "What was the other part or parts?"

Hugh didn't see a point in hesitating. "Me."

"What do you mean?"

Knowing that she would just keep digging if he tried to be surface level about things, Hugh elaborated. "Jack is Alvin's father, so naturally, he's got an issue with me if Alvin does. You know that I killed Edie, his mate." Zoie nodded. "The abridged version of what happened..."

Zoie interjected, "I don't want the abridged version. I feel like I already have the abridged version."

"You ask a lot of questions," Cayden pointed out as they poured some syrup on — or, more honestly drowned — a stack of waffles.

Quickly, Zoie retorted, "Well, I live in a different world today than I did yesterday, and I have a right to know what that is."

Cayden shrugged. "I think you're getting involved in something that you're never going to understand and that you really shouldn't be so heavily involved in anyways. But you do you."

Hugh rolled his eyes. "Get up on the wrong side of the bed, or...?"

Cutting a triangle piece into the stack of waffles, they shrugged again. "I just feel like we're treading on dangerous territory right here, Hugh. You know what the consequences are. You know what they'll do to her."

"I won't let that happen." Hugh grumbled.

Cayden let out an exaggerated sigh. "If you think you can stop them, fine. Continue on. But the three…" then they pointed at Zoie, "…and a half… of us can't stop the powers that be from handing out a sentence for the kind of crimes we are going to commit here."

"What are they talking about?"

Ignoring Zoie all together, Hugh replied, "It may not be a problem for long. We can solve this."

"What may not be a problem?" Zoie asked.

Cayden didn't even bother to swallow the next bite and started talking. "You can't predict that, Hugh. You don't know when they are going to figure out what's going on here. I love you, Brother, but I'm not about to be an accessory to this crime, and you *know* what kind of position that puts Stevie in."

"What kind of crime?" Zoie asked. When Hugh went to speak over her again, she lifted her mug and slammed it down on the counter. When everyone turned to look at her, her eyebrows were furrowed. "Don't talk about me, right in front of me, like I'm not here."

Cayden stood up. "Fine." Pointing behind them with their thumb towards the patio door, Cayden ordered, "Hugh. Outside. Now. Just us." Frowning, they looked at Stevie. "The conversation that Hugh and I are about to have is a *wolf thing*." In other words, they were ordering Stevie to occupy Zoie for the time being.

Hugh kissed Zoie's cheek. "This won't take long."

"You'll tell me later?" She asked.

Since he didn't want to even start to lie to her, he just kissed her cheek.

"You coming?" Cayden called from the patio.

Hugh stepped outside and shut the door. He realized that Cayden had walked down towards the water's edge. They really didn't want Zoie to hear what was about to be said.

As soon as Hugh was beside them, Cayden flatly said, "You know what will happen if we tell her that she has magic before she was supposed to realize it on her own, right?" Hugh didn't respond. "Hugh, the witches on the council can sense that shit and they will come for her and, unless there's the unlikely event that she's hella naturally powerful, they will imprison her. We'll all be imprisoned as gargoyles, too, for helping, and rumor has it that sucks *just a little*."

"Then we find a way to have her find her magic herself."

Cayden shook their head. "Yeah, Stevie let me know that you had discussed this." They tightened their jaw. "Are you sure this is what you want to do?"

"Cade, she's my mate. The sooner that she realizes that she's truly a part of this world…"

They interrupted. "Why did you talk to Stevie about this instead of me?"

Hugh scoffed. "Is that what this," he motioned up and down at Cayden's posture, attitude, entire self, "is all about?"

They threw their hands in the air. "A little. You're like a brother to me, and you didn't even discuss this with me. If Stevie didn't tell me everything, I would be basically clueless."

Hugh shrugged. "You didn't seem receptive to it when I brought it up the morning after the concert."

"Of course I didn't seem receptive; I was exhausted. I shifted the night before. I wouldn't have been receptive to anything. Hell, how either one of us is awake right now and pleasant is a shock to me."

Hugh took a step back. "Pleasant? You think that you're pleasant right now? Fucking Hell, Cade."

"Okay, okay. Fair assessment." They stood in silence for a moment. "Hugh, why did I have to hear about this from Stevie? Why didn't I hear about it from you?"

He shrugged. "I don't have an answer for that. I just... I enlisted her help because she's the most knowledgeable about the others." He added, "I'm sorry. I should have told you."

Cayden paused for dramatics. "I suppose I can forgive you." Then they added, "Just don't get me turned into a gargoyle for this."

"I'll do my best."

They started walking back towards the house and then stopped. "I'm also jealous, Hugh."

"What?"

They admitted, "I'm jealous that you've found your mate. I haven't. And," they looked down at the sand. "And, beyond that, as a wolf, I know that means that your loyalty belongs to her now. We've been the two of us for so long..."

"Stevie..."

Cayden shook their head. "It's not the same having her here with us. I would choose you — our friendship — over Stevie. She's not my mate." They frowned. "Until you met Zoie, you would have chosen me and our friendship over anything. But I know what this means."

"She wouldn't ask me to leave you behind..." Hugh was confused.

"I know. She wouldn't have to." They explained, "If we were in a situation where you could only save one of us, you would choose her."

"That's not fair, Cayden."

Cayden replied, "I didn't say it was, Hugh. It's just true. I can already see it in the way you protect her, even from my little jabs and jokes."

Hugh ran his hand over his beard and then looked to the sky as if there was an answer there. "She needs time to adjust to this world. I'm sure that once she's taken all of this in…"

They chuckled. "I'm not asking for anything here. I just was telling you how I'm feeling about this entire situation." They motioned back to the house. "Let's go back in there." Hugh caught up with them and Cayden put their hand on Hugh's chest to stop them both. "Please don't tell the ladies that I'm jealous of your connection with Zoie or that I'm scared about being turned into a gargoyle."

Hugh laughed. "About the jealousy thing: I would never. About the gargoyle thing: You'd be a fool to not be scared." He admitted, "It terrifies me as well."

Cayden teased, "Oh, I'm just scared. You're the one that's *terrified.*"

As he approached the patio door open, he heard Zoie say to Stevie, "…do you think she'll be upset that she needs to replace the headboard?"

Stevie laughed, "Nah. She's had to replace ours more than once before." She nodded her head towards Cayden and Hugh to signal to Zoie that they were back just as the door opened.

Zoie whispered, "Do you think they heard that?!" Stevie laughed and nodded. Zoie buried her face in her hands. "I should just go crawl in a hole and die."

Hugh walked up and put his hand on Zoie's back and kissed her cheek. "I only heard you mention the headboard, so whatever you said before that I didn't hear."

"Oh, thank god!" Relief washed over her. Then she asked,

"How far away can you hear?"

"Depends on how much I'm paying attention. But if I really wanted to, I could have possibly heard you from... hmmm... probably if I walked out into where the water is up to my knees." Her eyes grew wide. He laughed, "What did you say that you don't want me to know about?"

She blushed and looked down at her plate. "Nothing. It was nothing." Then, she smirked and added, "It was a *girl talk thing*."

"Oh, you're clever, using the *wolf thing* between Cade and I against me." Hugh still considered teasing her because he could tell from the look on her face that it was nothing bad. But he knew that she wouldn't appreciate that. Part of their mating bond was his role as her protector, so part of that was an unspoken promise to never intentionally embarrass her. But that wouldn't stop him from asking later when they were alone.

"Okay, where were we?" Stevie asked.

"Hugh was about to explain why Jack and Alvin just won't let go of Edie's death after over a century," Cayden replied. "Oh, hey, can I get more of these waffles? The ones I had before are soggy now."

Stevie nodded. "Yeah. They're right over there. Go get 'em." She looked over at Hugh. "Now, I know that Edie was Alvin's mate, so that makes sense that he just can't let that go. But you said there was more to this?"

"So, the reason that I killed her was... political? Maybe that's not the right word. But..."

"I didn't know you were interested in—"

Hugh put his hand up. "Let me stop you right there, Stevie. I'm not. I'm not interested in sitting at that big table with your parents and the witches and vampires. I never was, and I doubt I ever will be."

"Then why did you kill Edie?" Cayden asked, shoving a huge bite of waffle in their mouth.

Hugh took in a deep breath. "Did you ever wonder why Alvin is nearly 400 years old and then I'm the next oldest wolf shifter at about 200?"

Stevie let out a quiet "Huh" and then nodded. "That is interesting. Alvin *has* been on the council a very, very long time. The only reason his father — Jack — is not, well, it's because he's always drunk."

"Where did all the wolves between him and me go?"

Zoie asked, "You can't tell me that the gene lay dormant for more than two centuries because not a single person carrying it died a violent death. *Especially* with the Rising in Scotland, which, undoubtedly some of your ancestors fought and died in."

"Right. There were plenty of us, but as I was nearing the end of my training with Alvin and Edie, I overheard a conversation between them one evening, where they were discussing how they had eliminated all of the other threats — wolves that could overpower them and take Alvin's spot on the council."

"They took them all out?" Stevie's jaw dropped. "I mean, I know plenty of people that have killed to get to the top, but they killed them all?"

He nodded. "Well, most of them. They wiped them out to the point where the numbers were so low that your parents were considering removing his spot as a representative because there weren't enough of us to even represent."

"What did they do when they found out that you knew?" Zoie asked.

Cayden guessed, "They tried to kill you because you knew too much?"

Hugh nodded. "So a few days later, I got up the courage to approach them and discuss it. That's when Edie decided to send a spell my way. Alvin knew he couldn't beat me on his own, so she tried to stun me." He looked down. "I changed into my wolf form, and when she tried a bigger spell, I killed her." He frowned. "I'm not proud of it, especially since I threw her head at their seven-year-old son's feet." He looked at Zoie. "You know him. Miles Irving. You had a class with him."

"Miles?!" Confused, she asked, "He didn't come after you at school?"

Hugh laughed, "Only when I gave him a C that he *barely* earned in a class that is a deep dive into *Beowulf*." He added, "I think he was just there to watch me. You know, learn my habits and things so that his father could find the best time and place to attack."

"Did you know the entire time?"

He nodded. "We sense each other. All of us do."

"I'm sorry — I'm backing up." Zoie asked, "Why did they want to kill you and all the other wolves? Like I get that you maybe knew too much. But what was the purpose of killing off so many?"

Stevie interjected, "So that no one would be strong enough to fight and kill him. So he could stay in power. Forever."

"But why is he coming after you again? Why now?"

Hugh shrugged. "He holds a massive grudge? I don't know." He added, "When we've run into each other — maybe three times since then — it's always dramatic. I try to walk away, but there's always a fight."

"He really sought you out at the Vulcan though," Cayden pointed out. "The other times, we would be at Lunar or some totally random place. It was obvious that he was at the Vulcan to confront you."

"I wonder… No, that's silly." Stevie decided to pour herself some coffee to distract herself as she talked to herself.

Cayden looked at Hugh and shrugged. "No clue what she's muttering about."

"Stevie, spit it out," Hugh ordered.

"I think that he showed up now because of Zoie."

"Me?! What did I do?"

Hugh ran his hand up and down her back. "Nothing." He returned his attention to Stevie. "Do you think he'd come for her as revenge on me for what I did to Edie?"

Cayden nodded. "It's possible."

Stevie agreed. "Think about it this way, Hugh. If he eliminates her, he gets two things out of the deal. First, he gets that revenge he's wanted for so long. But, also, he would stop you from even being a threat."

Zoie then asked, with some sternness behind it, "I've heard the word 'mate' thrown around more than once. What does that mean?"

Stevie and Cayden both about snapped their heads off of their necks when they looked to Hugh for how to answer.

He took a deep breath. "Do you remember last night when I explained my feelings for you as 'innate'?" She nodded. "That's because they are."

"Excuse me?"

"Now, I don't want to scare you or make you uncomfortable, but we have a connection. It's…" Searching for the right words, he paused.

"Is this like imprinting in Twilight?" Zoie asked.

Hugh shook his head. "Absolutely not. Two mates can know each other their entire lives, but they won't feel the connection until both are adults."

"What does the connection feel like? Like, how do you know?"

Hugh smiled. "Electricity, every time we touch." He shyly admitted, "Do you remember when you handed me the apple the very first time we met?" She nodded. "That simple touch sent electricity from my hand through my arm and then shot out to the rest of my body."

"Our meet-cute?" She laughed, "That was a lack of humidity."

He shook his head. "No. That's not even remotely how it feels."

"Then why don't I..." she put her hand over her mouth.

He smiled. "Don't feel bad. I know how you feel about me." He continued, "Only those who have discovered their supernatural selves can feel it."

"And we won't know if I have magical powers until I die?"

Stevie interjected, "Well, not necessarily." She explained, "I told you that I was born into magic and knew it my entire life, remember?"

"Yes."

"So, not all of us have to die."

"Well, I'm obviously not a mermaid."

Stevie pressed her lips together and looked to Hugh. Then she said, "Most people show bits of magic in their mortal lives. For example, Hugh, didn't you say that you were always an abnormally strong tracker? Like you could find things by scent in the air?"

He nodded. "I could always hear really well, too."

Stevie continued, "That's only become more enhanced since his violent death."

"So maybe I just need to..."

Hugh protested, "Absolutely not. I will not risk your life just to see if I can keep you longer." He shook his head. "That could take you away from me prematurely." Before anything more could be said, Hugh continued, "We will have whatever life together that we

117

are destined for, and that's that."

Knowing that Hugh desperately needed this topic to change, Stevie looked at a clock and said, "Oh, I had best be getting to Maui to get you some clothes and some other supplies."

"If it's not too much trouble, I still would like to pick my clothes and try them on so that you don't have to return them if I don't like them or they don't fit."

Stevie smiled gently. "Bless your heart. Hugh's basically turned himself into someone from *old money*. Keeping an outfit that you don't like isn't going to make a difference at all."

"That's not what I meant, though." Zoie was very cautious and diplomatic with her explanation. "It's a couple things. First of all, I don't like waste. Fast fashion is really wasteful. Secondly, and most importantly, I don't want to give up my life just because I know about your world. I'm not going to go into extreme witness protection."

Hugh understood that this was all very sudden and new to her. He slid his hand down her arm and took her hand in his. "Can we compromise? Perhaps, you could be extra cautious for the next two weeks, and we could reassess then?" She looked apprehensive, so he added, "You were threatened just, what, two nights ago? Then last night..." He continued, "I realize that it's been 100% *my* decisions that have gotten us here, but..."

She squeezed his hand, gently. "Okay." She looked up at him. "Two weeks. I will give you two weeks of witness protection without a fight." She playfully tugged on his beard. "Two. Weeks."

"Thank you." He knew he couldn't eliminate Alvin's threat in two weeks, but it did give him time to find out, perhaps, what he had planned and how to fight back. It also gave him time to figure out what kind of magic Zoie was most attuned to, and then he could start planning how to get her to discover it on her own.

Stevie pulled a soft tape measure out of seemingly thin air. "Now, let me take your measurements so that I can get you some good stuff!"

—Zoie—

"This is the bathing suit you chose for me?" Zoie wanted to hide — she had never worn anything that wasn't a one-piece with a skirt in her life. She was always desperate to blend in and cover up.

"Zoie, the orange goes so well with your hair, and the bottoms are high-waisted. Shows off your curves. I don't know why you mind?" She pulled her perfect black curls into a ponytail and took out her earrings. "It's just going to be the four of us out there on the boat. No one's going to see."

"Hugh will." She searched for a coverup in the pile of clothes.

Stevie was visibly confused. "He's seen you without…"

"I know." Zoie knew she was being overly lacking in the self-confidence department. "My mom… she used to tell me I would be so pretty if I would lose weight in my thighs, so it's a bit of sensitive spot for me to look at. That's why I always wear pants. She told me I didn't have the legs for skirts and stuff."

Stevie frowned. "Are you joking? You would be so cute in a little pencil skirt." She hugged her friend. "And, you can wear whatever you want. Whatever makes you happy in the moment." She went back to admiring herself into mirror.

She pulled a black coverup over her head. "I'm good now," she smiled, reaching for her sunhat.

"Let's go." Stevie smiled. "You're going to love seeing the water from the boat. You can see pretty far down, too."

Stevie started off towards the door, but Zoie held back for a moment. "I have one more thing to do. I'll be along in just a second." Stevie nodded, and then Zoie opened a little box of assorted witchy items that she'd asked Stevie to pick up for her. She pulled out a candle to use for her protection spell. She only had white candles in this little kit, but that was okay — white candles could substitute for any candle in witchcraft. She grabbed some cumin from the kitchen and sprinkled it on the candle. Lighting it, she took her necklace and charged it in the smoke.

Necklace, be my protection;
Be charged with my intention;
Cast a shield in my direction.

She looked up into the mirror to make sure she didn't put the necklace on with the pendant turned the wrong way, only to see a dark hooded figure standing behind her. Zoie gasped and turned around — nothing was there. She looked back in the mirror to find nothing. "Shadows playing tricks on you," she whispered to herself.

She shook hit off and walked out to the patio door, where Hugh had her flip-flops ready and waiting.

—Hugh—

"You two ready to go?" Cayden called out, getting ready to start the outboard motors on the walkaround boat. They made a fake gagging sound at the sight of Hugh and Zoie as they stopped every couple of steps to kiss. "Get a damn room," they said under their breath.

122

Stevie elbowed Cayden. "Do you not remember how we behaved when we first started dating?"

"Ouch!" They rubbed where Stevie had connected with their body. "We certainly weren't that all over each other."

She kissed their cheek. "We were worse. So be nice."

Hugh helped Zoie onto the boat. "When we turn on these engines, it's going to be loud for a second, okay?" She acknowledged this kind warning, and he and Cayden kicked on all the engines.

The boat started to head out beyond where the waves would break, and Hugh took a deep breath in. He could swear that it helped him breathe better. He glanced over at Zoie and smiled to himself as she held her sunhat on against the wind while laughing at something that Stevie must have said to her.

Suddenly, she stood up and went to the other side of the boat, pointing excitedly. "Is that?!" She didn't have to finish, as a whale decided to wave at them as they sailed on by.

They sailed a bit farther and then finally got to a place to stop for a while. Cayden and Stevie worked together to drop the anchor, which was more or less automated so it wasn't a two person job.

Hugh stood behind Zoie as she looked out over the water. He wrapped his arms around her and rested his chin on her head. She giggled a little, and he changed position as she turned around to face him. "This view is really incredible."

He looked in her eyes and replied, referring to her, rather than the scenery, "enchanting." He kissed her forehead.

Suddenly a steady spray of water hit them both, and Hugh looked to its source and let out a loud laugh, all the way from his chest, immediately. Cayden was standing across the boat, holding a water gun that was more like an uzi. "I thought you two needed to cool off a bit."

Zoie chuckled and then removed her sunhat and now-wet coverup. Hugh smiled and thought about how gorgeous she looked. He stopped himself from commenting about it, though, because he didn't want to objectify her or even give that impression. He told her very often that he found her beautiful, so he felt certain that, even when he didn't say anything, she knew he was attracted to her.

Walking quickly — but never running on the boat — Stevie came over to stand next to Zoie. She excitedly asked, "You ready to swim out where you can't touch the bottom?"

"No way!" Zoie stepped back away from the edge of the boat. "There's sharks and other wild creatures under the surface!"

Hugh laughed. "They stay away from me and Cade, even though we can't swim too well." Zoie's expressive face let him know that she was confused. "We can only doggy paddle," he joked. "Wolves aren't the strongest swimmers. I never see the bears swim; the birds — not at all. The big cats, however, are excellent swimmers. Not like Stevie, of course, but definitely the best of the shifters."

Zoie shook her head in protest. "There's still those same creatures down below. And your magic can fail, and I could be eaten by a shark."

"Have you ever been diving?" Stevie asked.

Nervously, she shook her head. "No. I could get stuck in some small place." She added, "I've seen all the movies."

"Real life isn't like movies," Cayden laughed, ready to jump in but waiting for their friends.

Zoie looked around at the three of them. "I'm living in a new adult supernatural romance right now." She laughed and shook her head.

"That's fair," Stevie said, nodding. She waved her hands and suddenly three large bubbles rose from the water and were floating in the air. "Would you like to see what's down there?"

"Excuse me?"

With a wave of her hand, Stevie directed the bubbles to each of them, floating right in front of their faces. "Allow me to put these on you, and we'll all be able to dive deeper than you thought possible."

Zoie's eyes moved back and forth with uncertainty. "What about the water pressure…?"

"We won't go that far." Stevie snapped her fingers, and the bubbles surrounded their heads. She looked at Zoie. "Do not touch the bubble; it will disrupt the magic and, well, Zoie, that wouldn't be good." Moving to the edge of the boat, Stevie dove in.

—Zoie—

"I thought it was purple?" Zoie pointed to Stevie's fin.

Stevie splashed water up onto the boat with her bright pink fin. "My bathing suit is pink. It goes by what I'm wearing."

Zoie shifted her eyes back and forth, wondering if she's the only person that would have the gall to ask what she was thinking. "What if you were skinny dipping?"

"Then I would just be all one color." She then added, "and if I'm wearing lots of colors, they are all featured."

Cayden did a cannonball into the water, bubble still intact after slamming the water. Hugh took Zoie's hand in his. "Want to jump in together?"

She shook her head. "I want to be able to do this on my own." She was trying to seem braver than she actually was. Comfortable with Hugh and not a fan of lying, she admitted, "Truly, I'm worried that you would accidentally pull me down farther than I'm comfortable with."

"Oh, bless your heart," Stevie teased.

He acknowledged her reasons and didn't try to push her any further. She was a little surprised that he didn't wait for her — he just dove right in. Zoie was pleased to see that his bubble didn't pop either.

She looked around the boat into the water to see what predators were in the area — and she realized that it was true that her companions gave off major predatory vibes.

She stood on the edge of the boat and squeaked. Then she stepped back again.

"Get in the water, Zo!" Hugh treaded water like it was nothing.

"The water's warm, Sugar! Come on in!"

Cayden was floating on their back without a care in the world. Zoie wondered if they would even care if the current took them away.

Zoie stepped up on the edge of the boat again and then jumped — screaming until she felt the water touch her body. She cautiously opened her eyes, even though she was under the water, to see if bubble was still there.

When she realized it was, she let go of the breath she was holding. She was simultaneously relieved and disappointed that there were no creatures in the water. Sure, she didn't want eaten by Megalodon, but she would like to at least see a starfish or something.

"You okay, Zoie?" Stevie asked.

Zoie looked around. "We can talk in these things?"

"Well, yeah. Sound travels pretty well in water…" She stopped. "Shhh… there's a whale song… it's miles away, but you can hear it. Listen."

Zoie smiled as she heard something much more beautiful that Dory's whale-speak in *Finding Nemo*. She was lost in the sound when she was suddenly yanked farther down towards the ocean floor.

She started to kick and scream; her arms flailed as she tried to swim to the surface of the water, however she was getting farther and farther under the water. She knew that if she hit her magic bubble that she was done.

She tried to remain calm, but it was pointless. The water was getting a darker blue, and she started to panic that she was never going to get away.

"No! No!" She started to cry, and then just shriek. "Nooooo!" Her heart was going to pound out of her ribcage.

Then, as fast as her descent began, it was over, and she found herself in Hugh's arms. *Finally — what took him so long?* She wondered. She just sobbed as she tried to catch her breath.

—Hugh—

Laughing, Hugh turned Zoie around so that she was facing him. "You're okay. I was just playing."

She punched him in the shoulder. "Asshole!" He immediately let her go and she swam away from him instinctively.

Stevie took Zoie's side instantly, grabbing her wrist and pulling her just behind her in the water. "That was a real dick move." She added, "I should snap away your bubble and let your ass drown."

"For fuck's sake, he was playing with her." Cayden swam over to Stevie, but she slapped them away with her fin.

They rubbed their arm. "Ouch! How did that even hurt?"

She smirked at them. "Did you forget that the water doesn't have the same power of resistance over me? Yeah, I'll smack you to hell and back if you try to pull something like that on me, and I'm native to the water."

"Promise?" They wiggled their eyebrows. Stevie rolled her eyes, disgusted by the immaturity.

Hugh swam to Zoie's side. "I'm sorry. I shouldn't have done that. I know how anxious you were." He reached out to take her hand.

She didn't accept his hand. "Can we go back to the boat?" Hugh could hear her heart pounding as the sound traveled through the water.

Hugh nodded. Wrapping his arm around her waist, he started swimming upwards, pulling her right along with him. At first, she tried to push away from him, but she stopped resisting when it was obvious that he could get her above the water more quickly than she could herself.

He helped her onto the boat and then apologized again. "I feel like I ruined everything." He took a fistful of the bubble, popping it — and, essentially, teaching Zoie how to remove the spell without patronizing her.

She took both hands and pulled from either side of her bubble, bracing for the break to send saltwater into her eyes. "I think you forget that I'm new to this world and…"

"…and mortal."

"That, too." She frowned. Opening the cooler, looking for a few seconds, and then shutting it without making a selection, Zoie sighed. "Are you sure there's no way?"

"We're born this way, Zoie. I'm sorry, but I can't make you like us." Hugh hated disappointing her. He hated it even more that he had to keep it to himself that she very well may be able to have this life with him. He just didn't know when — or even if — she would have that moment when she had to use her powers.

—Zoie—

She heard two splashes of water — that distinct splash of

128

someone exiting the water, so she looked over at Stevie, wanting to watch how her fin would change into legs, but decided to turn away. Zoie considered how that might be a private moment for a mermaid. She didn't want to intrude.

She walked over to the edge of the boat. "As much as it scares me down there, I wish I knew what was at the floor of the ocean."

"Do you want to find out?" Stevie toweled her hair off. Just as she finished, Cayden shook off like a dog and drenched her again. She shook her head, chuckled, and then toweled her hair off again.

"I mean, yeah, but I'm not sure that even you all have a submarine at the ready." She laughed and then finally selected a sandwich out of the cooler.

Stevie smiled. "Bless your heart."

"That wasn't a nice 'bless your heart'; that was a 'what an idiot'. So please tell me what I've missed." She took a bite of the sandwich and then added, "I mean, did I miss the sub tied up at the dock?" She looked around, almost sarcastic with her movement.

Hugh and Cayden laughed. Then Cayden added, "Zoie, you were just went diving without scuba gear. Do you underestimate Stevie's abilities?"

"I... I'm sorry..."

"Don't listen to Cade. You're new to our world."

"Do you think you could do it?" Hugh asked.

Stevie looked around the boat and thought for a moment. "I've done it before, but never with..." she motioned towards Zoie.

"I won't touch anything." Zoie sighed loudly. She was used to all of it already. The inexplicable suddenly having rational — if it could be called that — explanations. The secrets. The magic, and her being told to not interfere with said magic.

Stevie frowned, noticing how Zoie was feeling singled out. Still, she felt the need to explain the reason she had to give the warning. "This time I'm going to create a bubble around the entire boat, so, Zoie, yeah, if this bubble breaks and we're too low, not only will you be crushed by the pressure, but so will Hugh and Cade."

Stevie placed her hands in front of her as if she was holding a big beachball and closed her eyes. The boat shook ever so slightly and then the water started to rise above the sides of the boat.

Terrified that they were going to take on water, Zoie latched onto Hugh's arm. She watched as either the water continued to rise above the boat or, maybe, the boat was sinking below the water.

As the water arched over their heads and created a ceiling, a fish fell at their feet. "Do I release it back or will that be an issue?" Zoie picked it up and waited for the signal — a nod from Stevie. Then she tossed it back towards the wall of water before it wiggled out of her hands.

The boat travelled further down into the depths of the ocean, slowly at first — as Stevie gauged Zoie's potential reaction to increased pressure around the boat. The water grew a darker and darker blue until the only light was what was held in their own bubble.

Zoie was standing at the edge of the boat, holding the railing, when she saw a small light. She leaned forward to get a better look. Squinting her eyes, she tried to make out what was holding the light. She leaned further forward only to be inches from the wall of water — and inches from many rows of giant, pointy teeth.

Jumping back, she gasped and placed her hand over her mouth. "What was that?!"

Cayden belly laughed. "Anglerfish — judging by the size, a female." They continued to laugh, but admitted, "I did the same thing the first time that Stevie brought me down here."

Hugh waved Zoie over to the other side of the boat. "Check this out."

Zoie's eyes lit up as she saw long strings of light all meeting with a soft pink light in the form of a round pillow. "Jellyfish?" Hugh nodded, and she then pointed excitedly to its right. "There's an orange one."

"Aye, there's creatures down here that haven't even been discovered yet."

Stevie had been quiet most of the ride down, concentrating, but she happily spoke, "Welcome to The Abyss," as their vessel sunk further below what had appeared to be the ocean floor, but was actually just a thick cloud of sand.

Cayden smiled. "Glad to be home, Stevie?" She returned the smile with a nod.

"It's beautiful." Hugh smiled, looking out beyond the front of the boat.

"I don't see anything," Zoie whispered to Hugh.

Pointing to his left eye, Hugh replied, "Night vision, remember?" He pulled her close, placing a gentle kiss to her ear through her hair and whispered, "You'll be able to see soon."

After only a few moments, light — every color of light imaginable — came into Zoie's view, and she noticed that they were entering an enormous cave. "W-O-W," Zoie exclaimed slowly, as if every letter were its own syllable. "Stevie? This is where you're from?" She replied with a smile and a nod, and Zoie simply said, "No wonder you dress like the entire crayon box. Like, the 128 pack." She stood in the middle of the boat and turned, taking in everything. "Incredible."

—Hugh—

Hugh stood back and watched Zoie spin, and wiped a single tear from the corner of his eye before it could betray him. Watching his Zoie experience sea magic for the first time was an emotional sight for him. Perhaps her connection to it meant that she was a Moon witch — controlling water and air better than the Sun or Earth witches could.

Cayden elbowed him in the ribs. "Pull yourself together. Loser."

Hugh could never comprehend how Cayden evaded emotions so easily. Their ability to suppress emotions — to show just enough emotion to not seem cold — was impressive. But he did as suggested and focused on something else so that Zoie wouldn't see him crying over something as silly as her little dancing on the boat deck.

The boat came to a halt and slowly became engulfed in the larger overarching dome that protected the city. Hugh's desire to try and see things through Zoie's eyes — the child-like eyes of someone experiencing something for the very first time — allowed him to notice that the structure of the dome was more like that of hexagons placed flush against each other, rather than a smoothly rounded shape that he had remembered from his last visit to the Abyss.

He helped Zoie disembark the boat and continued to hold her hand as they walked from the dock into the town.

"Everything is so vibrant!" Zoie spun, still never letting go of his hand. "I mean, I have questions, though."

Stevie giggled. "Ask away."

"Aren't you afraid that the water mixed with the electricity of the lights…"

Stevie put her hand up like a stopping signal. "I'm gonna stop you right there. That's bioluminescent algae, Zoie."

"What?!" Zoie basically dragged Hugh over to get a better look at one of the store signs. She reached up to touch it, but Hugh grabbed her wrist and pulled it back. "Hey!"

"That can be deadly to humans." He turned her to face him, put his hands on her shoulders, then slid them down her arms, and took her hands in his. "Zoie, we aren't in Birmingham anymore. We're not even on the island. Everything here... Humans are curious but scared of the depths because things down here can and will hurt you or kill you." He added, "I once saw a vampire lick that stuff on a dare, and his mouth and tongue were swollen for a week!"

Zoie's eyes grew huge, like frightened moons. "Oh. I will stop touching things."

"Thank you," he replied, with exaggerated relief. He pulled her close to him and put his arm around her. Kissing the top of her head, he added, "I care very deeply for you, Zoie. If something happened to you, I would never forgive myself."

—Zoie—

As they walked further down the street, Zoie watched as Stevie greeted everyone. Everyone. Like, every single person — merfolk? — that she encountered.

"Why are they all nodding so politely at her?" She looked over at Cayden for an answer.

They smiled. "She's..." But before they could finish speaking, the answer presented itself.

"Shhh." Hugh bowed a little, so Zoie followed suit.

"Welcome home, my sweet girl," the woman, grey-haired but somehow still youthful, greeted Stevie, hugging her tightly.

"Missed you, Momma," she replied.

"That accent!" she exclaimed. "Where have you been all these years?"

Just as Stevie opened her mouth to speak, the man, bald (with a perfectly shaped head), still carrying that same youthfulness, suggested, "Why don't you and your friends join us for supper, and you can tell us all about your adventures over the last few decades?"

Stevie excitedly agreed, and the group of them followed the

pair of them back towards a large black building lit up with more of the bioluminescent algae.

"Madam?" A woman motioned to Zoie to follow her. "Let me show you to your room. You can relax for a bit. We'll have some clothes brought up for you."

Zoie looked to Hugh for guidance, and he nodded, albeit cautiously, that it was okay. "Can he not come with me?" Her voice was nervous.

"Oh no, madam. He'll be joining the King for some drinks once being made more presentable himself. Their Grace, Cayden, will be joining as well." She ushered Zoie down a long hallway.

As she opened the door to the room, revealing what was actually a suite, she asked Zoie if it was to her satisfaction. Zoie nodded. "I'm sorry, what's your name?"

"Clarice, if it pleases you, madam." She curtsied.

"Oh, you can call me Zoie. I'm no one special." She waved a dismissive hand.

"Yes, ma — Zoie." She nodded. "May I take your measurements so that I can send someone out for a more appropriate dinner outfit?"

"Oh, I guess I can't be going to dinner in my bathing suit," she laughed. "Yes."

Zoie decided to go wash the salty sea off of her the best she could the moment that she was alone. As she looked in the mirror, she hoped that she could wipe some of the sunburn away as well. It wasn't tomato red, by any means, but *sun-kissed* was an understatement.

She turned on the water and thought to herself how incredible it was that there was plumbing in this kingdom under the sea. She also noticed that the water seemed to be freshwater, rather than saltwater. Zoie made a mental note to ask about the mechanics of this later. Touching the water, she determined that the temperature was perfect, so she stepped out of her bathing suit and set it in the sink, making a mental note that she needed to rinse the saltwater out of it.

She stepped into the shower and let the water cascade over her and actually let out a bit of a moan because it felt so good to rinse the salt off of her body and out of her hair. She had a momentary panic when she realized that her shampoo and other products weren't with her, but she turned around to see that the shower was stocked with items. Of course it was. This was a castle.

Zoie didn't sing while she was in the shower: she thought. Sometimes it was thinking about conversations she had in third grade and how she could have handled them better. Sometimes it was what she would say as she accepted an award — usually for her incredible screenwriting (that she had never even attempted a career in). And, sometimes, she thought about the events of the day. As she shampooed her hair — twice because it was that filthy that the shampoo wouldn't even lather — she thought about how Stevie lived in a literal castle. A huge castle. Under the water. At the bottom of the ocean. Technically under the ocean floor. She was the real-world equivalent of The Little Mermaid. She made a mental note to ask Stevie why she never told her that she was a literal princess.

As she ran the conditioner through her hair, she started to think about how a week ago, she'd had no idea that this part of the world even existed outside of the books that she read and the stories that she wrote. She reminded herself that it was possible that instead of Hugh interfering at that show, maybe one of those men pushed her to the ground, causing her to hit her head. Maybe she was in a coma, dreaming all of this up.

She finished her shower and reached for a towel and realized that a cotton T-shirt was hanging within reach. Zoie wrapped her hair in that to dry, so that her waves wouldn't become overly frizzy, and then dried off lightly, put on the aloe-infused lotion that was nearby, and then grabbed the fluffy robe, also nearby.

She then went over to the sink and rinsed her bathing suit out with cold water and then hung it in the shower to dry. She walked back over to the sink to brush her teeth — and, as she had since she was a little girl, she started to growl like a rabid dog as the toothpaste frothed.

She leaned over to rinse and then, as she stood upright again, looked in the mirror. It was then that she noticed that black-hooded figure behind her again. She turned around and saw nothing, and then turned back to the mirror, and it was over her shoulder again. This time, the figure let out an evil, distorted snicker.

Panicked, Zoie turned around again, but the figure was gone, and when she turned back to the mirror, it was nowhere to be found in the reflection, either. Breathing heavily, she left the bathroom and sat on the bed.

Maybe it was too much sun, she thought. *Maybe it was something in the water or something I touched. Maybe I'm exhausted. Yeah, that's it.* After changing into the pajamas that were laid out for her, she lay down on the bed and closed her eyes, and she fell into a deep sleep as soon as her head hit the pillow.

—Hugh—

Hugh didn't really want to join the King for drinks. He didn't even want to take the time to get cleaned up, to be honest. What he wanted to do was sneak across the palace into Zoie's room. He didn't like to be separated from her. Under normal circumstances, he wouldn't follow what was expected of him, but he felt that it was better if he did this time. Better for Zoie. Safer for her. She still hadn't been registered since she had yet to discover her magic. Any upheaval, and the Abyss could decide singlehandedly on punishment for Zoie and him. They were the oldest, most powerful civilization, and were the tiebreakers in any impasse. Plus, the law was clear.

He opened the closet and was pleased to see that the clothing that he had left from a previous visit was already in the room for him. The team that worked the palace was always so quick to complete any request.

After getting a shower and changing into something more appropriate, Hugh realized he still had a little time to spare before joining the King for the usual drinks and cigars — which Hugh actually loathed — so he made his way across the palace to Zoie's room.

As he neared her room, he could hear her feet rustling the sheets; he knew she was sleeping. Still, he opened the door very quietly and peeked in on her.

He still went all the way in to be extra sure that she was okay. He closed the door very slowly and quietly, not even allowing it to click when he released the doorknob.

She was hugging a pillow, and he just had to see this much more closely. He quietly walked over to the bed, and gently pushed her hair behind her ear. She gasped at the touch but immediately went back to her normal breathing pattern.

He looked over at her dresser and noticed that there was a pen and paper, so he took the time to write her a little note and put it next to her glasses on the bedside table. He left just as quietly as he arrived.

On his way to meet with the King, he ran into Cayden. "Ready to do this?"

"Ugh, yes. I hate this part of it. But I do it for Stevie," Cayden admitted. "I don't think her parents like me much. I've visited here a few times, but I still get the impression that they would rather her make a match with another underwater civilization's royal family."

"Why do you feel that way?"

Cayden frowned. "Just the impression that I get."

Hugh didn't press the matter, but he had a feeling that Cayden would open up after they left the Abyss.

They approached the room where they were meeting the King, and both Hugh and Cayden took a deep breath just before entering.

"King Reon," Hugh greeted the King before taking a glass.

"Hugh; Cayden," he smiled. "Cigar?"

Both declined politely.

The King got right into it. "Davies, I hear you caused quite the stir recently in Tenatoria."

Hugh about choked on his drink. "Beg your pardon?"

"Alvin Irving's father. Jack. I heard you two had it out. I'm sure he was just confused." He took a puff of his cigar. "He's been... off... since before he had to raise that little boy on Alvin's behalf."

"Miles." Hugh was fairly certain that Reon knew this, especially since he worked directly with Alvin regularly. He looked at Cayden to try to determine how to proceed, but Cayden just shrugged.

"Ahh, that's right, little Miles." Reon took another puff of his cigar. "I guess he's not so little anymore. He's about 100 or something."

Hugh took a sip of the whiskey in his glass. "He's about 150 or more, I believe."

Reon smirked. "You would know, wouldn't you? You threw his mother's head at him when he was a child."

140

Hugh swished his whiskey in the glass. "Reon, what are you doing here?" He put down the glass and took the time to pull his hair back.

"Whatever do you mean?" He took a drink. "I just was stating facts." Reon added, "I just wonder if you have it out for the family is all."

Hugh tightened his jaw. "Of course I don't. I stay away from them as much as I can. I prefer to not engage in any conflict in my life, if at all possible. The incident with Jack was a simple misunderstanding. That's all."

"You know, Alvin didn't say what Jack said the argument was about…"

"King Reon," Cayden interjected. "Jack Irving is senile and a drunk. I'm sure whatever reason he started the argument for was just made up in his mind."

Reon smirked again. "So, my daughter's — what are you again? She calls you her partner, but I don't see how you could be. She is far above your station, you know?"

Cayden took a deep breath. "Stevie doesn't see it that way, and you should respect your daughter's decision."

"Stephanie will someday have to take over as Queen of the Deep. Are you prepared to take the place seated next to her? Are you ready to rule? Our people wouldn't even respect you. You're a shifter and have never even lived in the Deep."

"I will be ready when the time comes." Cayden's hand was shaking, so they put their glass down.

"I'm sure you believe that." Reon turned his attention back to Hugh. "So, this Zoie. Was she the cause of the *misunderstanding* between you and Jack?"

"She was new in Nightbrooke, er, Tenatoria. He didn't

141

recognize her and he wouldn't leave us alone. It was just a big misunderstanding." He downed the rest of his whiskey. "Speaking of Zoie, though, I would like to escort her to supper, so I'm going to go meet her at her room." He looked at Cayden. "Perhaps you would like to escort Stevie as well?"

Cayden nodded. "Would be my honor."

They exited quickly, and as soon as they were out of earshot, Cayden growled, "I hate that guy."

Hugh sighed. "Yeah, me too. But we're guests in his home, so we both need to harness our tempers."

—Zoie—

"It looks lovely, Miss Zoie," Clarice smiled. "It's very simple, but you make it much more than what it is."

Zoie smiled shyly. "Thank you." The dress was plain, just as Clarice had said. A little black dress with a pencil-skirt bottom that stopped right below the knees. The top had a deep V-neckline and the waist had some criss-crossing that made her look like she had an hourglass figure.

Clarice turned around and then presented a pair of earrings. "These pearls are from the underwater civilization off the coast of Japan. Princess Stephanie stated that she would allow you to borrow them if you would like."

"Oh!" Zoie was pleased to see that they were just studs. She rarely wore earrings, so anything larger would have perhaps been uncomfortable for her. "I'm shocked to see that Stevie — Princess Stephanie — has anything so..."

"Plain?" Clarice laughed. "Yes, she rarely wears these. It's usually very flashy or she just won't be satisfied." She then pulled out a necklace. "And here is the matching necklace."

Zoie shook her head. "No thanks. I always wear my crescent

moon."

Clarice nodded. "Yes, Miss Zoie." She then asked, "Bracelet?" When Zoie declined that, Clarice showed her where the shoe options were.

"Are there no flats?" Zoie asked.

Clarice was confused. "Miss Zoie, the ladies at court never wear flats. And while this isn't..."

"But..." Zoie whispered, "I *can't* walk in heels, Clarice." He cheeks flushed. "I sprained my ankle when I was younger and it never healed properly. I've never been able to walk in heels. What am I going to do?"

Clarice thought for a moment. "I'll see if one of the other lady's maids has a pair of black flats that you can borrow."

Zoie thanked Clarice and suggested, "They don't have to be black. Just because the dress is black, they don't have to be black. In fact, it may be better if they aren't, so that we don't have to worry about the blacks matching." Clarice nodded and exited.

Anxious that she was going to be forced to make a fool of herself in heels, Zoie went over to the bed and picked up the note that Hugh had left for her and read it again.

Zo —

Since meeting you, the

magic has returned to my life.

Love,

Hugh xx

She smiled and hugged the note to her chest. There was a faint knock at the door, so she sat the note back down quickly. "Come in."

"Miss Zoie, I was able to find these." Clarice presented three pairs of flats: black, red, and nude.

Zoie thought for a moment. "I'll take the black ones. They have a pointed toe, and I like that best." She put them on and looked in the mirror. "Yes, they will do just fine."

Zoie heard another soft knock at the door. "Zo?" Her heart skipped a beat at the sound of Hugh's voice.

"One second." She checked herself again in the mirror, admiring herself. She hadn't worn a dress in a really long time, and she wanted to take this moment to build her confidence. She took a couple of deep, cleansing breaths.

She then nodded at Clarice, who opened the door. "I'll leave you two alone."

Hugh shut the door and then put his jacket on a chair. He turned back to Zoie. "You look... very... wow."

Zoie wanted to tell him that he looked wow as well, but instead she replied, "What? Did the professor that has so many 'different words for beautiful' run out of words already?"

He laughed. "Yes. Yes, I did. There are not enough words to describe you right now." He presented a single flower. "This is for you."

She cautiously took it — after everything she had experienced in the past 48 hours, she wasn't sure what was truly safe for her to touch. After a moment's thought more, she realized that Hugh would never give her something that would harm her. The flower's stem was so white that it almost looked like it was radiating light itself. The petals were long and pointy. The pink hue actually pulsated at the veins in the petals and then radiated out towards the edges. "This is really... I've never seen a flower like this before."

"It's only grown here. I don't remember what it's called." He touched her chin very gently, so that she would look up at him. "I'm going to kiss you now."

She took his tie in her free hand. "You don't ever have to ask or

145

warn me." Then she tugged it playfully.

The moment that his lips met hers, she felt each burning flame of desire that had been lying dormant in her stomach wake up and announce its presence. Zoie thought about the electricity that Hugh felt when they touched. *Was he feeling it now? Was it painful? Why didn't she feel it, too?*

She was brought back into the moment when she felt his hand slide to the zipper on the back of her dress and start sliding it down.

She let out a laugh. "Hugh, I'll never get back in this dress if you take it off now."

Their lips were still touching, and she could feel his mischievous smile. "Not seeing the problem." He gave her another quick kiss and slid the zipper down farther before sliding it back up.

"You're so bad!" She laughed.

He fixed his tie in the mirror. "I'm pretty sure that's part of what you like about me."

She felt her cheeks get warm, so she turned away. "Why do you do this to me?"

"Because I think you're cute when you blush," he admitted as he put on his jacket. He offered her his hand. "Now, I've come to escort you to supper, Miss Zoie."

She placed her hand in his, feeling the warm touch of his skin once again. She took in a deep breath, as even such a simple thing could cause the flames to ignite around again.

The corridor was ridiculously long — the walls were overstuffed with expensive-looking art, but she could tell from the blank spaces that the walls were a very dark blue — almost black. The floors were the same color. The lighting was more bioluminescence; Zoie was nearly mesmerized by this phenomenon.

As they neared the dining room, Zoie stopped for a moment.

146

Hugh turned to her. "Everything okay?"

She took in a deep breath. "First of all, thank you so much for slowing down to walk beside me the entire time. You've always done that and you're the first man in my life to ever do this." She added, "There's such a big difference between our heights that I know that it is likely difficult for you..."

He smiled and kissed her hand. "My place is beside you. I wouldn't want to be anywhere else." She returned his smile, and he asked, "Was there a 'second of all'?"

She nodded. "I'm terrified. What if I use the wrong spoon?"

He chuckled. "Zoie, don't worry about it. Queen Zhenga is really nice and patient." As they started walking again, Hugh added, quietly, "King Reon is a fucking dick, though."

Zoie didn't have time to react because they were entering the dining room at that point.

The very first thing that she noticed was that the table — and the room — was absolutely enormous. They could seat probably 50 people at the table, but there were only six place settings all down at one end.

Then she saw Stevie, who was wearing a long dress that was dark purple with gold accents. Her hair even had a gold barrette in the shape of coral pulling back her hair on one side.

At the head of the table was, of course, King Reon, and to his right was Stevie, while to his left was Queen Zhenga. They, too, were dressed in purple.

Of course, next to Stevie was Cayden, and Zoie assumed that Hugh would be sitting between her and the Queen. But when they approached the table, the Queen motioned to the chair next to her and sweetly said, "Zoie, you're going to sit next to me." She explained, "I know it's out of the norm, but you're the only person here that

I don't know, and I would love to get to know you." She added, "Stephanie tells me that you've been a wonderful friend to her."

"Oh, Stevie's, er, Stephanie's really been the wonderful one."

"You can call me Stevie," she explained. "You don't have to use my proper name just because they do." She sighed. "Momma and Daddy are the only two that call me by my full name."

"It's a beautiful name, and the one we gave you," Zhenga gently teased her daughter. She turned to Zoie, "But, yes, you can call her Stevie."

Reon interrupted. "Let's get onto supper. I'm famished." He then gave a little speech of sorts.

Zoie wasn't paying as much attention as she should have been because Hugh had put his hand on her thigh, and she was doing everything she could to not react or even blush — as if she could control that.

"...so let's toast to my beautiful daughter, who has returned to us after such a long time of traveling."

Zoie had never had champagne before — let alone champagne from deep under the sea, so she had no idea what she was expecting. However, she was very pleasantly surprised to taste apple. She loved the flavor of apple, but didn't want to drink much more, as she had never drunk before and wanted to be able to keep her composure. She made the decision to stick to water for the rest of the dinner, if at all possible.

"So, Zoie," Zhenga asked, "Is this your first time at any of the Deep civilizations?"

Zoie took a deep breath. She knew, based on the conversations that she had overheard or had with Stevie, Cayden, and Hugh, that she needed to behave as if she belonged in this world. But she also knew that maintaining the closest possible answer to the truth was also vital. "Yes. This is the first time."

"Oh! What an honor that you chose the Abyss as your first! So tell me, what do you think?"

Zoie got excited. "It's *sooo* beautiful. I'm very much interested in the bioluminescent lighting, and, oddly enough, the plumbing."

Zhenga laughed. "Our plumbing?! What an odd thing to take an interest in. Are you a plumber when you are blending in with the mortals?"

Zoie shook her head. "No, no. I used to work in accounting, but, presently, I'm attending graduate school for creative writing."

Reon interjected, "Davies, isn't that what you do? Writing?"

Hugh politely answered, "Presently, I'm a Professor of Literature. That's where Zoie and I met."

"Dating one of your students, eh? You ol' dog, you!" Reon laughed. Zhenga tried her best to hide her disgust at Reon's reaction, but Zoie still caught it. He then asked, "Is that common practice in the mortal world? We don't allow that here." He added, "Just another reason we should stay away from those mortals. We really should. They are below us."

Hugh paused before answering. "To answer your first question, Zoie did not take any of my classes, so, no, she wasn't my student. And, no, it is not common for professors to date their students. In many places and institutions there are laws and policies against it." He put his hand on Zoie's leg again. "And, Reon, you know my feelings on our living amongst the mortals. I don't see what the issue would be."

Reon took a sip of his champagne and then sighed. "Davies, Davies, Davies. This is why Alvin Irving will not step down from his seat on the council. He feels that your beliefs in this area are too radical to give his seat to you."

149

Zoie felt Hugh tense up. "We know what the real reason is." The staff presented the next course, and Hugh took the opportunity to pull his hair back.

Zoie looked to Stevie for a moment, unsure of what to do, and then she just put her hand on Hugh's thigh, hoping to signal to him calm down.

"What reason is that?" Reon motioned for another glass of champagne.

Hugh cocked his head to the side ever so slightly, squinted his eyes, and asked, "Are you going to make me say it?" Reon motioned for him to continue, so Hugh said, "All right. You know he's power hungry. He just likes being in power."

Zhenga interjected. "Gentlemen, gentlemen. I think that's enough of the political talk. We ladies find this subject just an absolute bore. Are you with me? Stephanie? Zoie?" Both nodded in agreement. "Then it's unanimous. Let's talk about something else." She looked to Zoie. "Now, how long have you known that you're a witch?"

—Hugh—

Hugh's heart stopped, and he nearly choked. He hadn't prepared Zoie for this — and Zoie didn't know that she was a witch yet. He realized that he should have told her when they were alone in her room some story about it. That Stevie had told her mother that Zoie was a witch to keep the peace.

Barely missing a beat, Zoie replied, "Oh, not long. Maybe a week or so." She turned to Hugh. "Are you all right, *Dear*?"

He knew that she hated lying and that she also needed help. He nodded, and then added, "We aren't even sure yet what kind of magic she has her strength in."

Zhenga turned towards Zoie. "Well, isn't that exciting? I've

150

always taken a really big interest in witchcraft." She smiled. "I never told Stephanie this, but if I wasn't a mermaid, I would want to be a witch. A Moon witch, of course. Because they can manipulate water." She asked, "Do you have a preference on which you would hope to be?"

"Momma," Stevie interjected. "That's a lot of pressure to put on her. She's still learning about magic and things. She doesn't even know what they really do yet." She continued, "She just found out that magic exists."

"Forgive me." She then added, "But you're wearing that necklace. Maybe you secretly prefer the moon?"

"Or maybe it's a symbol for the howling dog next to her," Reon muttered under his breath.

Hugh closed his eyes and took in a deep breath. Under the table, Zoie took Hugh's hand. Then she chose to ignore Reon's comment, and she replied to Zhenga. "I have always loved the moon. In fact, I have always wanted to travel beyond Earth and find other civilizations, but then this past week happened, and I discovered that there's more to learn about this world right here."

Reon nodded and then asked, "Now, I assume you share the same views as your... as Hugh about the mortals?"

Zoie adjusted her napkin on her lap and replied, "Now, King Reon, with all due respect, the Queen has asked us not to engage in that topic at the supper table. I feel that we should respect that."

He smiled and looked to Hugh. "She's much more diplomatic than you are. Perhaps she can be a good influence on you. Help prepare you for the life that follows if ever Alvin Irving decides to take his leave from the council."

Hugh looked at Zoie, taking her hand under the table again, and replied to only the parts of Reon's statement that he wanted to. He never took his eyes off of Zoie. "She does make me a better man."

Hugh was taken out of his fixation on Zoie by the sound of a playful slap on Reon's arm. Zhenga smiled, "Now, why don't you look at me like that, Reon?"

Reon took another drink. "I think we have just found Mr. Davies' weakness."

"I disagree," Cayden interjected. "I think you've found his strength."

Stevie rose a glass in the air. "I'll drink to that!"

Zhenga agreed. "Yes, yes. To new love." Then she looked to Reon, "and love that still feels new after centuries." After everyone drank, she said, "Girls, after supper, perhaps I'll tell you how to keep…"

Stevie interrupted her. "Momma, I'm going to stop you right there. I don't even want to think of you and Daddy like that…"

Zhenga put her hand to her mouth in shock. "Stephanie, I meant nothing of the sort. I, young lady, am a queen, and would never discuss such improper things at the supper table. I was suggesting how to keep them in line when they act up."

Stevie looked at Zoie. "*Suuuurrrreeeee* she was."

Zoie giggled and reached over to Hugh again. As soon as her hand hit his leg, he felt the electricity shoot through him. He was starting to realize that the manner in which they touched determined the amount of electricity between them. If their contact was one that was more of a signal, it would be minimal, but if their embrace was loving or full of desire, it would radiate throughout his entire body. This difference would prove very useful as they lived their life together and encountered different situations — some that might even be dangerous.

Reon began to ask Stevie to share what she had been doing

since her last visit, and she began telling stories about how she met Cayden and then Hugh and about living in the Deep South. Hugh didn't pay much attention to the stories because he was focused on Zoie and getting through the rest of this ridiculous meal with 17 spoons without an all-out argument with Reon.

The staff brought them each a bowl of chocolate ice cream, and Hugh thought, *Finally. Dessert. We're almost done with this.*

"Zoie," Zhenga stated, "This chocolate ice cream is an Abyss specialty."

Zoie smiled. "This is exciting! I love ice cream."

"I'm interested in if you can determine what the secret ingredient is." Zhenga took a big spoonful of the ice cream and let out an *mmmmmm* sound. "I swear, sometimes this ice cream is better than…"

"If you say *sex*, I swear to Triton that I will never return to visit ever again," Stevie said. "Ever."

Cayden, who was mostly silent during the entire supper, busted out laughing. "I'm sorry; I'm sorry!" They kept laughing. "I don't know why that was the thing that… hahaha."

Hugh chuckled. "Was it the swearing to *Triton* or the overall theme of the statement?"

Cayden was still laughing. "I don't know." They waved off their face. "I think that paired with the earlier statement that was *allegedly* about keeping your man in line."

At this point, Reon was staring at the pair of them, but Hugh really didn't care. If he had said it once, he had said it a thousand times: he hated that guy.

Suddenly, seemingly out of nowhere, Zoie announced, "Seaweed!"

Zhenga clapped, excitedly. "Yes! That's the secret ingredient.

153

How did you know?"

"I love sushi, and seaweed is part of the wrap." She took another bite of the ice cream.

Reon put his spoon down. "So you eat fish and other sea creatures, Zoie?"

Her eyes grew wide, and Hugh felt her heartbeat increase speed even without touching her. He put his hand on Zoie's back. "Reon is just joking." He glared at Reon. "I've had many meals with him where he's eaten shellfish."

"Daddy, that was mean," Stevie protested.

He chuckled, "She's fine. I can tell that she's tough and will rebound quickly." Then he looked over at Zoie. "I was just teasing. It means I like you. If I stop doing that," he looked at Hugh, "then you should be concerned."

Hugh rolled his eyes. "I think we should retire soon, Zoie."

"You're staying in the palace again, right?" Stevie pleaded.

"Do stay!" Zhenga encouraged. "In fact, you should stay for a bit so Zoie can develop her magic. I've always wanted to see how a witch learns her magic." She turned to Zoie. "I insist."

"Oh, I don't know. I wouldn't want to impose." She turned to Hugh, her eyes wide with concern.

Hugh had to navigate this carefully. For one thing, he knew that Zoie was concerned because she didn't know that she had any supernatural abilities and was afraid she couldn't keep up the charade. On the other hand, it would be a great place for her to learn about magic. "Perhaps a few days wouldn't hurt anything. I really think that you would love learning about the Abyss and the magic down here. You could at least explore water magic."

"Then it's settled!" Zhenga clapped. She called over her lady's maid. "Please make sure their rooms are all fully stocked." She added, "I believe Hugh and Cayden have clothing and other essentials here, but Miss Zoie does not. Her lady's maid has her measurements."

"Oh, I can't…" She looked at Hugh. "I can't just have them get me more clothing." She turned back to Zhenga. "Please tell me how much the items are…"

"Oh, how is it that you say it, Stevie? *Bless your heart?*"

"Yes, *Bless your heart.*" Stevie explained to Zoie, "My mother is offering you a gift, and it would be rude to not accept a gift from the Queen." She then added, "Your money, from America… it's no good here, Zoie."

"Oh."

Zhenga took one of Zoie's hands. "You are just precious. I am thrilled to have a new witch staying with us." She added, "I never got to grow up mortal and have that ripped out from under me. It must be quite the maelstrom of a journey, and I'm looking forward to learning all about it."

Reon rolled his eyes and groaned. "It's getting late, Zhenga. We should let Stephanie and her friends do whatever it is that young people do in the evenings nowadays."

As soon as they were excused from the dining room, Hugh loosened his tie. He looked over at Zoie as they walked towards her room. "You did very well tonight." He added, "Reon liked you. That's actually pretty rare, especially since you're not from the Deep. But be careful. He's not to be trusted, and he can change his opinion in a second."

As soon as they got into her room and locked the door, Hugh threw his jacket and tie onto the chair. He watched Zoie contort her body to try and unzip her dress. "Zo." She turned and looked him. He smiled and motioned for her to come over to him. "Let me help." She stood with her back to him and moved her hair. He kissed her neck and slowly slid down the zipper.

"Why does Zhenga think I'm a witch?" She asked.

He took in a deep breath. "Stevie told her that because you shouldn't be here if you aren't." So, he was going the route of lying, despite not wanting to. However, in interest of protecting her, he knew it was the only way. He began to slide the straps of her dress off of her shoulders. "Do we have to talk about this right now?"

She turned around and started unbuttoning his shirt. Well, she unbuttoned the top button. "I think I'll be distracted if we don't." Then the second one. "You know me and all my questions."

He paused. "Ask. Anything that is distracting you. Get all of the questions out right now." He kissed her. "I have thought about nothing more than getting you out of that dress since I first saw you in it, so ask quickly, please."

She smiled. "Oh?" She pretended to think hard. "How am I going to continue to pretend to have magic while down here, if I don't have any?"

"Just really, really try. Act as if you believe you have magic and try." Not only was this good advice for trying to keep up the act, it could actually help them figure out if they could eliminate or, even better, solidify, Moon magic as her magic source.

She unbuttoned one more of his buttons. "And what happens when I can do nothing?"

"Then you don't have Water magic. They'll believe that."

She unbuttoned another. "What about the other kinds of magic?" She pushed him so that he would sit on the bed.

He pulled her closer. "You couldn't possibly do Sun magic down here. The Sun's rays don't reach down here, so you'd have no way to harness it."

Another button.

"And they don't know how to do Sun or Earth magic anyways." He slid her straps completely off of her arms, dropping her dress to a pile on the floor. "I get to ask a question."

"Okay."

"Are you going to keep stalling much longer because wolves are not known for our restraint." He pulled her closer, kissed her neck and growled in her ear.

She shivered at his low growl. "I like having this power over you." She tried to walk away from him, but he pulled her back and quickly flipped them over so that her back was on the bed and he was over her.

"Do you still feel like you're in charge?"

She looked into his eyes. "I know I am." She pulled him into a kiss. "You would never hurt me."

"Sure about that?" He kissed her and then bit gently on her lower lip drawing a moan out of her.

Then she giggled. "You win. You win!"

"Zoie." He looked in her eyes. "I hope you know that this — us — it's forever for me." She bit her lower lip and looked away, so he rolled onto his side, facing her. "What's wrong?"

—Zoie—

Zoie took a deep, shaky breath in. "Is it just because of this mating bond you feel, or would you choose me without it?" She had to be sure. Even if she didn't fully understand things, she needed to know if he felt like he would have chosen her if his body didn't command him to.

"The mating bond makes everything move faster emotionally for me, but Zoie," he pushed her hair out of her face, "I would get there without it." He ran his fingers up and down her arm. "Getting to know you — even in this completely abnormal way that we have — I know that I would fall for you without the mating bond."

She closed her eyes. "Hugh, I… I moved to Birmingham because I never wanted to fall in love again. And I thought if I got away from everything and started over, I could do that. That I could be independent."

"Hey," he took her hand in his. "I will go as slowly as you want." He added, "and I would never dare take away your independence."

Her lip started shake. "What if I never get there?" Then she started to cry. "Or, worse, what if I do and then you realize that you were wrong and you find someone else? Or, even worse, when I get old, you fall out of love with me because I go grey and get wrinkles…"

"It doesn't work like that, Zo." He put her hand on his chest over his heart. "Do you feel that? That heart? It's yours. Forever."

"But what about if I don't look like this forever? I could…"

He smiled. "What? Gain weight? Lose weight? Age?" He chuckled, "Get a scar or two? I think it would be hypocritical of me to hold an imperfection against you. Don't you?" He stared into her soul. "Zoie, I think it's pretty obvious that I think you're gorgeous and that I want you. But the outside parts, they aren't everything. I mean, they don't hurt, and, while I love looking at you, the stuff in your head and your heart — that's the stuff that I am falling in love with."

Hugh pulled her closer. "You are so, so, so brave. Do you realize that you are in the deepest part of the ocean? Deeper than the rest of the world knows even exists. Humans don't come here. They can't. And if they could, the vast majority would decline because one tiny little leak in their vessel and they're done. You are bold; you essentially told a king — in his own home — today that you didn't care what he wanted to talk about, you were not accepting his topic." He added, "That was really hot by the way." Hugh pulled her closer again and then rolled onto his back so that she was on top of him. "I will love and protect you until the day I die…" he laughed, "Well, the day I die *again*."

The fire that she felt for him started to burn stronger. "You promise?" She held her pinky out.

He hooked his with hers. "I promise."

She unbuttoned the last two buttons of his shirt. "Show me."

"Gladly."

———————

Zoie woke up to the sound of a knock at the door. She went to get out of bed, but Hugh held her close, restricting her movement. "Let them knock. Stay here next to me." His eyes were still closed.

Another knock. "Zoie, it's Stevie."

"One sec."

"Let us sleep!" Hugh called out.

Zoie threw on the first articles of clothing she could find and opened the door just a little bit. "Good morning."

Stevie pushed her way in. In an angry but hushed tone, she said, "Hugh, you are *not* supposed to be in here. My father would throw a fit if he knew you were in here."

He laughed. "Is he worried about her virtue?" He rolled his eyes. "Can you turn around so I can get dressed?" He sarcastically added, "I mean, I know I'm a … how do you describe that actor you like, Zoie? A super mega hottie? Regardless, Stevie, all this is for Zoie's eyes only."

Stevie rolled her eyes and turned around. "Yeah, you aren't my type." She continued to talk while looking at the door. "So, Zoie, today we're going to go to walk around the city a bit, so you can see the Abyss, and while we're out and about, you and I will talk about how to proceed with the magic part of things."

Hugh interjected, "Stevie, I had forgotten to tell Zo before dinner that you told your mom that she was a witch. But I told her after." He added, "Oh, you don't have to look at the door anymore. I'm decent."

Stevie nodded slowly. "Oh! Yeah, Zoie, I'm really sorry I didn't give you the head's up on that one. It's just better for everyone all around that she believes you're a witch."

Hugh pulled Zoie close. "I'll see you later. Enjoy your day with Stevie." He leaned over to kiss her, and she got on her tiptoes to meet him. As he grabbed the doorknob, he turned to Stevie. "Take care of her." He looked back at Zoie again. "I will see you this evening."

There was another knock at the door. "Miss Zoie?"

Zoie opened the door. "Good morning, Clarice."

"Just getting out of bed at this hour? You must have been exhausted after your trip yesterday."

Stevie laughed. "Clarice, you don't have to be proper in front of me. We all know she was up late with her boyfriend, thanks to that killer dress you got her yesterday."

Clarice smiled. "It's not my place to say anything." She turned to Zoie. "I brought you some more comfortable choices for the next three days." She then showed her the shoes and smiled proudly. "No heels."

"Thank you so, so, so, *sooooo* much!" Zoie laid everything out on the bed and started to make her decisions.

Clarice asked, "I don't think that you will need me for any of these. May I take my leave at this time?"

"Oh, of course. I appreciate all that you do." Clarice exited and then Zoie turned to Stevie. "Okay, so what is the weather like out there? So I can pick the correct outfit."

Stevie shifted her eyes back and forth. "The same as it was yesterday. We have climate control down here." She then asked, "How long do you think it will take you to get ready?"

"Honestly? 45 minutes?"

"I'll see you at the front door in 45 minutes then."

—Hugh—

As he made his way from Zoie's room to his, Hugh ran into Cayden. "Where were you? Wait! Did you stay in Zoie's room all night?"

Hugh waved Cayden off. "Your girlfriend already gave me the lecture." He added, "Besides, it's not like we haven't slept in the same room before."

Cayden shrugged. "True. But you're already on thin ice with Reon."

"What's he going to do? Kick me out of his house? Ooooh. *Scary.* If he does, I will just take the portal and go home." He added, "And I would take Zoie, and that would make Zhenga upset. And, let's face it, while Reon's a hard ass, we all know that Zhenga is in charge down here."

"True. She does get everything she wants." Then they asked, "What's the plan for today?"

"Well, I was going to sleep the day away with Zoie, but Stevie killed that." He rubbed the sleep out of his eyes and then grabbed his doorknob.

"We need to figure out…"

Hugh grabbed Cayden by the wrist and pulled them into the room. "Shhhhh." He checked the hallway and then shut the door. "We need to be careful. I don't trust anyone in this city, and it's actually against my better judgment to let Zoie out of my sight while we're here." He let out an annoyed sigh. "We're lucky that Zhenga sensed the witch in Zoie and even more lucky that Zoie handled that properly."

"Well, maybe we should figure out sooner rather than later how we can test her. The sooner we find her magic, the sooner that we can get her registered and put this mess behind us." They walked over to the window of the room. "Every time I visit here, it feels like... I just don't feel welcome here."

"Is this about Reon and the shit he said in the study? Ignore him."

Cayden turned around. "Hugh, you act like he doesn't scare you, but he has to. You're more afraid of him than you want to admit or you wouldn't have yanked me into this room like a rag doll." They reminded him, turning around, "How many times have you and I stood in the center of NightBrooke and watched Reon stand on that stage and turn someone into stone?"

Hugh knew, deep down, that Cayden was right. Reon was to be feared, and Hugh would be foolish not to recognize that. "He can't make that call alone."

Cayden scoffed. "Hugh. C'mon. The witches help him every time. The Vampires are more strict about the law we've broken than anyone else besides maybe Reon himself, and he obviously has Alvin in his back pocket. Be logical about this. He can and does." They added, "When was the last time that Alvin voted against Reon? Right there, it's at minimum a tie, and Reon gets the tiebreaker vote because their civilization is the oldest."

164

"It's a stupid way of doing it."

"Doesn't matter. It's the way it's done." They walked to the door and grabbed the doorknob. "If you want things to change, you need to get Alvin out of the way." Cayden left quickly.

—Zoie—

"Why do you keep everything so... dark... here? Everything is black or dark blue. The floors, the walls, the ceilings. Everything. The only colors are the bioluminescence." Zoie inspected a unique fruit at one of the carts in the market.

Stevie thought for a moment. "I think it has to do with how everything this far down is that color out there because there's no light." She reminded Zoie, "Remember when we were coming down here?"

"That was incredible, by the way. How you did that — it was... just... incredible." She was at a loss for words. "I wish I could do that."

"Aw, thanks. That was the first time I attempted something on such a great scale," she admitted. She turned to Zoie. "I was actually petrified doing that. I was afraid that I would lose concentration and, well, that would have not been good."

Zoie wanted to help her friend's confidence a little. "You seem to have the magic thing well under control, Stevie. Have you always been able to harness all of your power so well?"

Stevie laughed and nudged Zoie with her elbow. "I'm not even all that powerful. I had to practice a lot. For decades. That bubble thing? You remember that?" Zoie nodded. "That took me like five years to perfect." She frowned. "My father used to get really frustrated. Apparently magic came easily to him."

"I wish I could do some magic," Zoie pouted.

Stevie stopped. "Zoie, I believe that every woman has a little bit of magic in her."

Zoie blew the comment off. "That's ridiculous."

Stevie pointed over to the bakery. "Do you see the baker behind the counter? That's Mona. She really doesn't have a lot of magic in her. She can barely bend water. But somehow, if her dough is too dry, she can make the water multiply to the *exact* right amount. She can remove water if it's too wet." She continued, "I once saw her remove some of the liquid in an egg white because it was three drops of wetness too much."

"That's really cool, though."

"But she can only do it when she's baking," Stevie explained. Then she pointed at a woman who was working in a crane on some bioluminescence. "Jo can only manipulate the liquid within bioluminescence." She pointed at another woman who was pushing two children in a stroller and holding the hand of another. She got really close to Zoie and whispered, "That's Francesca. She doesn't have any water magic, but she sure as hell has some sort of magic over the men in her life and she knows the secret to staying perfect. She has three more children at home. She doesn't have a single grey hair or wrinkle. How does she do it? It has to be some sort of magic."

Zoie rolled her eyes. "She probably is up moving all day running after children and never gets a chance to eat and secretly loves it."

She looked at Zoie. "I bet if we tapped into your very core, you would have some little bit of magic too. I'm telling you, all women possess magic."

Zoie laughed again. "Stevie, I know you're trying to humor me." She looped her arm with Stevie's. "I appreciate that you know how badly I want to have an extraordinarily long life with Hugh, and I think it's sweet that you're playing into that." She added, "and for his sake — and you and Cade's — your safety, I will play with the little charade with your mom."

"Zoie, if you don't actually put the effort in and try to believe you can do it, my mom is going to know that something's up. We have to be as convincing as possible." She asked, "Don't you want to have magic? To have all those candles and stones and herbs mean something? To truly believe that water that you charged in the moonlight holds some power?"

Zoie sighed. "You know I do. But you also know that if I can't do it — I'm sorry, *when* I can't — I'm going to be disappointed." She looked down at her shoes. "Heartbroken." She took a seat on a black bench that was against a black storefront. She adjusted herself so that her right leg was bent and her ankle was under her left thigh. She placed her hands in her lap.

Stevie sat down and put her hand on top of Zoie's. "What's wrong?"

Zoie actually burst into tears. She yanked her hands from Stevie's and put them to her face. "It's so much pressure."

"Zoie, what do you mean?"

"I have to convincingly pretend to really try to do magic, and I don't even know what that feels like or how to behave." She looked up towards the ceiling of the black dome to try and stop crying.

Stevie shook her head. "Everyone does magic differently, and learning how it feels is a part of the training. My parents will never know that you're not..."

"Legitimate." She started crying again.

Stevie put her hand on Zoie's shoulder. "What's *really* going on?"

"I think I'm just sleepy," she lied. Zoie just didn't want to admit the silly reason she was upset.

Stevie didn't buy it. "There's something more going on here."

Zoie tried to regain some composure, but it just made her more shaky. "If I can't do this — if I can't make this happen — I just think about in *Twilight* when Bella says to Edward that he won't want her when she looks like a grandmother…"

Stevie put her arms around Zoie. "That's just a story, Zoie."

"Is it?" Zoie dramatically waved her hand out towards the world around them. "A week or so ago, I would have agreed with you."

"So, more or less, you're telling me that you, deep down, hope that something is triggered in you while we're playing this charade?" She asked.

Zoie nodded.

"And it's because you're afraid to age beyond Hugh?"

She nodded again. Hugh had reassured her the night before, and, as much as she wanted to believe him — in fact, she did believe him — it just didn't win the battle against her own self-image.

"Zoie, if you want to do this just because you're worried that Hugh will fall out of love with you, well… First of all, you're wrong. And," she forced her friend to look at her, "most importantly, you'd be doing it for the wrong reasons."

"What would the right reason be?" She pulled her sleeves down over her hands and started to rub the tears off of her cheeks.

"I could easily come up with several. Because you have dozens of books on witchcraft in your house. Because you made me buy you candles so you could do a protection spell before we went out on the boat. Because you manifest things according to the moon. Because you've actually charged water in the sun. Because, Zoie, you actually believe in this shit." She added, "You want to act like it's all fun and games for you. That it's something silly. But you don't really feel that way, do you?"

168

She shook her head very slightly. Almost unnoticeable. "No," she said quietly. "No, I don't feel that way."

"Then let's get up and go to the pools behind the castle. My mother likes to spend time there, and I'm certain that she would love to tell you about water magic." She stood up and offered Zoie her hand. "But first, we gotta get you a different shirt and fix your make up. You look like you are an early 2000s emo teen."

Zoie tried to laugh, but her breathing still had that weird sob breath that people did even after they had stopped crying. "I used to want to marry Gerard Way. You know, from My Chemical Romance?"

"Ew, really, Zoie?" Stevie asked. "He looks like a vampire."

"What's wrong with that?!"

Stevie about gagged. "They aren't even alive. Like... they are the only supernatural being that is kind of true to their folklore."

"So a vampire could bite me and I..."

Stevie cut her off. "No. That part's not true." She thought for a moment while they continued to walk back to the palace. "To be honest, becoming a vampire's actually quite romantic. Someone has to be dead — like really, really dead." She looked totally serious. "Like. Dead."

"Okay. I get it. Dead as a doornail."

"Deader." She hummed a little tune while she thought. "You know Sleeping Beauty and Snow White?"

"Yeah?"

"They weren't dead enough. BUT!" She put her finger in the air as if she just had an idea. "But the theory is similar. True Love's First Kiss."

"What?!" Zoie stopped walking.

Stevie motioned for Zoie to come along. "People here don't like hearing about them. There's stories of other underwater civilizations that the Vampires have wiped out. Let's walk and talk, okay?" Zoie nodded and started walking again, so Stevie continued. "Anyways, the only way that a vampire can be created is if they are kissed by a vampire — on the mouth — after they are dead. Like, gross, am I right? Something about the venom and the lips being such a thin membrane. I don't know the science of it."

"Okay so can we maybe find one of these vampires and maybe have them agree to..."

She shook her head. "No, it doesn't work that way. They actually have to be bonded with the person that they are making."

"Like me and Hugh?"

She nodded. "It's so weird. Like, how do you know if you're bonded with a corpse?" She quickly said, "And I know your next question — but be real. What human is really going to hang out with a Vampire? They are their *food*." She then quickly added, "Don't say Bella Swan."

Zoie just shrugged. Off the top of her head, she couldn't think of any other character — but she thought about how, if Hugh was a vampire, against her better judgment and as much as she hated to admit, she could picture herself clinging to him, even though she would be his food.

They made their way back through the little market and two the palace. "We'll just take the path around the side," Stevie suggested. "It's really pretty once we get towards the back."

As they made their way around the left side of the black palace, Zoie actually felt as if she was being led to her death. It was difficult to see anything in front of her because there was no bioluminescence to light their path.

But just as soon as it got darker than Zoie thought it could get, everything became bright again. The flowers were illuminated like the one that Hugh had given her before dinner. The pulsating colors flowed in such a way that Zoie imagined that they were dancing to a secret song that they could only hear.

The path led further behind the palace to a large pond of water silver with shimmers of rainbow that it looked like liquid metal mixed with a little bit of oil swirling around on the ground.

Zhenga sat on a stone bench, reading a book. She was so engrossed in it, she didn't even look up when Stevie sat down next to her.

"Momma?"

"EEK!" Zhenga's book went up in the air. "Stevie!" She put her hand on her chest. "You scared me!"

Stevie shrieked with laughter. "You should have seen your face!"

Zoie tried to keep a straight face, but she couldn't. So she took it upon herself to walk behind the bench to pick up Zhenga's book. She smiled when she saw that it was a romance novel — one that she recognized from her mom's shelf: *Lovestorm*. She did her best to stifle a giggle.

Zhenga wasn't even ashamed. "I've read this one dozens of times," she admitted. "Stevie makes fun of me." She swatted her with the book. "What kinds of books do you like to read, Zoie?"

"Oh, all kinds. But I really like…" she trailed off for a moment. "I really like stories about werewolves and vampires and other creatures." She blushed slightly.

Zhenga smiled. "Well, I imagine you were surprised when you not only found out that they were real, but also that you were a part of that world!" She then asked, "Do you know the legends and history of water magic?"

Zoie shook her head. "I mean, I don't think that I do. I know the stories I was told growing up." She tried to think about what she knew. "But I don't think any of the stories I've ever been told the parts about how magic came to be."

"Aaaahhhhh." Zhenga turned towards the pond and waved her hand three times, pulling one large ball of water out and two smaller ones, floating them in the air above the water. "As you probably know, all life started in the sea on this planet. That life evolved and eventually left the water, creating the dinosaurs." The large sphere of water started rotating, and the two smaller ones started circling it. "But what they don't tell you is the true story about what ended the dinosaurs."

"Well, I don't think they know, but they have several theories," Zoie stated.

Zhenga shook her head. "No, we know." She explained, "The most powerful Sun witch is able to manipulate time enough to go back to see what caused that mass extinction."

"What? Sun witches can manipulate time?" Zoie asked.

"Sun witches can manipulate time and space and also harness fire." She clarified, "Most sun witches can only go back or forward a few minutes. Usually not even that far."

"Oh," Zoie replied slowly.

Stevie interjected, "I never thought — Zoie, do you know about the different kinds of witches and what they do?"

"No, I honestly don't," she admitted.

The Queen smiled. "Well, you certainly are in the right place to find out. I've studied witches extensively." She asked, "Would you like for me to continue with the history or take a brief detour and explain the types of witches' magic?" She didn't even wait for an answer. "You need to know it all. As you just found out, the Sun witches mess with time and space and also fire. So déjà vu? That's a bit of witchcraft."

172

"Really?!" Zoie's eyes got huge.

Zhenga nodded. "Yes, if you've ever experienced that or maybe walking into a room and forgetting why you were there — it's because a witch manipulated your mind."

Zoie sat down on the bench. "Tell me more."

Stevie's smile beamed from ear to ear. "I'm so excited you want to learn about this, Zoie."

"Yes." Zhenga clapped a little out of excitement. "I'm so thrilled that I may be able to help you find what kind of magic is yours."

Zoie's smile fell. She hated lying. Especially to Zhenga, who had been nothing but kind to her. She had opened her home and also was willing to take time out of her day — which had to be busy as a queen — to teach magic to Zoie, and it was all under false pretenses.

"What's wrong, Zoie?" Zhenga asked.

Snapping back into reality, Zoie responded, "I just don't know how I will know which magic is for me?"

"Well, the witches can do all types of magic, but they are drawn to one more than others and they can wield it much better." She explained, "For example, if you're an Earth witch, you would be able to create potions with ease and manipulate the plants and trees to do your bidding. That being said, you would still be able to, I don't know, manipulate water, but it just wouldn't be as powerful or easy for you." She took Zoie's hand. "I secretly hope you do Moon magic because you would be able to manipulate water like us mermaids." She giggled a little. "Now, back to the history."

Zoie nodded. "Please."

She pointed their attention back to the three floating spheres of water that had never stopped rotating the entire time they were talking. "Back when the Earth had formed, there used to be two moons. I'm sure you know that the phases of the moon possess different strengths for magic?"

Zoie nodded. "I do know that. Back before I knew," she hesitated, trying to think about a way to not lie but still stick to the story. "Well, back before I became a part of this world, I was very interested in moonology and astrology."

She smiled. "Wonderful! There's a base to start with." She continued. "Well, as you know the moon — well, in this case, moons — were satellites to the Earth. But much like the moon we know now is slowly separating from our planet, the other, slightly smaller moon, was being pulled in."

"Really?" Zoie knew the science that she had been taught, but she loved a good conspiracy theory. With that being said, her reality had changed very quickly over the past week, so she wasn't counting Zhenga's story out.

Zhenga nodded. She twisted her wrist very quickly, and one of the small spheres started slowly getting closer to the large one with each rotation around it. "Eventually, it couldn't fight the gravity from the Earth, and, well…" She moved her index finger slightly, and the smaller sphere collided with the large one, causing a large splash and ripples. "The moon collided with the Earth. Some of the debris spread into the air and onto the lands of Pangaea, while the rest flew into the Great Ocean."

"And that moon rock created…" Zoie spoke cautiously, concerned that she didn't fully understand the story.

Zhenga smiled. "The pieces on land provided moon magic to land creatures that eventually evolved into the Moon witches we know today. The pieces that went into the Great Ocean — well, those are what created what would become the perfect creatures that you see before you." She flipped her hair a little, intentionally being jokingly dramatic about her beauty. She then waved her hand downward, knocking the spheres of water back into the pond.

"So, Stevie had mentioned to me that you all can manipulate water, but do you have the power over the air, too?"

She shook her head. "We do not have that power."

Stevie interjected, "I believe it's because our ancestors were underwater so long that the power over air never had an opportunity to develop, so it was lost."

"Very good point, Stephanie." Zhenga nodded. She turned to Zoie. "If you don't work with your power and practice, you will lose it, Zoie."

"Are you ready to try?" Stevie asked.

Zoie's jaw dropped and her eyes got huge. "I mean, I don't even know where to draw the power from."

Zhenga stood and motioned for both ladies to stand with her. "I think that everyone draws their power from a little bit of a different place, but any time I've ever spoken to someone about it, it usually seems to manifest somewhere from the shoulders to hips." She seriously said, "Never the head or brain."

"If they are stuck in their brain, it will never be right," Stevie reinforced, subtly telling Zoie to get out of her head.

Placing her index finger on her lips, Zhenga concentrated for a moment. "Let's start with something very simple. Just a little test to see if water magic is a strength for you." She reiterated, "I promise, this is beginner level."

—Hugh—

After lying on his bed and staring at the ceiling for what seemed like half the day, Hugh sat up. He couldn't spend one more minute trying to find a way to change the rules of their world. The solution that kept coming to him was not one that he even wanted to explore. He pushed it to the back of his mind and walked over to the window in his room.

It overlooked the large silver pond behind the castle. He smiled as he saw Zoie standing between Zhenga and Stevie. He selfishly wanted her to discover her magic down here so that this whole thing could stop. He would take her to get registered in their secret city, and then avoid any fear.

But he had a feeling that her magical talents lay elsewhere — in a type of magic that she would have to explore above the surface of the water.

Hugh wanted to go see what kind of progress they were making down there at the pond — and he wanted to be present at the moment that Zoie discovered her magic. If it was Moon magic, she would discover it with that silver water, which meant he had better get down there.

Opening his closet door, he looked at his choices. Several suits for those pretentious dinner parties that he would have to sit through basically screamed in his face. He sifted through them to finally find a pair of jeans and a black V-neck T-shirt. He found in a back corner a handkerchief of his clan's tartan — which he knew that Stevie or Cayden must have acquired and hid for him at some point over the past few decades of their friendship. He shoved it in his back pocket and found shoes and headed down to the garden.

He approached slowly, as to not interrupt, and, if he was honest with himself, to spy.

"...so when I was learning, I would rub my hands together really hard and fast and then pull them apart." Stevie demonstrated. "You'll be able to feel your magic then."

Zoie did it and then giggled. "That's just friction and..."

Zhenga shook her head and waved her finger a little. "No, no. I think we have a non-believer in our little circle here."

"Zoie, I told you: All women possess a little magic." Stevie encouraged her to do it again.

Hugh stepped closer, still hiding behind a brightly illuminated bush.

"...If you need to close your eyes, do it," Zhenga suggested. "It may help you clear your mind right now. But don't get used to doing that. It's not safe in battle."

"Imagine that you're grabbing the water with your hands and lifting it — imagine that it will keep its form as you lift." Stevie demonstrated. "Feel it somewhere in your core."

"But like..."

"Get out of your own head," Stevie encouraged. "When you sat at home, and you made a little spell — anything — that candle at the beach house and whatever you did with that. Where did you

178

feel it when you tried to make it real?"

Do not push her too far, Stevie. Hugh thought. He feared that pushing her too hard would cause Zoie to admit the lie. That would lead to not only punishment for the group of them, but it would also cause Zhenga to admit that she sensed Zoie's magic. While that would have some positive effects, it wouldn't take away their punishment — and Zoie's would go from being a quick, albeit still painful, death to the torture of being forced into gargoyle form for all of eternity.

He heard Zoie take a deep, peaceful breath and then he saw her move her hands out in front of her. Zhenga reminded her that it was okay to close her eyes in the beginning, and Hugh saw Zoie nod. He watched as the water in the pond rippled a little, but no real effect.

He smiled a little — this lack of any real effect meant that Water magic, and therefore Moon magic, wasn't Zoie's strength. But that little effect of the ripples meant that she had enough magic at this point to make Zhenga believe.

He hid better behind the bush and looked up at that ceiling of the dome, silently thanking whatever higher power there might have been for making this work.

"Hugh?" He heard Zoie's voice — still far enough away that she couldn't have possibly walked up and discovered him. He knew that he was well hidden.

Stevie's voice chimed in. "I don't see him?"

Then Zhenga's. "I don't see him either."

He considered staying hidden to see if she would trust her own feelings. It was the mating bond growing stronger that helped her sense him, and her exploration into magic was actually helping. But Hugh didn't want to be sneaky, so he walked over and made himself known. "I'm right here."

"Why were you hiding?" she asked, closing the distance between them.

"I didn't want to distract you during your practice." He took her in his arms. "How did it go, overall?"

She shrugged. "I couldn't make it happen."

Zhenga interjected, "Are you bonded mates? For you to be able to sense him like that… That's different than sensing that another supernatural being is near."

Hugh feared that telling Zhenga that they did have the mating bond would actually get that information back to Reon and subsequently Alvin. Alvin had threatened Zoie, but that was just his being hot headed and wanting to get a rise out of Hugh. He feared that Alvin would retaliate in a bigger way if he knew they were mates — in a similar way to how Hugh separated Alvin from his mate Edie.

But a lie would hurt Zoie and confuse her. "Yes." He smiled at Zoie, looking deep into her eyes. "Yes, we are."

Zhenga brought her hands to her heart. "How romantic! It must be nice not having other people trying to get into your way, Zoie."

Zoie took a little step back. "I'm sorry, what do you mean?"

"Well, I'm sure you know by now that, well, as a wolf, Hugh is naturally very loyal; that's part of their nature. But when you add the mating bond in — as long as you're alive, he'll never even turn his head at another person." She continued, "Even in the magical world that level of love and devotion is rare."

"Oh? You and Reon have been together for… well you said centuries at supper last night."

Zhenga picked up her book. "Let's make our way back inside."

Then she answered the question. "Well, yes, but we are not bonded mates. In fact, when he was just a prince, he was betrothed to some duchess or whatever." She waved her hand dismissively. "I was a mere baroness. I had prospects, of course," she admitted, "but they weren't going to gain me much position in society."

Stevie rolled her eyes. "Momma, do you have to tell this story?"

Zhenga tapped Stevie with her book. "I don't have to, but I'm going to." She looked back over at Zoie as they walked. "So, anyways, you know how politics and things are; everyone is always looking to get ahead."

"They were engaged to be married but you somehow got her out of the picture?" Zoie took Hugh's hand as they walked.

Zhenga nodded. "A woman has her ways, but let's just say she poses no threat whatsoever."

"Ooooh, a scandal?"

She shook her head. "No. Well, at least it did not appear that way." She quickly added, "And that's all I have to say about that."

Hugh pulled Zoie closer. "Nothing can come between us."

Laughing a little, Zhenga stated, "Well, there's one thing that can."

Stevie sighed. "Momma, that's rude."

"Death," Zoie said. "I know it's death."

Zhenga looked at Stevie. "See, she's not some delicate flower. You don't need to treat her like she's fragile." The made their way into the great room. "This is where I will take my leave. I'll see you all at supper this evening?" They all nodded. She took a few steps away and then turned. "I'll try to talk to my husband about being a better host."

Hugh chuckled a little, and then turned towards Stevie and Zoie. "What now?"

"Where's Cayden?"

Hugh frowned. "We had a little disagreement this morning, so they may be hanging out in their room. I have not seen them since."

Hugh felt Zoie's hand rub his back. "I'm sure whatever it was, you will mend it quickly."

Suddenly, the sound of quick footsteps came from the large staircase in the room. "Well, I've decided to grace all of you with my presence now."

Stevie's face lit up. "Cayden." She jumped into their arms.

They lifted her up and flung her over their shoulder, causing Stevie to let out a shrieking laugh. "All right, where are we going?"

As soon as they were out of the palace and the doors were shut behind them, Hugh admitted, "I kind of want to get out of here."

Stevie smacked at Cayden playfully. "Put me down!" As soon as she had her footing, she asked for clarification. "Do you mean just a break from the palace or to leave the Abyss?"

Hugh shrugged. He meant leave the city, but he also didn't want to hurt Stevie's feelings or cause the King and Queen to be offended; that could cause greater problems in the future.

"Well," Zoie said, "I want some more of that delicious chocolate ice cream from last night's dessert."

Before anyone could answer, all three of their phones buzzed. "Ugh," Hugh groaned. He pulled his out before anyone else could and read the alert. "Oh, it's just a reminder that there are parole hearing slots available for those that want to argue on the behalf of those they have imprisoned." He rolled his eyes.

"As if it matters," Cayden added. "No one ever gets freed, and sometimes even those that requested the hearing end up imprisoned for," they added finger quotes, "questioning the decision of the council."

"Then why do they do it?" Zoie asked.

"To make the council look like a fair governing system." Hugh pulled out his wallet and handed it to Zoie. He pointed across the street. "There's the ice cream you like. Go get some."

"Is the money complicated here?" She asked, blushing.

He chuckled. "No. The coins are based on size. They have looneys like the UK. No pence though." Then he added, "I think I only have bills in there. They are clearly marked." He kissed her cheek. "Get a really big ice cream. Biggest you want."

"Okay," She giggled and went off towards the shop, almost skipping like a child.

Hugh felt a smile build starting in his heart.

"Hey, Loverboy," Cayden whacked Hugh in the arm.

"Oh!" He turned back to Cayden and Stevie, falling right into the conversation that they were having, despite not really hearing it. "So we know that Moon magic isn't it."

Cayden asked, "How?"

Stevie answered, "Momma and I tried to teach her water magic. She couldn't do it. Only made some ripples — but she doesn't know that because she had her eyes closed." Then she looked over at Hugh, "Though I think she was distracted."

He ignored the last bit. "We can't test the others down here, so I think that we need to get her to the surface."

Cayden nodded. "I agree. But where should we take her? Where's safe?"

"Do you think maybe somewhere out in the country where we need not worry about hurting someone while we're testing this?" Hugh asked.

"But we need to find someone that's an expert like my mom is," Stevie suggested. "I think Zoie felt comfortable with me and

Momma because we knew how to encourage this specific type of magic."

"Sun witches are extremely rare," Hugh stated, shaking his head. He wasn't sure what the next step was.

"But Earth witches are as plentiful as Moon witches," Cayden responded. "If we find an Earth witch and she has that magic: awesome; we can stop looking. If she doesn't: awesome; she has Sun magic, and we can stop looking."

"But she will need training," Hugh added.

Stevie bit at her thumbnail. "What if…"

Cayden took Stevie's hand away from her mouth. "What are you thinking?"

"What if we let her pick where we go next? Maybe that will offer some clue. Maybe the way that she activates the lock or the destination provides something or awakens something in her?"

Hugh nodded. "I think that may be a good idea." He looked to Cayden, who nodded.

"I'll message my mom and tell her we're going." She got out her phone, but Hugh waved his hand for her to stop.

"Let's stay for dinner and go in the morning. Your staff probably has already prepared for us to be there, and I really don't want to cause the palace coup." He added, "Your father already hates me."

The bell on the ice cream shop door jingled, so Hugh looked over to see Zoie with her bowl of chocolate ice cream with whipped cream and sprinkles. "Here." She handed him his wallet. "Thank you."

He put his wallet back in his pocket. "Give me my spoon."

"Ummmmm…" She took another bite of the ice cream and then shifted her eyes back and forth. "Was I supposed to bring one for you?"

Hugh chuckled and shook his head. "No, I am teasing you. Enjoy your seaweed."

They started to walk and Cayden asked, "Hey, Zoie, how did you feel about your magic lesson today?"

She shrugged as she took another bite of the ice cream. "I mean, I feel bad because I can't do it and, well, I feel like I'm... well, I am lying." Stevie went to speak, and Zoie cut her off. "I know you say that you believe that all women have magic, Stevie, but I just don't think that's going to happen for me." She frowned.

"I don't like to see you frowning," Hugh said. He suggested, "Take another bite of ice cream."

She did as told and moaned. "Mmmmm. It's sooooo good."

"That's the most satisfied I've ever heard Zoie," Cayden laughed.

Hugh rolled his eyes and took in a deep breath. Before he could respond, Zoie interjected, "Let it go. They're just jealous because without a big, dramatic production from Stevie, they'll never know if she's satisfied." She continued eating her ice cream, still looking straight ahead.

Hugh looked over Cayden. "I think she actually won this round."

"Savor it, Zoie. It doesn't happen often." Cayden chuckled. Then, trying to be discreet, Cayden leaned over to Stevie and asked, "You're, y'know..."

She rolled her eyes. "Let it go. Yes, we work well together."

Cayden stopped walking. "Work well together?!"

Stevie stopped and turned around, throwing her arms up. "Don't you see what she did? She's going to have you all in your head, and it's going to mess with you for days." She turned to Zoie. "Thanks, Zoie. My sex life is fucked for at least the next four days."

Hugh laughed loudly. "I think that's more of a figurative 'fucked' than literal, don't you, Stevie?"

She groaned. "You see, Cayden? They are just messing with us."

Cayden pouted. "I guess."

Ignoring them, Hugh looked at Zoie. "How'd you get whipped cream on your nose?" It didn't matter that she didn't actually have any whipped cream on her nose; he just wanted to tease her.

"What?" Her eyes got wide, and she blushed. "Where?" She tried to wipe it off with a napkin, but since she also had the spoon in her hand, she was struggling.

"Zoie, put your spoon down."

"No. You'll take my ice cream," she laughed. Then she thought for a moment. Touching her nose with a clean part of her finger, she realized he was lying about the whipped cream. "Oooooh, you evil man! You did just want my ice cream!"

He laughed loudly. "No, no! I mean, yes, it would be nice if you would share, but no, I did it to tease you." Hugh added, "and, if you didn't figure it out, I was going to use it as an excuse to kiss your nose."

"Aww, well, that's kind of cute. Forgiven." She took another bite of ice cream. "You're still not getting any of this."

—Zoie—

As she and Hugh walked into the dining room, Zoie noticed that the Queen had been standing at the end of the table, rather than her seat at the side from the previous night. She turned to Hugh, "Is King Reon not joining us this evening?"

Hugh shrugged. "I'm not sure."

If Zoie would have waited two seconds, she would have had her answer. Zhenga announced, "I'm sorry, Reon has been called away on some official council business. It will just be the five of us this evening."

"Oh, that's a shame," Stevie replied. "This is our last evening here, and I was hoping to say goodbye to him. I'm sure our guests were too."

Hugh spoke on their behalf. "Yes, as always, do extend our gratitude for his *hospitality*." Zoie could feel the sarcasm dripping from the statement as if it was being feed to her through an IV. She nudged Hugh very slightly.

Zhenga waved off Hugh's statement. "Oh, I won't even pretend that I don't realize that you and my husband aren't the best of friends." She added, "I know he's… difficult at times."

Stevie supplemented the statement. "He's just very old-fashioned, Hugh. But I'm sure that as our world changes more, he will, too."

"Well, regardless, do thank him for opening his home to us for a few nights," Zoie reiterated.

After taking a spoonful of her soup, Zhenga asked, "Why are you leaving so soon? I was enjoying having my daughter home." She added, "and, honestly, I thoroughly enjoyed teaching you of our magical history, Zoie. I hope you do visit again."

"Zoie needs to explore the other forms of magic, Momma," Stevie explained. "She can't do that down here."

Nodding, Zhenga replied, "I understand. That makes sense." She added, "Zoie, do you have any other questions about water magic that perhaps I could assist with?" She frowned a little. "It's a shame that you didn't pick up the water magic a little more strongly. I am sure that Stevie would have loved assisting in your training."

Zoie nodded and took a sip of her water. "I would have loved learning more from both of you."

"Well, once you find out what kind of magic you have and get a good handle on that, I'm sure we could show you a few tricks of the trade for you to use in a pinch."

"Of course."

During the switching of the courses, Zhenga asked, "Where are you headed? I don't think you mentioned."

Cayden actually decided to answer for the group. "We're actually going to let Zoie pick. She's never opened a portal herself, and we figured, why not let her have a go?"

"Oh? Zoie, do you have a particular destination in mind?"

Zoie was blindsided. She quickly answered. "Not yet."

"Oh! Kind of a portal roulette! How fun!" She began telling a story of the last time that she had left the Abyss, which was decades ago, and how she and her girlfriends just went from city to city just to see all the sights that they wanted.

Zoie was zoned out, thinking about how she was going to be in the clear with this charade come the next day. She was brought back into the real world when she heard a large crash behind her.

One of the servers had dropped a plate of dessert on the floor. "Oh! Now we'll only have four!" The server cleaned everything up with such urgency.

Zoie insisted, "It's fine. Hugh and I can share."

"Oh, are you sure? I can can give you mine and go without," Zhenga suggested.

Zoie shook her head, "No, I insist. I don't even think I could eat an entire piece. It would be wasteful."

Zoie took the first bite of the cake. "Mmmm. It's delicious." She put another bit on her fork. "Hugh, you *have* to try this." She went to feed it to him and intentionally missed his mouth, getting it on his mustache. "Oops."

She grinned at him. He shook his head and laughed as he wiped his face. "You did that to get back at me for the ice cream earlier, didn't you?"

Putting her hand to her chest in shock, she asked, "Whatever do you mean?" She took another bite of cake. "I would never do something like that, intentionally, at a formal dinner."

Zhenga smiled. "To be so young and in love, especially new love. Seeing this just warms my heart." She looked over at Stevie. "I would love to someday see you like this."

Cayden pushed their chair out and got up and walked away.

Stevie glared at her mother. "Why would you do that?"

"I just meant finding a bonded mate. That's what every mother wants for her daughter. Cayden is fine, really. I like them." She didn't even look as if she regretted anything she had said.

"You knew exactly what you were saying." She got up to leave.

Hugh offered, "Would you like for me to…?"

Stevie slammed her chair into the table. "No, I've got this." She stormed out.

Zhenga sighed and instructed the staff to clean up. She looked at Zoie and Hugh. "I am so sorry. Sometimes I just say the wrong thing." She looked to Zoie. "I'm sure that your mother has said the same thing to you in the past. She surely wants to see her daughter happy in love."

"Stevie is happy," Zoie replied, matter-of-factly. She looked at Hugh. "I would like to turn in for the evening." When he nodded, Zoie turned back to Zhenga. "Thank you very much for allowing us to stay here and also for teaching me the origin of Moon magic."

"Of course."

As soon as they were out of earshot, Zoie asked, "Do you think we should go and check on Cayden?"

Hugh shook his head. "I think they are in good hands right now."

They walked in silence for a bit, and then Zoie said, "I want you to meet my mom."

—Hugh—

Hugh smiled. "Really?"

"Yeah. But it's not for the reason that you think." She stopped in front of the door to her room. She turned to him. "My mom will never...she's just not supportive."

He opened the door. "Can I come in?" She nodded and led him through. He locked the door and then asked, "So, why do you want me to meet your mom, if it's not to get her blessing for the relationship?"

Zoie laughed, "First of all, this isn't the 1800s. We don't need that." She took the bobby pins out of her hair. "But secondly, and more honestly, my mother has only ever liked one person I ever dated, and he was this really rich, but entirely dreadful, person. So you have a pretty steep hill to climb because you are a good person."

"Okay. So why?" He asked a second time.

"Because I want her to see that I've found happiness my own way. That I could do it on my own, without her influence." She sat on her bed. "She told me that I wouldn't be able to do this — be on my own." She shrugged. "Maybe I'm not on my own. I mean, I'm here with you..."

He sat down next to her and took her in his arms. "You are extremely independent. You're not here because you're co-dependent. You're here because you want to be. You almost walked away from me at the Vulcan, remember?"

She smiled. "Yeah, but you came after me and looked at me with those green eyes of yours right into my soul and somehow convinced me to stay."

"You wanted to, Zoie. You were going to leave because my behavior didn't meet the standards you want in a partner." He kissed her cheek. "You know you're in charge, right?"

"Pfft." She sat up and turned so that she was facing him. "Like I could tell you what to do. You could overpower me in a second."

He shook his head. "No, Zoie. I wouldn't." He thought for a moment. As he removed his tie with his left hand, he said, "Give me your hand." He put his hand on her forearm. "Hold my arm like this." As he wrapped the tie around their hands and arm, he said, "In Scotland, we used to have a custom called hand-fasting."

Zoie let go of his forearm.

He chuckled. "Zoie, I'm not going to do *that* hand-fasting ceremony right now." She cautiously placed her hand back on his arm. He continued wrapping the tie. "Use your free hand to help me knot this, please."

They fumbled to get it knotted. "We probably should have used our right hands to do this part and wrapped our left."

He laughed. "You're probably right." They finally got it tied, and Hugh took a deep breath and then looked in her eyes. "Zoie, the first night we spent together, you told me a pinky promise was like an unbreakable vow. I'm going to do my own kind of unbreakable vow with you."

She smiled. "Okay."

"Zoie, I vow…" he paused, and let out a deep breath that he didn't know he was holding.

"Are you okay?"

He nodded. "I didn't realize that when I decided to do this how deeply I mean what I want to say."

"Hugh, I know you care about me." She placed her free hand on his cheek. "You don't have to do this."

He shook his head. "I need you to know so that you'll never question your safety with me." He looked in her eyes. "I will never hurt you or ask you to do anything you don't want to do. I will use anything I have to protect you, and that includes my own life, if it comes to that. I surrender my entire being to you. And that is for however long our forever is. No — longer, Zoie. I surrender to you beyond this life."

She pulled herself towards him and as their lips met, Hugh felt the electric shock of their bond through his entire body. He felt her lips curl into a smile as their kiss broke. "What?" He asked, while their lips were still nearly touching."

"I don't feel that... electricity thing that you talk about, but..." She blushed and put a little space between them. "I feel this *fire*. I thought it would fade, but then you say things like what just said... or you just sit there, looking hot." She added, "Or you're just you. Sometimes it happens when you hold my hand."

He smiled and pulled her close. "That's our bond, Zoie."

Her free hand made its way to his cheek, and she wiped a tear away. "You okay?"

"I'm just happy that you feel it." He added, "and that you indulged me with this. You could have blown it off." He kissed her again, and he felt her grab a fistful of his shirt with her free hand. "We're going to hurt each other if we don't untie this."

"I thought that we were supposed to leave it on until midnight?"

He smiled. "It's not that kind of hand-fasting, remember? Plus, my vow is like your pinky promises. Unbreakable. Taking the tie off won't change that."

She asked, "Can we try to get it off without untying the knot? I want to keep this."

He nodded and smiled. Then they worked together to get free from the tie, and Zoie put it next to some of her personal items. Hugh stood up and started walking towards the door.

"Where are you going?" She looked at him and then at the bed.

He laughed. "You haven't slept alone in several days, and that also means you haven't gotten enough sleep overall." He winked at her. "You need to rest because we are going to be traveling a lot tomorrow."

He touched the doorknob, and she quietly requested, "Don't go."

"Zo—."

"I just… I would just feel safer here if you were with me. It's still a strange bed in a strange room in a strange place…"

He removed his hand from the doorknob. "I'll stay."

"Thank you." She ran over to him and put her arms around him. "I feel much safer in your arms."

—Zoie—

Zoie didn't want to tell Hugh that every time she looked in the mirror, she was seeing this strange black figure over her shoulder. She just held him tightly and felt his heat wrap around her.

"Well, believe it or not, I feel safer in your arms too." He ran his fingers through her hair.

She laughed and put a little space between them. "I'm going to change into my jimjams, okay?"

He nodded. "I'm going to take this opportunity to go get my pajamas and other things I need. I'll only be gone a couple minutes. I promise."

She hesitated, but she knew that she had to let him do this or he would start asking questions. As soon as he shut the door, she quickly changed and then crawled into bed, being sure to face away from the mirror.

When he came back, in addition to his pajamas, he brought a few books. "Wanna read together before we fall asleep?" He put the books in front of her while he changed into pajama pants —

with squids on them. "Let me know which one you want me to read to you."

"Sure," she said, not even looking at the books. "You're really handsome, you know?"

"That title doesn't ring a bell," he teased, as he turned around. "I thought I brought *The Hobbit*, *Wicked Fox*, and *Wrinkle in Time* with me." He continued, "I don't remember — what was the title? 'You're really handsome, you know'?"

She tossed a pillow at him, but he caught it and put it at the top of the bed as he crawled in beside her. She put her head on his chest and he grabbed the books.

He held up the books for her. "Which one, beautiful?"

"Wrinkle in Time." She settled in, as he put his arm around her.

"OK. I think we were on page 84 or 85." He opened the book. "Yes, the Tesseract." Zoie loved when Hugh read to her because he did all the voices. "Yes Mrs. Which said Hheeee isss beeehindd the darrrknessss…"

She fell asleep to the vibration of his voice in his chest against her ear.

———————

The four of them, plus Queen Zhenga, met at the front door the next morning.

"It really was a pleasure meeting you," Zhenga said, embracing Zoie. "I do hope you come to visit again. I'm interested in what power you are able to harness." Zoie thanked her and promised to get her an update somehow.

Then Zhenga addressed Hugh and Cayden. "Always a pleasure." Hugh was polite about it, but Cayden rolled their eyes and grunted.

She then hugged her daughter. "Let's try to not stay away for

194

a decade or so this time, shall we?" She kissed her cheeks. "Love you dearly."

The moment that they vacated the perimeter of the palace, it felt as if the entire group let out a collective breath that they didn't know that they were holding.

"Okay," Zoie broke the silence. "Where are we going."

"Zoie," Stevie said, "We're going to let you pick where we go."

"Oh, I thought that was just something that we told your mom for our story," Zoie admitted.

"No, we really want you to select," Cayden replied.

Zoie looked at Hugh immediately for guidance. "How will I know where to pick?"

He pushed her hair behind her ear. "Pick from instinct."

He took her hand and they started to walk to the center of city so that they could head to the portal. Since the Abyss was a purely supernatural city, it wasn't difficult to find the portal to Nightbrooke; there was actually signage directing them right to it.

They took a left turn down an alleyway that was unusually lit up like the Vegas Strip. It led them directly to a large well.

Zoie peered over into the blackness within the well. "We're going to jump in there, aren't we?" Zoie took a step back and shook her head. "I don't know if I can do that, Hugh."

He took her hands in his and looked in her eyes. "You will be in my arms the entire time. Hold your breath until you can't hold it any longer, but then still hold it. Hold it until you get back to Nightbrooke." He touched the top of the well wall with his hand, opening the portal.

"How will I know?" Her lip started to shake. She was terrified. Not only was she petrified of heights, she was also claustrophobic, so the idea of this was giving her a panic attack.

195

He touched her chin. "We are going to come out into a pool as if this were a waterslide."

"What if…"

"I am not going to lie to you. This is going to hurt. You're going to feel a lot of pressure; and when you hit the water, it may sting; but you'll be okay. Just hold your breath as long as you can. I will be with you." He stepped onto the wall of the well and reached his hand out to her.

She took his hand and stepped up. "I'm scared of this."

"I know." He looked in her eyes. "I made a promise to you that I would protect you." Hugh put his arms around her. "Put your arms up here around my neck, and I will lift you up. Hold onto me, and together, we'll go through faster."

"What if I can't get through this because I'm mortal?"

He looked in her eyes again. "Do you trust me?"

"With my life, but…"

"Then actually trust me with your life. I would give mine for yours, Zoie." He lifted her up so she could put her arms around his neck. "I'm going on three. Get ready to hold your breath." She took in a deep breath. "One… Two… Three." He jumped off into the blackness of the well.

Hold your breath just a little longer. A little bit longer. Just a little bit longer. Her eyes were closed so tightly that she didn't have any clue what kind of supernatural terror she could have seen on the route to her destination. She realized that that she might need to open her eyes to know when she hit the pool, but she wasn't ready.

She felt the pressure that Hugh had warned her about. It got increasingly greater and greater. She felt like a boa was constricting around her body and as if her eyes were going to pop out of the orbital bones. But then, just as quickly as it had gotten to the point of unbearable, it started to ease. The pressure released suddenly, and then she hit water and heard the splash.

Instead of being pulled down again, she felt herself rise back up to the surface of the water and opened her eyes.

Breathe, she told herself. Then she encouraged herself to swim. She needed to get to the edge of the pool. Looking for a ladder or stairs, she was treading water in the center of the pool. She turned herself around to see a huge wave about to crack over her head.

Zoie was no stranger to the ocean or wave pools, so she just held her breath again and dove under the wave. However, her lungs were weak from her ride through the Wishing Well of the Abyss and all of the pressure that came with it. She barely made it to the surface of the water before having to gasp for air. She felt something grab her wrist, and then she realized it was Hugh, pulling her to the edge of the pool.

Hugh helped her up out of the pool, and she realized that she couldn't just walk freely through Nightbrooke. She was mortal — not a supernatural (so, a *natural? unsupernatural? nonsupernatural?*) being, and it was obvious because she was soaking wet. The shifters could shake the water off; the merfolx dried off the moment they exited the water; vampires barely touched the stuff in case it was *holy*; and witches could just manipulate the water to dry off. She needed to find a way to get dry.

Then it hit her. "Stevie, can I get a little help here?"

Stevie smiled. "Of course, Sugar." She placed her left palm up and then with her right hand she made a clockwise motion with her index finger over her left palm. Wind spun around Zoie, like one of those tornado machines with the money on a game show. In about 15 seconds she was dry.

She felt her hair. "Um, Hugh, can I have your ponytail holder?"

Cayden gasped. "If he gives it to you, how are we supposed to know when shit is about to get real — like really, real?!"

Hugh burst out laughing. "Because I started carrying two when I started dating Zoie." He handed her one. "Just in case this happened."

Zoie pulled her hair into a ponytail, and asked, "Does he really do that?"

"Fuck yes he does!" Cayden laughed. "I mean, I know you've only seen him get angry maybe three times, but it's the sign to get the Hell out of the way."

"I don't want my hair getting in the way, and I don't want anyone to be able to grab it. It's tactical." Then he added, "Also, I don't want to cut it. I've had long hair for over 170 years."

"Was it a clan thing?" Stevie asked.

Hugh chuckled. "No. It was a preference thing. And, to be honest, as a teenager it was just laziness and not wanting to sit for someone to cut my hair."

Zoie thought back to her memories with Hugh. "You pulled it back at dinner the other night..." Zoie asked.

"Oh, yeah, I was going to jump over the table at Reon. I had pretty much had it with his shit before dinner even started." Hugh shook his head, annoyed. "I fucking hate that guy."

"Hey!" Stevie protested.

"What is it that the kids say now? Sorry not sorry? Because I'm not." Hugh pointed out, "You're one of my best friends, but I fucking hate your father."

Stevie shook her head. "Wow." Then she turned to Zoie, changing the subject. "Use your spirit and pick where you want to go."

She started looking for different passageways and doors; she contemplated what her best options were. A big city? Or maybe a rural area where the people were nice and welcoming. But these portals weren't even marked. She didn't know where she would be going. She didn't even know *why* she would be going. Just for fun, sure. But *why* would she end up picking a place?

She started casually walking until she felt pulled somewhere. The first four or five paths just made her feel uneasy. The next one smelled of chocolate, and she felt like that was probably a trick. Hansel and Gretel style tricky. And then, she heard a saxophone playing and turned towards a large, yellow, bowstring bridge. At the end of that path was a steel door with three grooves etched into it. Two from the opposite corners at the top, wiggling towards the center of the door. The third came from the bottom of the door, curved to the right and came back to meet the others.

She stood at the beginning of the bridge and hesitated.

"Everything okay?" Hugh stood next to her and put his arm around her waist.

She turned to him. "The best and worst memory I had with my dad — the last memory I have of him..." She took a deep breath. "I was seven or eight. We had gone to a Pittsburgh Pirates baseball game. The parking is all across the river, and you walk over Clemente Bridge to get there. There was a man that played saxophone on that bridge for every game. Every. Single. Game."

She turned to Hugh and put her hands on his waist, taking his shirt into her hands, tightly making balls of the fabric in her fist. "They actually won the game, and that meant that my dad was celebrating hard. We had had so much fun at the game. He even put me on his shoulders so that I could see better. I didn't know it at the time, but he had been drinking and he drove us home anyways."

"Oh, Zoie," Stevie came over and put her arms around her friend.

"He missed a turn and hit a tree. He was dead instantly." She started to cry, and Hugh pulled her closer, and Stevie hugged harder.

She continued, "My mom said that the paramedics had no clue how I survived." She took a breath that sounded more like a sob. "I played that memory over and over in my head, trying to change the outcome, and nothing I did would change the outcome."

Stevie released Zoie and stepped back, and Hugh pulled her closer. "It's okay. It's okay."

"Zoie, did you say that you tried to change what happened?" Stevie asked.

She wiped her tears and nodded. "I mean, it was just a memory."

"Tell me about that though," Stevie requested.

Zoie shrugged. "Just before the impact, I kept rewinding it my head and tried calling out to my dad about the turn or asking him to pull over. Nothing ever changed. You can't change a memory." She took a deep breath. "The doctors told me that it was my way to cope."

"Zoie…"

"Not now, Stevie." Hugh ordered. He looked in Zoie's eyes. "Are you sure this is the door that you want to take?"

She nodded. "I told you that I wanted you to meet my mother, and this door will lead you to the closest city to where she lives." Zoie took Hugh's hand and started walking over the bridge. The saxophone music got louder and louder the further she went.

As she approached the door, Zoie hesitated. She didn't know how to activate the door. She dropped her hand from Hugh's and got closer to the door. She didn't ask Hugh or her friends for directions. "You're just going to have to figure it out," she told herself, quietly. As she reached her hand towards the point where the three grooves met, water started to flow in each one, creating three little streams on the door.

She turned and looked at Hugh and jumped a little. Placing her hand at the center of the streams, knowing with absolute certainty where this door was going to lead, and pushed it open.

Stepping out from the trees, Zoie knew where she'd ended up the moment she felt the sun as it fought its way through the grey clouds. The park that she was in came to a point, as if it were a triangle, and three rivers met at the edge of it. "Point State Park!" She did a twirl with her arms out in the middle of the grassy area.

She smiled as she looked to her left. "The Incline." She spun around and saw a row of yellow bridges and then the tall UPMC building. "Pittsburgh!"

Stevie pushed passed Hugh and took Zoie's hands. "Zoie, do you realize what you just did?"

"A twirl like a child in open public?"

"No, before that."

Hugh's loud voice overpowered Stevie's. "Not right now, *Stephanie.*"

Stevie turned around and faced him. "No, you listen, she already had her moment. She already has this, and it's not dangerous anymore."

Zoie looked back and forth between them as they argued.

Cayden walked over and stood next to Zoie with their arms folded. "Who do you think will give up first?"

"Hugh is much more stubborn than she is."

"I'll take that bet." They reached out their hand.

"What are the terms?"

They shrugged. "Bragging rights?"

Zoie nodded and shook their hand. "Good enough for me." Then she asked, "What are they arguing about?"

Cayden glanced over at her. "Does it matter?"

"Good point."

"…could have dangerous ramifications!" Hugh spat forcefully back at Stevie.

"Fine. I'll wait!" She growled. Then she took a deep, cleansing breath.

Cayden conceded, actually shocked. "You were right."

Zoie admitted, "I won't brag too hard about it."

"You know, when he didn't pull his hair back, I thought for sure she was going to win this one."

"Zoie?" The voice was familiar. Too familiar.

As she turned, before even seeing who had called out to her, she knew. She knew it was someone she didn't want to see. She knew it was one of the reasons she left Pittsburgh to begin with. But she also knew that she was part of the reason that Zoie wanted to return.

"Zoie? Is that you?" Zoie didn't even have a chance to react before her mother had her wrapped in a hug.

"What are you doing downtown?" Zoie asked. "You hate the city."

"Bradshaw is tailgating over at the field. The Buccos are playing." That explained the black and gold get-up. "You should join us. I'll skip the game if you want. Or maybe Bradshaw can get you a ticket." She looked at Zoie with a combination of confusion and disgust. "Why on earth do you have your hair in a ponytail? You know it makes you look like an alien. Who are your friends?"

Zoie started the introductions. "These are my friends, Stevie and Cayden."

Her mother apprehensively shook their hands and looked them up and down.

Then Zoie took Hugh's hand. "And this is my partner, Hugh."

He reached out shake her hand, but she stepped back to get a better look at him. "Your *partner*? What are you a cop now? Do you work together?"

Zoie rolled her eyes. "He's my boyfriend, Mom. But we're both a little too old for that term."

She scoffed. "Sure he is."

Hugh pulled Zoie closer. "I am."

"Whatever." She waved it off and started walking back towards the tailgating area.

"Mom, I was wondering…"

Her mother, Carol, interrupted her. "What are *you* doing in the city? Did things not work out in Birmingham?" She started ushering her daughter towards the stadium parking lot, ignoring the rest of the group. "I told you that it was too far from home. You would just get homesick."

Zoie just let Carol talk. She knew that the only way to get what she wanted — a chance to let Hugh get to know her life before Birmingham, and what made her into the person that he fell in love with — was to let her mother have free rein to say whatever she wanted.

"…you look like you've gained a few pounds since moving down there. I'm sure the food is good. But remember, you'll never land a man — at least a good, worthwhile one — if you let yourself go." She smiled at Zoie. "But you have such a pretty face, so maybe that will salvage things."

Zoie rolled her eyes. "Mom, Hugh's actually wonderful. He's very successful, and he's kind and patient with me."

"You always see your *partners* through rose-colored glasses." She added, "I'll make a judgment on him myself, thank you very

203

much." She paused for a moment, and then she quickly added, "Though, I will say he's quite the hunk. If you want to hang onto him, do like I said, lose some weight and stay looking youthful."

Zoie looked up to the sky, asking the Sun Goddess to grant her the serenity to get through this. "Mom, I really wanted to bring those closest to me in Birmingham — the man I care very deeply for and my two best friends — to meet you." She added a little white lie. "You helped make me into the wonderful person I am today, and I wanted to bring these two parts of my life together."

"That's wonderful, dear," she replied, not even paying attention. Suddenly she was mingling with everyone they passed in the parking lot. She no longer cared about Zoie's presence. It was more about being the most popular person at the tailgating event. In fact, when they got to the truck and saw Bradshaw, one of Carol's *gentlemen callers*, she didn't even acknowledge Zoie. In fact, her first words were, "Are they complimenting my meatballs?"

Zoie waited patiently for Carol to even acknowledge her to Bradshaw. She knew that she wouldn't dream of introducing her friends.

Bradshaw looked up from the grill. "Zoie! Hey, how are ya? We didn't expect to see you here."

Zoie walked up to give Bradshaw one of those one-armed hugs from the side. "It was last minute."

As an attempt to appear like she gave even half a care, Carol turned to Bradshaw. "Do you think we could get tickets for Zoie and her friends?"

"They can come up in the box with us," Bradshaw smiled. "It's air conditioned and there's plenty of free food. The seats are excellent." He picked up his phone and called the box office to get their names added on the list.

Bradshaw was one of the nicest of Carol's boyfriends. He was a bit of a geek, but he never bothered Zoie. He never *accidentally* walked in on her while she was changing or did the *reach-around* when giving her a hug. He didn't have any children of his own, so he didn't have anyone to force Zoie to hang out with or share her room with when they came over.

Was Zoie bitter? Yes. While all of those things boiled up and created pressure, there was one thing that pushed Zoie to decide to get far away. And she had vowed she would never come back.

It was when Zoie told Carol that one of her gentleman callers had assaulted her, Carol asked Zoie what she did to lead him on. Carol didn't believe that Zoie was just getting ready to go out to a movie with her friends. Virgil would *never* try to force himself on anyone. Never mind all of the instances that Zoie decided not to come forward with where he would walk in on her in the shower or changing. Carol wasn't having it. She accused Zoie of attention seeking.

Bradshaw started breaking down the tailgating setup and Hugh and Cayden joined in to help. Carol was busy speaking to Stevie — exchanging stories about how much charitable work she'd done over the last few months, it sounded like.

"So, how's Birmingham?" Bradshaw asked Zoie. "I did some research after you moved down there and found out that the Sloss Furnaces is one of the most haunted places in the country. That's nearby there, isn't it?"

Zoie smiled. Bradshaw would have been the one to check out the area, masquerading as if he was checking out *cool stuff* to actually make sure that it was safe. "It is! I went there once but didn't go in because it just felt creepy." Remembering what Hugh had told her about the dark alleyway near the fountain in Five Points South, she wondered if Sloss Furnaces had been bewitched for the same purpose. "Birmingham is good. I did well in all of my classes."

"That's wonderful!" He turned to Hugh and Cayden. "Are you keeping her out of trouble?"

Hugh laughed. "She keeps me out of trouble." He winked at her.

After they got everything loaded into the truck, Bradshaw pulled Hugh aside. "Now, Zoie's not really my daughter, but I've been dating her mother for over a decade, so she's *like* a daughter to me."

Hugh nodded. "Yes, sir."

"If you hurt her in any way, I may not look like much, but I do know some people who could really take you to the cleaners."

Hugh looked Bradshaw in the eyes and said, with sincerity, "She is precious to me, Bradshaw. I will protect her with my life."

"I will hold you to that." They shook hands, and then Bradshaw finished making sure the truck was locked up.

Hugh walked over to Zoie and took her in his arms. "Bradshaw just gave me 'the talk' about how to treat you."

Zoie blushed and put her head in his chest. "I'm so sorry."

"I actually enjoyed it. I've read about that and seen it in films, but I've never actually experienced it." He noticed that Bradshaw had started walking towards the stadium. "We'd better go."

They started walking, and Zoie reached her arm behind him and hooked her thumb on his belt loop. He put his hand in the back pocket of her jeans.

Zoie heard Carol whispering loudly to Bradshaw. Her voice carried back to them. "How old do you think he is? He looks older, don't you think? I wonder why he can't get a woman his own age?"

She loudly responded as they walked. "He's 36. He's interested in me because we are into a lot of the same stuff. Like, we have similar hobbies. He doesn't want a woman his own age because, in Birmingham, they are all catty, like you."

Cayden and Stevie snickered from behind, and Carol stopped and turned, putting her finger in Zoie's face. "Listen here, missy. You will not talk to me that way. I am the mother here, and you will respect me."

Hugh stepped forward, just a half of a step. "Zoie's a grown woman, and she deserves to be treated with respect as well, *Carol*. I don't know how Zoie's previous beaus reacted to the disrespect you have shown her all day so far, but I will not stand by and watch you belittle her." She glared at him, but he didn't back down. "Your daughter is incredible. She's independent, intelligent, brave, kind, and a fucking goddess in bed." Zoie yanked on his belt loop. "I've waited a helluva long time to find someone that sets my heart afire the way that she does. You may be her mother, but you are not mine, so I have no problem telling you how it is." He pulled his hair up. "Now, kindly, take your finger out of my girlfriend's face before I move it for you."

Carol took her finger down and looked at Zoie. "I don't think I like him."

Hugh didn't miss a beat. "The feeling's mutual."

"Did you really have to make the comment about me in the bedroom?" Zoie whispered. "I'm mortified."

He smiled at her. "No, I didn't. But I figured it would piss her off to the point that she wouldn't know what to say, and that's what I was going for." He slid his hand back into her pocket. "Plus, it's true."

—Hugh—

The elevator ride to the club box was silent and the tension could only be cut with a chainsaw. Still, Hugh did not regret standing up to Zoie's mother. He had a feeling that Zoie wouldn't do it herself and, beyond that, no one had ever done anything like that on her behalf before.

They were shown to their private box and then Bradshaw addressed the group. "Okay, so this is my company's box. The way we behave in here reflects upon…" He laughed. "Just kidding. Enjoy as much food and drink as you want. There's about twenty seats on the other side of that glass that are all to us. There's a couch, as you can see, and our very own private bathrooms. You can set the thermostat at whatever makes you comfortable. It's just the six of us, so have fun."

"Bradshaw's cool!" Cayden clapped and rubbed their hands together. "Show me to the foooood."

Carol and Bradshaw immediately made their way to the front row of the box seats. As soon as they were comfortably seated, with Bradshaw's arm around Carol, Stevie turned to Hugh. "Are we going to talk about how you nearly ripped Zoie's mother in half, or are we just going to let that go?"

"Zoie and I talked about it on the way up here, and everything is fine." He grabbed a drink and then sat next to Zoie on the couch.

"I don't want to speak for Zoie…"

"Then don't." Cayden immediately regretted speaking and went back to crunching on some nachos.

Stevie turned and glared at them. Then she turned back to Hugh and Zoie. "Hugh, Carol is Zoie's mother, and you should really make an attempt. Zoie brought us here to meet her mother. And, while I love the fact, Zoie, that you want me and Cade here," she looked back at Hugh, "you, Hugh, are the most important to Zoie."

Hugh looked at Zoie. "Would you like me to make nice with your mother?"

She turned so that she was sitting sideways on the couch and took Hugh's hands in hers. "She pisses me off, and I love, love, LOVE that you stuck up for me. But, yes, I would like it if by the end of this game — which will take about three hours —you to at least come to some common ground." She put her hand on Hugh's cheek. "After all, you both care about me, so you have that in common."

Hugh felt his heart soften. "She has a funny way of showing it. But," he held his pinky out, "I pinky promise to *try* to smooth things over." He added, "I have a feeling that it isn't going to be easy with her. She seems stubborn."

Zoie chuckled likely. "She isn't the only one."

Pretending to be shocked, Hugh reacted, "Me? Stubborn? I don't think so!"

"Yeah, and water's not wet," Cayden said, piling more nachos on their plate. Everyone stared at them. "What?" They paused mid-nacho-placement. "Bradshaw said we could eat as much as we wanted."

"Yeah, but Bradshaw didn't know that you and I change into nearly seven feet tall wolves and could consume a village of people if we didn't control ourselves." Hugh added, "and he didn't tell us how to get more."

Cayden corrected Hugh, "I only get to 6'3"; you're the monster that is like 6'10". Oh, and there's a sign right there on how to order more." They pointed to an 8x10 framed sign that explicitly stated the steps to get more items.

Hugh shook his head. "I'm going to sit outside and watch the game. Zoie, join me?"

Zoie declined. "I'm going to take a nap right here on this couch. You enjoy the game though."

"Do you want me to—"

Stevie, Cayden, and Zoie, in unison, all said, "No!"

He backed up to the door with his hands up. "Okay!" He looked at Zoie, "I'm not sitting next to your mother right now, so if you think that this is the way to get me to become her 'bestie', it's not." He even did the finger quotes around 'bestie.'

Hugh made sure the glass door was shut and then made his way to the second row — on the opposite side from where Bradshaw and Carol were sitting.

He sat there for a few minutes and just watched the Pirates completely blow the game by the end of the second inning. Then he heard Carol say something to Bradshaw — he hadn't been paying attention, so he had no idea what. But then she was making her way over to the seat next to Hugh.

"May I sit here?"

He nodded. "If you want to."

She sat down and placed her purse in her lap. Both she and Hugh stared straight ahead for a few moments. Still looking at the game, Carol broke the silence. "My daughter has always been… different. A little difficult."

Hugh turned towards her a little. "Well, Carol, each one of us is different from the other. But, please, do elaborate on how Zoie has been *difficult.*" The disgust in his voice was intentionally not subtle.

"Maybe that's not the right word."

Hugh tightened his jaw. "Maybe you should try to explain what you mean, and I'll help you find the right one. I am a literature professor, so I can help you find the word you're looking for."

She laughed. "Fine, Webster." She thought for a moment. "She always fought everything. Any injustice she saw. Any injustice she felt was against her. Any inequity for another person. She fought me on anything I ever told her to do or any punishment I wanted to hand out." She added, "Zoie has never taken the easy route."

"Well, there's a lot of words for that stuff." He smiled. "Compassion. Kindness. And even grit." He felt his heart beat a little faster. "These things you described are why I love her."

She rolled her eyes. "You love her? You haven't known her long enough—"

He cut her off. "Carol, I admit that I don't know everything. But I do know, without even the tiniest doubt, that I love Zoie."

"If you say so." She sat in silence for a few moments. "She moved away because of a broken engagement."

"Is that supposed to bother me?" He added, "Everyone has a past."

Carol took this as the chance to dig in and find any of Hugh's past indiscretions. "What about you? What about your past? Why aren't you married? Have you ever been married? You're a good-looking man. Why are you still available?"

Hugh cleared his throat. "I see where Zoie gets her ability to ask 100 questions in thirty seconds." Carol did her best to stifle a laugh at that. Hugh smiled very slightly and then answered the questions. "Never been married because I just recently met the right woman, and I've not asked her yet." He then looked directly at Carol. "And let's not pretend you don't see the massive scar down the entire left side of my face. A lot of women say that they want a rough, bad boy, but when it comes down to it, they don't. So I'm not that *good-looking*, Carol, but thank you."

211

"What are your hobbies?"

"Reading, writing, tea — drinking it, learning about it, just everything about tea. Um, I'm sure you're looking for something less wholesome, so," he paused and thought for a moment. "I ride a motorcycle." He then added, "and she rides with me."

"Really? That shocks me to hear about her." She turned towards him and squinted at him a little. "Tell me about your family."

Hugh took in a deep breath and thought about how to answer this. "I am an only child, but my parents died when I was very, very young. I don't really remember them."

"Oh." It was the first time that she actually showed some genuine concern or care for him. "I'm sorry..." Then she added, "Zoie's father died when she was very young."

He nodded. "She told me recently."

"She had a really rough time of it afterwards. For months she kept saying that she tried to stop it and couldn't. I don't know what a seven-year-old thought she could do." She looked down at her lap. "He failed her — her father did. Sure, he left us so much money that we didn't know what to do with it, yes. But he failed her. He made that awful decision, and then he abandoned her because of that choice."

That was the core issue right there. He'd finally found it. Hugh frowned and then turned towards her. "Carol, I will never abandon Zoie. I promise."

She smiled. "I know you believe that. But something will separate you. She'll be difficult — and before you interrupt me: I know you haven't seen that side of her, but you will. Or you'll see another woman that turns your head more than she does." She paused for just a moment. "Or you'll make a bad decision and end up in a ditch."

Hugh turned back towards the game. "Well, Carol, as much as I would love to spend the next two hours trying to convince you that I am not going anywhere, you're not the one that needs to be convinced, are you?" He moved in preparation to stand up.

Carol put her hand on his arm. "I suppose I could let you date my daughter."

He stood up. "You don't really have much choice in the matter, do you? You said it yourself. Your *difficult* daughter really does her own thing, doesn't she?"

She called out to him. "I just don't think you're good enough for her."

He turned around before opening the door. "Well, you're right about that, Carol. I, most definitely, am not."

—Zoie—

Startled awake by the touch of Hugh's lips to her temple, Zoie gasped. "What year is it?"

Hugh laughed loudly. "We're still at the game."

"Is it over?" She sat up and rubbed her eyes.

"It is for the Pirates, but, no, there's still… I think five or six more innings." He sat down next to Zoie, and she felt the warmth from his body radiate around her as he pulled her close.

"Where's Cade and Stevie?" She looked around confused.

Suddenly a loud bang and thud came from the bathroom next to the couch. Both Hugh and Zoie laughed quietly to each other.

"Did you talk to my mom?"

Hugh let out a deep sigh. In fact, it was the deepest sigh she had ever heard in her life.

"It went that well?" She crawled onto his lap and put her hands on his shoulders.

She felt his warm hands on her back, and he looked in her eyes. "I think I have a long way to go before I'm her favorite person in the world."

Zoie couldn't help but be disappointed. Not in Hugh. Even

if he only half tried, he knew that any stubbornness was on her behalf. Her mother was another story. Nothing she did was for anyone else's behalf. But she didn't expect anything else, so how could she be disappointed?

He ran his hands up and down her back. "I'll try harder." Another loud thud from the bathroom was accompanied by some moans, so Hugh stood up, still holding Zoie with his left arm. He slammed on the wall with his right fist. "Highly inappropriate!"

The glass door opened just as Hugh sat back down, still holding Zoie.

While Bradshaw ignored what he saw, Carol just couldn't help herself. "Have you considered entering yourself into one of those strongmen competitions, Hugh? Lifting Zoie, with one arm at that, and making it look easy — she's not light. You didn't mention weightlifting as one of your hobbies when we were talking earlier."

Zoie felt Hugh's chest rise slowly as he took in a cleansing breath. She felt a low growl in his chest, but he didn't react any further. Still, she took the opportunity to sit properly on the couch in case he had a change of heart.

He couldn't, actually, because Cayden and Stevie came out of the bathroom — Stevie was giggling, and Cayden was wiping their mouth. They stopped dead in their tracks when they noticed the four sets of eyes staring at them.

Bradshaw broke the awkward silence. "Well, that's certainly not the first time that those bathrooms have been used in that manner."

"Please, for the love of all that is holy, tell me you aren't referencing you and my mother." Zoie gagged a little.

"No, no, no, no, no!" Bradshaw tried to fix it as quickly as he could. "I meant that I know other people that have. I swear, I would never…"

"You would never?!" Carol hit him lightly with her purse. "You definitely will never now."

Bradshaw went to speak again, but Hugh cut him off. "I would leave it. You're just going to dig yourself a very deep grave if you keep going with it. Anything you say now will be twisted. Just let it go." He stood up to get some food. "I feel like that situation was very similar to 'does this dress make me look fat?' You know?"

"When I ask you if something makes me look fat, do you lie?" Zoie asked.

He turned and looked her in the eyes. "Zoie, I would never lie to you." Then, he turned back around and, jokingly, mouthed *totally would lie* to Bradshaw. Zoie threw a pillow at Hugh, but he must have sensed it because he caught it, even though his back was still to her.

—Hugh—

Hugh's phone buzzed and made a swooshing sound, and then Stevie's and Cayden's followed. The three of them tried to ignore it the best they could — because that notification sound meant only one thing: someone had broken a major law in their world and the entire registry was being notified of it. The purpose was letting the entire world know who it was and what the reward was for turning in the criminal.

Stevie's phone beeped twice more — text messages. "Ah, umm, oh, this is not good." She grabbed Cayden's arm and pulled them outside of the club box.

This prompted Hugh to actually check his phone. "Shit." He looked at Zoie. "I'll be right back. I'm going to step out with them."

"Should I…"

He shook his head. "No, just stay right there." Quickly exiting the club box, he met Stevie and Cayden out of earshot for Zoie.

"What is this?!"

"Hugh, I swear I didn't know anything about this," Stevie said. "But I just got two messages from my father — he's livid that I brought an undocumented witch into the Abyss. He says it makes him look soft on the laws."

"How did he find out?" Hugh growled.

Stevie glared at him. "How am I supposed to know?"

"I bet this was his sudden council work that he had to do," Cayden grumbled.

Stevie's phone rang. "It's him." She answered and sweetly said, "Hi, Daddy." Hugh couldn't make out what was being said on the other end, but Stevie winced a couple times. "Daddy, I was unaware that she wasn't registered... Jack who? Jack Irving?" She looked at Hugh. "I don't know how he knew and I didn't, Daddy... right, but... I understand." She gasped. "No, I will not turn them over to you!" She frowned. "No, not even her. She's my friend." She hung up, pressing the screen with some force.

"So?"

She took a deep breath. "So, apparently after your fight, Jack Irving went to his son and explained that the argument was over some strange girl. Alvin took the opportunity to look into it a little. Apparently, he has friends that have been tailing us." She continued, "They found out Zoie's name, looked her up in the registry and couldn't find her." She added, "We're actually lucky that we went to the Abyss and my mom sensed she was a witch, otherwise this would be a throw-Zoie-into-fire sort of spectacle."

"Hugh, what should we do?" Cayden asked. "If we walk her into NightBrooke right now, the bounty hunters and anyone looking to make a quick buck will be all over her. You'll never be able to wait in that long-ass line."

Hugh looked at his phone again. "Don't you think it's a little strange how high the price is?" He showed Zoie and Cayden the alert on his phone. "100,000 for her and 125,000 for me? The last time this happened, wasn't it like 8,000 and 10,000?"

"Maybe it's a typo?" Stevie suggested.

Cayden shook their head. "This is personal. Alvin's behind this."

"I agree. He wants to get back at me." Hugh paced.

"Hugh, I think you should also consider the political gain that Alvin will have here if this ends poorly for you." Cayden pointed out, "You could probably snap him in half, and, after he threatened you *and* Zoie at the fireworks, he knows you'll be after him."

"Yeah, he may have just waited for you to mess up so that he could take this action." Cayden looked at Stevie. "And your dad wants Hugh out of the way, too."

"Maybe we should consider telling Zoie about her powers now," Stevie suggested. "She's a Sun Witch, Hugh. That's incredibly rare, and she's been one since childhood. Maybe she could pick it up quickly."

He shook his head. "Or maybe she's let her powers lay dormant so long that she can't do it at all."

"Hugh, she needs to be able to protect herself," Cayden pleaded on Zoie's behalf.

"I can protect her."

Stevie rolled her eyes. "No you can't. Not from all of this. There's going to be a lot of people after her, not to mention skilled bounty hunters." She added, "You didn't even know someone was following us."

"Yes, I did. Someone's been following me and Zoie since we met at the concert. At first, I thought it was just a random witch, but they showed up again when we were in the Abyss." He added,

"I think Zoie's felt their presence. She didn't want to be alone at all last night, and it wasn't… It wasn't like *that*. It was about her safety. She specifically said that she just felt safer with me there."

"Hugh, brother, she's your mate. How do you want to handle this?"

He thought for a few moments, taking deep breaths. "I think we should go to her mother's as planned for a few days and decide while we're there. I'm fuming right now, so I don't think making a decision at this moment is the best course of action." He turned to Stevie. "I am choosing to trust you throughout this, despite your father's part in this. Don't make me regret it."

"Hugh, I won't. She's my friend, and you've been my friend for as long as I've known Cayden." Stevie frowned. "I'm sorry that he didn't give you a chance to explain."

"How are you going to explain this to Zoie and her mom?"

Hugh ran his hands down his face and actually pulled on his own beard. "We'll just tell them it was a work thing. Something about the university. I'll fill in Zoie later." He motioned towards the club box. "We should head back in."

"What was that about?" Zoie asked.

Hugh replied, "Work thing. Confidential, but pretty big."

"Oh…" Hugh could tell that Zoie knew that he would tell her later, and she didn't really have to play it up because her mother wasn't overly perceptive. "While you were out there, Bradshaw called a car service for us, since he brought the truck today."

—Zoie—

"This was way more comfortable than riding in the bed of a truck for 90 minutes would have been." Stevie stretched out on one of the seats in the limo.

"It's ostentatious, don't you think?" Zoie rolled her eyes. "Bradshaw did this to look good. Usually her men are trying to impress me. But, of the five or six of them, last time I checked that was the current count, anyways, of all of them, Bradshaw is the one I like the best. I really think he was trying to impress Cayden — or at least stay cool." She laughed.

"Whoa!" Cayden called out as they turned into a long driveway. "This is where you grew up, Zoie?" Cayden rolled down a window and stuck their head out. "This place is like... the size of Stevie's... where Stevie grew up."

Zoie laughed. "It's not that big, but yes, this is where I grew up."

"Just you and your mom?" Cayden asked.

"Well, yeah, and our cocker spaniel, Buffy." She added, "The house may look impressive, but it was lonely. Especially after Buffy passed away."

When they entered the house, Carol and Bradshaw were in the

221

kitchen having some late-night French toast and wine. They were laughing loudly, and Carol called out. "Webster! Webster! Get over here — we have a vocabulary question."

"Oh. My. God. How wasted are you?" Zoie shook her head.

Carol gave Zoie a kiss on the cheek. "Webster! We have a question about the pl— the pl— What's that word Bradshaw? You know — for more than one?"

"Plural?" Hugh answered on Bradshaw's behalf.

"That's it!" She yelled. In fact, she was so loud that when she pointed at Hugh, even *that* was loud. "What's the *plularrr* of moose? I say that it's *mooses*, and Bradshaw says it is *moose*. Now how does that make sense?"

"It's meese," Zoie answered as she got herself a glass of water. Cayden and Stevie laughed to themselves.

"I was asking Webster!" Carol laughed.

Zoie slammed her glass down on the counter. "His name is Hugh."

"Oh, hush. You should be happy that I'm joking around with him." She continued, "Though, I will say, he's such a hunk. If he wasn't such an asshole, I might have tried to steal him away from you." She slurred, "Remember when I stole your boyfriend that was in your college calculus class?"

Bradshaw quietly apologized, but Zoie barely even acknowledged it. She was completely frozen in place, not sure how to react.

Hugh put his arm around Zoie to lead her away. Before leaving the room, he said, "The plural of moose is meese, Carol." He looked at Zoie, "Show us all to where we'll be sleeping?"

Carol called out, "Steve and Aiden will be in the first guest room on the left. Webster cannot sleep in your room with you, Zoie. You're not married." She hiccoughed. "And I don't believe this

222

nonsense about you being a golden god in bed. You've never been able to keep a man satisfied. That's why they all cheat on you!"

Zoie turned around to head back in the kitchen, but Hugh stopped her. "Are you sure that it's worth it, Zoie? She's wasted. She probably doesn't even know what she's saying."

"She knows. Drunk words are sober thoughts." She turned around to keep heading towards their rooms, knowing that Hugh was right. "This is you guys. There's a en suite bathroom and everything. If you need anything, my room is down at the end of the hall on the right."

Her room looked the same as when she had left it, including her autographed Hanson poster hanging, framed, over her writing desk. In fact, there was still a boombox on top of her dresser. A dresser that was white with pink daisies panted on it. She had painted those daisies when she was fourteen and her mother had been livid about it. Zoie had been spanked and then grounded for a week over that.

She sat down on her bed and grabbed a pillow and put it over her face as she screamed.

Hugh took a seat beside her and rubbed her back. "I'm sorry that I wasn't able to protect you against the things that she said." He added, "I failed you because I didn't prepare for the possibility of having to protect you against words like that. Especially from someone who is supposed to love you."

She crawled on his lap and let him hold her. "You didn't fail me. You kept me from going back and making things worse." She tried to make herself closer to him. "Thank you for telling her meese."

He smiled. "It was the least I could do. I hope she insists that it's correct at her next wine and cheese party or whatever it is that rich, miserable, middle-aged women do, and gets embarrassed."

223

"I can't believe she brought up my college boyfriend. That was so mortifying." She started to cry again.

He ran his fingers through her hair. "She should be embarrassed. What mother not only takes her daughter's boyfriend but is actually proud of it?"

"She's right about other stuff. Almost all of my boyfriends have cheated on me. My fiancé even did. That's why I broke our engagement." She cautiously asked, "am I not..."

He put his finger to her lips. "Don't even question that." He suggested, "This has been a really long day for all of us, so how about we fall asleep in each other's arms?"

"Sounds good to me." She crawled under the blankets with him and took in that familiar scent of tea and old books.

"So, this was your room when you were growing up?" He patted on the bright pink comforter.

She laughed. "I used to really like pink, okay?" She added, "But, yes, this is the room where I spent the vast majority of my time as a teenager, and even when I was in undergrad."

"Because you were in trouble? Your mother mentioned that you were difficult as a teenager." He continued, "When I was a teenager, if I was in trouble, I would have to manage different things on the farm — usually the less desirable tasks, such as hauling manure around — while waiting for my father to come home to use his belt to punish me."

"Oh, that's horrible — that last part. I mean, it sucks to have to do work as punishment, but at least that's character building."

He shook his head. "No, that's what was done back then. Would never happen now, though."

"Should have never happened. But I guess things were different in the 19th century." She then went back to his initial question.

"No, I spent most of my time in here because I wanted to be alone. I was bullied in high school, and my mom was just... her. Even back then."

"Do you remember a time when she wasn't like this? Like, what's your best memory with her?"

Zoie thought for a moment. "Well, after my dad died, things changed drastically. She doesn't act like it, but I'm pretty sure that she really loved dad. That may be why she has an endless supply of men that she never really commits to." She sighed. "But I remember right after dad died, when the doctors were suggesting that I needed to go to a psych hospital, she wouldn't let it happen. She fought for me, really hard, because she felt that therapy for the both of us would be better than sending me away. I remember her saying that she wouldn't let me feel abandoned by both of my parents. They still tried to take me away from her, but she had the backing of my dad's corporate lawyers and friends, and the support of one of my dad's aunties, so she got to keep me."

He ran his fingers through her hair, and Zoie cuddled closer to him. "That's your best memory?"

"Well, she kind of abandoned me anyways, don't you think?"

"Sure, but... think harder. There has to be a time of joy for you, even if it was before your dad died." He started braiding a small piece of her hair.

Zoie searched her memories, closing her eyes. Her brain rewound through her entire life, sometimes pausing to try something different to change her own behavior to find a different outcome. Her eyelids flipped open. "When I was sixteen, I was getting ready for the prom. Mom had paid for this professional to do my hair, but she had never worked with wavy hair before, so it ended up a disaster." Zoie laughed. "I mean, it was lopsided and just looked horrible." She hopped out of bed and went to her closet.

"What are you doing?"

She pulled a photo album out of a box. "I have pictures of it before and after." She flipped through a couple pages. "See? Horrible."

"That's... interesting..."

She laughed. "No it's horrible." She turned towards him. "But Mom rinsed my hair as soon as she left and started over. She somehow was able to fix it even better." She turned the page to show the photos. "We laughed a lot and worked together to get everything right. Then she even did my makeup and everything. It was a big success."

"That's really lovely." He added, "And it proves that you two can get along and communicate." He flipped through the photos. "Who took these photos?"

"My great aunt Lettie," she replied. "She started coming around after dad died. She's one of the few from that side of my family that I know. Mom didn't like her much because even though she was much older, she looked really pretty and young."

He pointed to a figure in a mirror, with long, wild red hair and lots of bangle bracelets on her left wrist that didn't match the long dress she wore. "Is that her?"

"Yeah, but why?"

He looked at Zoie. "I know her."

"Oh that's neat that you met my auntie!" Zoie put a little space between them. "Did you know me when I was a child?"

Hugh shook his head. "No. The first time I ever met you was on campus when I dropped my apple." He looked closer at the photo. "Yes, that's definitely her." He asked, "Do you still have contact with her?"

Zoie bit her lip. "Um… she died five or six years ago. I was 18 or 19." She held her necklace up. "She gave me this and told me that she would always be with me as long as I had it."

He shook his head. "Are you sure? I saw her about two years ago at …"

—Hugh—

As soon as it came out of his mouth, he regretted it. "Maybe it was someone else. You know, they say everyone has a twin." He closed the photo album and put it on the bedside table. He reached out to pull Zoie close, praying she would just fall asleep and forget about this.

Zoie retreated from his touch. "Hugh, did you date her or something? You seemed really excited to see her."

He grimaced. "We were friends for several years and tried to date, but it didn't work, and we remained friends for years afterwards."

Zoie jumped out of bed. "Did you sleep with her?"

Hugh laughed, "No, no! It was like two dates. More like one and half?" He cringed. He contemplated how to move forward. "On the second date, she told me that she… um… she said that she felt as if I was destined for someone else." He had to be very cautious with his words.

She squinted at him. "Are you sure you're being honest with me?"

A way out of this awkward conversation. "Zoie, I told you that I've not been with anyone besides you for over a century."

Zoie got back into bed with him, albeit cautiously, and put her head on his chest. He smiled as he felt her soft, cool skin against his.

Just as he was about to fall asleep, Zoie sat up, startling him away from dreamland.

"You said you just saw her two years ago. Where?"

He waved the question off. "I've lived a really long time. I'm probably wrong about the length of time it's been." He lightly pulled on her pajama top. "Come on. Let's go back to sleep."

Putting his hand on Zoie's back, he could actually feel her heart racing. Then he felt the weight in the bed shift and heard her feet on the wood floors. Even though the lights were out, he could still see her clearly in the dark, pacing.

She started muttering to herself. Then she went over to her closet and turned on the light in there and started digging through more boxes.

"Christ, Zoie. Turn off the light." He tapped his phone. "It's two o'clock in the morning and we still haven't slept. Can you shut the light off in there and maybe we can talk about this after some sleep?"

Zoie started flipping through more photo albums. "I remember when I was 17 or 18, during my senior year, mom and Auntie Lettie had a huge argument. I don't know all the details, but it had something to do with my future and education." She continued to flip through the pages of her albums. "Mom ended up telling her that she was no longer welcome in our home. She died just after my next birthday, and in her will, she left me this necklace and a letter." She pulled out a piece of paper, aged and written in calligraphy and obviously, the tool was definitely not a ball point pen.

Hugh swallowed hard — he was trying to swallow a secret that was just a matter of time before Zoie figured it out. He needed her to figure it out herself. He just didn't know how much he could encourage.

She piled five dusty photo albums in her arms and threw the letter on top. She carried them over to the bed and turned on her beside lamp. "Okay, this album is from when I was about ten." She flipped through. "There's Auntie Lettie... there... there... and there." She pointed at several photos. She opened another one. "Here — at my 8th grade graduation... she's there. And she looks exactly the same. Exactly. The. Same."

Hugh took a deep breath in. "What are you getting at, Zoie?"

She looked him dead in the eyes. "Don't lie to me. How long ago did you date her?"

"It's been long enough that any romantic feelings we had have long gone, if that's what you're worried about." He took a deep breath in, because if he knew Zoie at all, he knew that answer wasn't sufficient.

She groaned a little. "That's not what I asked you, Hugh. I want a year — or at least a decade."

Looking over at the tie that Zoie had hanging out of her purse, he was reminded of his vow to her and knew he couldn't lie any longer. He braced for this. "It was the 1930s, and it was when I was living in Canterbury in England."

Zoie shook her head. "No. That's not possible. She wouldn't have even been of age at that time..." She started doing math on her fingers.

He watched her mind work and smiled to himself. He didn't want to give her any clues. She needed to come to this conclusion all on her own.

Her eyes grew wide. "Is she... is she like you?"

"A werewolf? No." He bit on his thumb a little.

"No, is she immortal like you?"

He nodded slowly.

"She's really pretty, so is she a mermaid?" Zoie asked.

He chuckled. "No. Mermaids don't have the monopoly on pretty." He poked her side to tickle her a little. "You're really pretty, and you're not a mermaid."

She took her pendant in her hand. "Is she a witch, Hugh?"

He smiled. "Yes, she's a Moon witch." Now Zoie just needed to figure out the rest, entirely on her own, and maybe they could work on getting this bounty eliminated.

"Oooh, this is really exciting! Is there a way that I can see her?" She moved all of the photo albums to a pile on the floor and crawled into bed.

He nodded. "But can we get some rest and talk about it after?" She agreed and placed her head on his chest. Hugh was pretty sure that Zoie was going to struggle sleeping, but he definitely felt more relaxed since Zoie had gotten several steps closer to figuring out that she was a witch.

—Zoie—

Zoie sat up quickly, pulling her hair from where it was stuck to her cheek. Her mouth was dry, but the shoulder of her pajama top was soaked. The space where Hugh had been sleeping was cold. She looked at the digital clock on the bedside table. "Holy shit — NOON?" She grabbed a hair tie and pulled back the mess of hair on her head as best as possible.

As she made her way towards the kitchen, she was painfully aware that there were no pictures of her among the photos of her mother and friends — and lovers — from her travels. In fact, there were pictures of Buffy, their dearly departed dog, all over the house. None of Zoie.

That, combined with the memory of her mother sending Auntie Lettie away, reminded Zoie of the constant anger she held in her heart. The anger that she had suppressed since leaving for Birmingham — until last night.

She saw her mom, looking quite rough, sitting at the dining room table with Hugh, Stevie, and Cayden. Hugh stood up when she entered the room. He met her at the refrigerator and gave her a sweet good morning kiss on the cheek.

231

"You didn't wake me?" She pouted.

He ran his hand up and down her back. "You looked so peaceful, and I figured that you may have needed it."

"Zoie, can I speak with you?" Carol asked, motioning towards the study, as it was more private.

Zoie shut the refrigerator. Gathering some confidence, she replied, "Anything you have to say to me, you can certainly say in front of, at the very least, Hugh."

Carol threw her hands in the air. "Fine, if you want to embarrass me further, I'll do it right here." She sighed. "I wanted to apologize for my behavior last night."

"Thank you. I appreciate that." Zoie started putting some French toast on her plate. "This your French toast, Stevie?" Stevie nodded.

"Well?" Zoie's mother asked.

Zoie put her fork on the counter firmly. "Well, what?"

"Don't you think that you owe me some sort of apology?"

Zoie took a step back. "Excuse me?" She looked at everyone else. "Did I lose some time from last night? I don't remember what I did yesterday to warrant having to apologize? Please, tell me if I'm incorrect." She looked at her mother. "Can you, please, tell me what I did that offended you?"

Her mother straightened her posture. "Well, for starters, you showed up, unannounced — with guests. Then you did have quite the attitude yesterday at the game and when we came home. Much of what I said was merely a joke."

Zoie let out a deep sigh. "And there we have it, folks. The backpedaling." She rolled her eyes. "The only thing I am going to apologize for is showing up with unannounced guests. This is my home as much as it is yours. Dad let half of everything to me, and

that includes this house. So, hmmm, now that I think about it…"
She paused for dramatics. "These guests were not unannounced, because they came with me to *my* house." She took a bite of her breakfast. "Ergo, no, I don't have an apology for you."

Her mother scoffed. "And here I thought living in the south would make you a little more gentle."

"You mean submissive." Zoie waited for her response, but it never came. "I'm going to be *difficult* for the rest of my life."

Carol snapped at Hugh. "That conversation was between us."

Zoie rolled her eyes. "First of all, what planet are you on that you think that this man isn't going to tell me everything? Secondly, you've called me difficult for my entire life. It's no secret that you feel that way."

"What do you want from me, Zoie? Do you want me to admit that I'm a terrible mother?" She threw her hands in the air.

Zoie shook her head in disbelief. "Look, Mom, I am sure it was difficult after Dad died. There's no manual on being a parent, let alone how to be a single parent after being widowed. I. Get. It." She continued, "But you have to stop acting like your choices are my responsibility to get right with. If you have regrets, that's on you. Not me. I have enough of my own consequences to face for my own choices." She went to eat more breakfast and stopped. "Also, if you ever make a comment about my weight or appearance not being up to your standard again, you will not see me again."

"You'll understand when you're a mother to a daughter."

Zoie pressed her lips together. "Maybe I will. And, if that's the case, maybe I will come and apologize to you." She added, "But I wouldn't hold your breath for that moment."

"You're so damn stubborn." She pointed back and forth between Zoie and Hugh. "You and Webster seem to be a perfect pair to drive each other insane." She walked away, her heels clicking the entire way until she reached her bedroom at the far end of the house.

Zoie let out a breath that she didn't know she was holding and turned to Hugh, burying her face in his shirt as she cried. He wrapped his arms around her. "It's okay. I'm here." He quietly added, "You were very brave to stand up for yourself, and I'm proud of you."

Stevie and Cayden got up and surrounded Zoie with a group hug. "We're really proud of you, too," Stevie echoed.

"Thanks." Zoie started to regain her composure. "That was just built up over the last 24 years."

"Are you going to be okay?" Stevie asked.

Zoie nodded, and then Cayden stated, "Good. Because we have some serious shit to talk about."

—Hugh—

"Geez. Let her finish her breakfast first." Hugh turned to Zoie. "Would you mind if I went and got one of your photo albums. What we talked about last night will be pertinent to what we need to talk about today."

Zoie smiled. "Yes, that's fine."

In order to not encounter Zoie's mother, Hugh actually used his enhanced hearing to find where she was and then he moved as quickly and as quietly as he could.

Upon getting into the room, he found the album with the most recent photos of Lettie. He was about to leave when he noticed the letter from Lettie to Zoie laying on the bedside table. He decided to read it.

Sweet Zoie,

I am sorry that I wasn't around much for you these past several months. Just know that no matter where I may be standing, I am always protecting you.

Enclosed with this letter is the crescent moon necklace of mine that you've always admired. Wear it and I will be with you.

Get yourself some white pillar candles and some cumin, and you can enhance the protection abilities that live within this necklace. You can create your own spells or take them from those that have come before you — just feel them with your spirit.

Your father would be very proud of you and all that you have accomplished, as am I.

Love,

Auntie Lettie

Quickly folding it back up, he placed the letter back where he had found it. Since there wasn't much in the letter, he regretted reading something so personal to Zoie. The only thing of worth was that it was obvious that Lettie did realize the powers that Zoie had within her, and she wanted to encourage this.

As he walked back into the room, Zoie turned to Hugh, holding Stevie's phone out. "Why didn't you tell me about this?"

He growled and put the photo album on the table. "Stevie, why didn't you wait for me before you did that?"

Cayden stepped between the two of them. "It was my idea."

Hugh rolled his eyes. "I thought we were going to find somewhere more private?" Then he looked at Zoie, "I didn't tell you because I wasn't sure how to handle it. I wanted to have a plan — or at least the early makings of one — before I worried you."

Zoie huffed a little. "You always underestimate me. I could be of use in making the plan."

Cayden clapped their hands together. "Okay, while your little argument here is *riveting*, we honestly need to figure out how to get you two out of this situation."

"They won't just drop it?"

Stevie choked on her tea. "OK, so, I know this isn't a movie, but, like, have you ever heard of someone just 'dropping' the bounty on someone without reason?" She threw her hands in the air. "Let's just give up!" She chuckled. "I mean, this is the supernatural version of *John Wick*, Zoie."

Zoie frowned and quietly replied, "I didn't know."

Hugh rubbed her back gently. "Do you think we could talk to your parents, Stevie? Make them understand?"

Stevie shook her head. "It's a crime, Hugh. It's one of the highest crimes of our world, and you know it."

"You're their daughter. Do you think—."

It was Stevie's turn to frown and get quiet. "They aren't speaking to me."

Zoie looked up. "What? Why?"

Stevie answered, "Because I refuse to turn you in."

"Wait a minute…" Zoie scrolled through and read the notification again. "What's this mean? 'Undocumented witch'? Maybe that's a loophole."

"No, Zoie, the law is that to get into NightBrooke, you have to register upon first entry," Stevie explained. "You didn't do that."

Zoie let out a little pfft noise with her mouth. "No. That's not what I mean. The information is incorrect. I'm not a witch, so maybe we can argue that the accusation is incorrect?"

Stevie placed her hand on Zoie's arm. "Then you both would be in for a worse punishment because you shouldn't have been in there at all."

"Hmmm."

Hugh then presented the photo album and opened up to the most recent picture of Lettie. "I think that she may be of some help."

With a shocked look on their face, Cayden asked, "You know Lettie Murphy?"

Defensively, Zoie asked, "Did you date her too?"

Cayden laughed. "No, but I really wanted to. She was always so much fun. Hugh, do you remember the time that you and Lettie—" They noticed the glare Hugh was sending their way and quickly said, "Y'know, now's not the time for that story."

Zoie sent a quick icy look Hugh's way. Then she stated, "Lettie is my great aunt. She gave me my necklace."

Stevie smiled. "Zoie, have you considered —."

Hugh cut her off. "I'm thinking that if we go and speak to Lettie, she can talk to the Shrews, since she's always been close to the Moon witch Chandra. Maybe she could speak with your father and convince him to call this off. Chandra's on the council."

"First of all, she's only one-third of a vote, with the Shrews all having to vote as one. Secondly, what can she offer my father that would be of any use to him?" Stevie obviously thought this was pointless.

"Maybe she could make a maelstrom over another civilization in the Deep and knock them down a couple pegs?" Hugh shrugged.

Stevie shook her head. "That's ridiculous. It's something he could do himself."

"Not really. I mean, yeah, physically he could, but that would be an act of war." Hugh continued, "He couldn't do that without the entire council behind him."

Zoie interjected. "Stevie, may I ask —"

Hugh pressed his lips together and then talked right over

her. "I just don't want to start running. It's ridiculous, and it will never end."

"So, what are our realistic options?" Zoie asked.

"We could take out some powerful people to get the bounty to go away," Hugh suggested.

Stevie narrowed her eyes. "Are you suggesting that we kill my parents?"

Cayden let out an annoyed sigh. "I mean, that's a way…"

"I've heard about people not liking their in-laws, Cade, but…"

"You can't be serious." Stevie stood up. "I know that I'm presently on the outs with them, but I will not be a part of that."

Zoie shyly added, "Me either."

Scoffing, Cayden replied, "You don't really have a say here, Zoie. You can't do anything. You're actually a liability." They very directly added, "You'll do as we instruct."

Zoie put down her tea with some force, splashing some liquid high enough to spill down the outside of the cup. "As you instruct?"

They didn't back down. "That's all you can do. You can't offer yourself as anything except for bait."

Stevie looked back and forth between each person in the room, speechless, waiting for the next person to pounce.

Hugh let out a low growl from his chest. "Watch your tone, Cade. She's my…" He tried to come up with a word other than mate, as Zoie had once told him that she felt it sounded like they were animals. "She's my…" He looked over at her. "Marry me."

—Zoie—

She looked up at him, and her heart sped up. "What did you just say?"

Hugh took her hand in his and knelt before her. "I know it's really sudden, and maybe it's not normal, but it would protect you

238

and solve the problem. They couldn't hurt you, and we've really grown close. I'm certain that we'll fall more in—"

She cut him off. "No."

Stevie's jaw dropped to the floor, and Cayden swallowed a chuckle.

"No?" Hugh made his way to the chair next to hers. "I just thought that since it would mean that I would need to update my little section in the register, since we have to update with marital status changes, birth of children, and stuff... I thought it would solve the problem. It would make us go into a different, shorter line in that god-forsaken office..." He began to trail off but then clearly said, "I thought that we both cared for each other."

A soft smile graced her face. "Hugh, I do care very deeply for you." It was her turn to take his hand in hers. "Marriage just isn't the answer here. I don't feel that we know each other well enough to make that sort of commitment to each other."

Stevie's wealth of knowledge about supernatural creatures kicked in. "Do you not understand the mating bond?"

Zoie straightened her posture and gathered her courage. "I don't care about the mating bond in this instance. I don't feel like it's the right decision for me." She added, "This feels akin to getting married just because we're having a baby or something. It's not the right reason." She was shaking on the inside, standing up for herself in this situation. "Find another solution."

Stevie blurted out, "Take out Alvin so you can take his place as the Shifter representative at the realm meetings."

Everyone was silent.

Zoie slowly broke the silence. "I thought we weren't killing anyone."

"No," Stevie replied. "We aren't killing my parents." She

explained, "This is the answer. One — Hugh, you've already got beef with this guy. He threatened you before at the Vulcan, remember? You killed his mate, albeit accidentally, right? Two — Alvin does this same kind of shit for political gain. He nearly wiped out the entire wolf-shifter race just to maintain power. Three — it's against the law to put a bounty on the head of another Councilmember or their mate, so once you take his place, they have to drop this bullshit."

"Commit murder?" Zoie quietly asked.

"This crosses into assassination territory," Cayden pointed out. Looking to Hugh, they asked, "Will they let you take his seat if you do this?"

Stevie replied, "There's no law or bylaw or obscure rule against this. In fact, it's how people get into power all the time."

Hugh thought about it for a few minutes, pacing back and forth. "I actually think this is the only way." His eyes darted back and forth as if he was reading some invisible, albeit wordy, sign in front of him. "I don't think that Alvin will stop coming for us unless we eliminate him, so, even if we did find another way to remove the bounty on our heads, his revenge will still be looming over us."

"It's a total power move and I know my parents will respect it. It's how my mom kind of got into power. She was in love with Daddy, but he was betrothed to that other woman — the duchess, and Momma took her out." Stevie took a drink of her tea.

"*That's* what she did?!" Zoie wasn't entirely comfortable with this plan — and they hadn't even gotten to the actually planning part. She didn't enjoy the idea of hurting another living being. She was fairly certain that her friends weren't overly excited about it, but they also weren't bothered by it.

"...I just don't know where to intercept him that will make

240

it easy to take him out." Cayden twisted an imaginary beard in their fingers.

"I mean, it would be easier to find that out if Zoie could harness her Sun powers. She could look to the future…" Stevie closed her eyes with regret the moment that it came out of her mouth.

"What do you mean?" Zoie asked, already knowing exactly what was meant.

Hugh glared at Stevie. "You just had to do this right now? We discussed waiting until the right time."

"It was an accident." Stevie's eyes grew to the size of moons as she watched Hugh pull his hair back.

"That is the second line you've crossed with her in the last hour without checking with me first." He leaned over the table, getting right in Stevie's face.

Zoie touched Hugh's arm as his muscles started to twitch. "Hugh," she said softly.

He sat back down next to her, regaining his composure. "This was not the way that you were supposed to find out."

"Why didn't you tell me?" She quickly added, "Don't say that you didn't have the opportunity."

Cayden put his hand on the back of Stevie's arm to direct her out of the room.

"No. You stay." Zoie pointed at them and then to some chairs. "Sit." They did as she commanded. "You've all been lying to me."

Hugh closed his eyes and breathed out. "We all lied to protect you." That didn't move Zoie to run into his arms and accept his indiscretion.

"Actually, to be fair, Hugh, Stevie's wanted to tell Zoie…" Cayden pointed out.

Hugh turned towards him and growled.

"Hugh." Zoie looked directly at him as he sat down. "You guys can't do that here. We've already said too much with my mother in the house." She looked outside. "Let's go out to the greenhouse."

As they walked through the huge backyard behind Zoie's house, Cayden asked, "Are we not going to talk about how if Zoie says your name, you calm down? I mean, I've never seen that before."

Zoie, still furious about being lied to, sarcastically suggested, "It's probably the mating bond."

Stevie quietly replied, "It is."

Hugh let out a deep sigh. "If you ever wondered if you had complete control over me, that mystery should be solved now."

Zoie turned to Stevie. "Explain. And don't leave anything out."

Stevie shrugged. "All I know is that with the shifters, there's three ways to get them to turn back to human. One is give them clothes; another is that they get so exhausted they fall asleep and transition back during their sleep; and the third is hearing their bonded mate say their name."

"You have to be careful with it," Cayden explained. "If you're in battle and call out to him, he'll change back and get hurt or killed."

"Hmm." Zoie said, opening the door to the Greenhouse. "It will get warm in here pretty quickly, so we need to be quick."

Cayden started looking at the plants. "Are these...?"

"Yes, my mom has a hydroponic weed farm." Zoie pointed out, "There's also tomatoes, peppers, lettuce, and basil." She went back to their conversation from the kitchen. "How long have each of you known that I was a witch?"

"I found out the day of the fountain at Five Points South," Cayden answered quickly.

Stevie went next. "The Vulcan. I had my suspicions but knew for certain when we were wiping the beer off of your purse in the bathroom."

Zoie looked at Hugh. "And you?"

He quietly admitted, "When you handed me the apple and our hands touched."

"Why? Why didn't you all tell me?" She tried to shove her way past Hugh to get to the door and he put his arms around her. "Let me go! You're the worst of all!"

"Zoie, you don't understand… I didn't know if you already knew at the time." He tried to hold her tightly.

"Why didn't you tell me after the concert? The night that you admitted to me that you were a shifter?" She added, "Why didn't you tell me last night?" She broke free from him. "You just tried to propose to me and you've been lying to me the entire time that we've known each other."

"Zoie, I'm sorry." He continued, "I promise I won't ever lie to you again."

She scoffed. "You promise? You made a vow to me, two nights ago. You called it unbreakable. And you did not hold to it."

"Zoie, it doesn't work like that in our world. He can't just tell you. None of us can," Stevie attempted to explain.

Zoie shook her head. "I thought you were my friend, Stevie. You were the first girlfriend I've had in my entire life. You're a part of this." She added, "You knew — more than anyone — how much I wanted to be a part of this world. How heartbroken I continuously was because I thought that I was just going to be a momentary event in his long life."

"Zoie, we're all doing what we thought was best for you. Letting you discover your magic in your own time," Stevie explained.

"What about what *I* thought was best for me?" She threw her hands up. "Like doesn't my opinion matter?"

"That's very fair, Zoie, and I should have considered that." Hugh stepped towards her and took her hand.

She yanked it back. "Don't try to smooth this over by agreeing with me for the sake of sparing an argument."

He reached for her hand again. "I'm not. I should have told you everything. You *are* right."

She rolled her eyes. "Tell me everything now."

Zoie listened intently as Hugh told her, supplemented by commentary from Stevie and Cayden, about how they had been trying to gently test out her powers, to find out what kind of magic she possessed. Hugh also explained that Stevie had confirmed his suspicions about someone following them. "…and I believe that it's the same person that was following us after the concert."

She pressed her lips together, considering her next words very carefully. Still feeling the past trauma of spending some time, off and on, since her father's death in the psych floor of the hospital, she worried that admitting what she's been seeing in the mirror would get her shipped right back to a hospital bed with restraints. However, she felt that it was necessary. "I've been seeing a black figure behind me in the mirror."

Hugh held his hand out to her. When she took it, he gently pulled her into a hug. "I thought that you had at least sensed something or someone." She allowed herself to feel safe in his arms.

"Zoie, why didn't you tell us?" Stevie asked.

She turned around in Hugh's arms, and he still rested his hands on her shoulders. "I thought it was just exhausted." She shrugged. "And… when I was a kid, I had some… I spent some time off and on in the hospital and it wasn't a good experience for me." She added, "but Mom and Auntie Lettie got me out."

Stevie looked Zoie directly in the eyes. "Zoie, you do realize that the memories from the night of the car crash with your dad — you were using the power to manipulate time to try and save him, right?"

Zoie shook her head. "No."

"You were," Stevie reiterated. "Do you know how rare that power is?"

Zoie started to shake a little and moved towards the door of the greenhouse. "I can't talk about this right now." She ran through the grass back into the house.

—Hugh—

"You should follow her, Hugh," Cayden urged him.

He hesitated. "I don't know. This was a lot for her."

"That's why you should go after her." Cayden pushed Hugh's shoulder a little.

Stevie added, "I think she really needs you right now." She continued, "Her entire life has been turned upside down repeatedly over the last several days."

He nodded and headed back in the house. When she wasn't in the kitchen, he went directly to her room. He quietly turned the doorknob. The door creaked eerily.

Zoie actually made a joke. "That door sounds haunted." Hugh heard a tiny chuckle between sobs. He noticed that she looked at him, but then she pulled the blankets over her head.

Softly, he asked, "Can I come sit with you?"

"Yes." Her voice, despite the shakiness from the crying, had an innocence about it.

He sat down on the bed. "Would you like me to hold you?"

She sat up, wrapping herself with the blanket, and nodded.

Faster than the speed of light, he was by her side and wiping her tears with his thumb. "I am very sorry for all that you have experienced today. I should have been a better partner to you."

She nodded. "This is true." Another sob forced its way out. "But that's not what actually has me upset."

"Wanna talk about it, then?" He put his arm around her and pulled her closer.

She nodded. "When Stevie mentioned that I was using my power..." she cried harder. "My dad." He held her a little tighter. "I didn't try hard enough to save him."

"No, no." He ran his hand up and down her arm as he held her. "Zoie, there are things that are fixed points in time. Usually, those moments when a witch uses her power the first time in a major way — those moments are usually fixed points in time." He added, "and, even if not, you were a child, Zoie. You were untrained."

"Maybe I can go back later, when I'm trained..."

"No." He touched her chin so that he could look in her eyes, even though she would fight it because they were red and puffy. "Fixed moment in time. Nothing can change it. You would not be the person you are today if your father had survived."

She went to speak, and Hugh knew what she was going to say.

"No, Zoie. You told me last night that your mother changed after your father died. That affects you. Also, Lettie never would have come to visit and taken such an active part in your life if you hadn't had that moment." He kissed her very gently. "You may not have moved to Birmingham, which means we may have never met."

"Do you think that Auntie Lettie knew it was me when she told you that someone else was meant for you?" Zoie asked.

He thought about it for a moment. "Well, she is a Moon witch, it's not likely that she has to gift of foresight. It's not impossible,

but just not likely. Foresight is usually reserved for Sun Witches."
He continued, "It could be a couple things. Maybe it was her way
of letting me down easy. Or, it could be that she had a very low-
level ability and it just manifested to her very slightly."

"Oh."

"Do you want there to be some big, epic romance novel destiny
for us to be together?" When she nodded shyly, he smiled and
replied, "Then I think the answer is that, yes, she knew. Maybe
Great Auntie Lettie is actually a more distant relative that's actually
a direct relative of yours — the one that gave you the gene." He put
his hand in her hair and stared into her eyes. "Maybe Lettie knew
that one of her several-times-great-granddaughters was destined
to be my soul mate."

"I like that."

"Me too." He kissed her, and then suggested, "I think you
should nap, okay?"

She agreed and lay down. Hugh turned the light off as he left
the room.

—Zoie—

Zoie gasped and sat up, startling herself awake. She reached over to Hugh's side of the bed. Momentarily confused by the lack of warmth, she finally remembered that she had been napping.

Not sure what really woke her, she decided to go to the bathroom and rinse her face.

After patting her face dry, she decided to look in the mirror, only to see the same dark, hooded figure as she had been seeing since the safe house on the island. She gasped and jumped back.

Then she turned around, slowly, to see who it was while thinking that she could keep one eye on the mirror, however impossible that it was. Nothing was there.

She turned back to the mirror, and the figure was back.

"Zoie." The voice was deep and distorted.

Putting on her bravest face, she warned, "Look, you had better do what you're gonna do and do it quickly. There are three supernatural beings in this house, and one of them would definitely die before he would willingly let anyone hurt me. They will come to my rescue at any vibration of trouble…"

She heard a small, albeit distorted, chuckle come from the black figure. "I'm not going to hurt you... today." Then he added, "Even if I planned to, they wouldn't be able to do anything. I've placed a hex on all of them." Zoie's fear and concern must have washed over her face because he added, "Don't worry. They — and your mother — are all just napping. I'll release them when I leave." He paused, for dramatics. "If..."

"If what?" She reached behind her for some sort of weapon on the counter, but all she could feel was the plastic bottle of hand soap.

He sighed. "If you stop doing shit like that." Snapping his fingers, he called the bottle of soap to him. "Don't try to fight, Zoie. I already told you I'm not planning to hurt you today."

"What do you want?" She swallowed her fear so hard that it actually hurt her throat.

"It's simple, really. I'm just here to warn you. The moment you are unprotected, I'm going to take you. I'm going to take you and torture you slowly." He added, "And not only will I ensure that there's video evidence of this torture, depending on how I do it, I very well just may send your body back to Hugh, piece by piece. Starting with your fingernails. Maybe an eye or an ear next..." He said it as if he was explaining how to boil an egg. *First, I put the eggs in the water — making sure to add baking soda so the shells don't stick when it's time to peel them...*

"Then why not just do it? Why not just kill me here? Why not kill them, too, right now?" She threw her hands in the air. "Why give up your chance?"

He, gladly, explained, "it's not what I want to do. I don't want to kill them. I don't even care about the mermaid and her pet. I don't even *want* to kill Hugh. I just want him to suffer. Suffer like I did when I watched my mother die when I was just a child. When he

252

tore her limb from limb. When he threw her head across the room and it landed at my feet. Suffer like I did when I watched my father deteriorate into depression to the point that my grandfather had to raise me until my father got his shit together."

Zoie went to ask another question, but he reached up and slapped her across the face. "Shut up." Continuing, he stated, "And, as if this revenge couldn't get any sweeter, there's the price on your head from the council."

He backed up to leave and then turned. "Oh, and don't even try to tell them about this. That slap — it was a spell. You'll not be able to tell anyone about this conversation."

"Hugh will never let anything happen to me."

"I think that's my favorite part about all of this." She could almost hear the smirk behind his mask. "Of course, Zoie, he's not going to *let* it happen. He's just going to be powerless to stop it." Another distorted chuckle. The wind came whipping through the room, and the black robes started flowing as he lifted off the ground. "See you soon, Zoie."

And just as fast as he arrived, he was gone.

—Hugh—

"...and then if we could just find a way to sneak into the event, we could..." Hugh stopped abruptly when Zoie entered the room. The right corner of his mouth crept up into a smile at the sight of her red hair disheveled and the sleep still in her eyes.

"Where's my mom?"

Cayden answered, "She had a hot date with not-Bradshaw."

"Not-Bradshaw?" Zoie laughed. "Do you like Bradshaw that much that all others will henceforth be 'not-Bradshaw'?"

Cayden nodded. "Pretty much. Bradshaw actually seems like a genuinely good guy."

"Yeah, we're all in agreement," Stevie laughed.

Zoie nodded. "I'll be sure to let her know the consensus." She stretched and squeak-yawned, walking directly to the refrigerator and pouring herself some orange juice. "How much of the assassination plot do you have written?"

"We have a weak outline," Cayden answered.

Pulling her hair back in one of Hugh's hair ties, Zoie took a seat at the table with them. "Tell me the plan so that I can poke holes in it."

Hugh gently replied, "Are you sure? You don't know as much as the rest of us about this world."

"Yep. That actually may make my analysis more valuable. I'll have a different perspective." She looked at Hugh. "I can't believe you didn't think of that. You had to do a doctoral dissertation and the dissenting side is always a part of that. It helps strengthen the debate."

"Thanks for joining us on this." Stevie placed her hand on Zoie's shoulder as she went over to the counter for more grapes. "So, I really think that the retreat for the realm representatives is the ticket."

"What's that?" Zoie asked.

"Hmmm…" Hugh slid his chair next to Zoie's. "You know the Illuminati?"

Zoie's eyes grew wide. "They are the Illuminati?!"

Hugh chuckled. "No. No. But they are like these ultra-powerful people that control everything in the supernatural world. So *like* the Illuminati. Every 50 years, they have a super-secret retreat to hang out and talk about their political plans. Get buy-in from each other, you know?"

"Let me guess," she said, "they meet this year?"

"This weekend," Cayden interjected. They glanced at Stevie. "Do you know where the retreat is this year?"

She nodded. "Romania. Bran Castle."

Hugh groaned. "The vampires are hosting?" Stevie nodded, and he let out a whiney "I hate vampires." Then, Hugh added, with a gag, "They all have this… smell…"

Cayden nodded in agreement. "It's like…" They moved their hands about as if they were going to generate the right word out of the thin air.

"It's not quite death… it's like… thick blood. Iron." He closed his eyes and held back another gag.

"Yes! Yes! That's it!"

Stevie busted out laughing. "Are you serious? I thought that was a made-up thing."

Hugh shuddered. "No, totally factual. They smell —"

She laughed again. "No! That wolves hated their smell."

"Totally true," Cayden replied. "They smell awful. They try to cover it, but we can smell it through their oils."

"Ohhhh kaaayyy." Zoie tried to get them back on topic. "Well, if they are hosting, there's going to be a lot of them, so how are you going to get past that… reaction to their *stench*?"

Cayden suggested, "Coroners use Vicks VapoRub under their noses to battle the smell of death in the morgue."

"They would smell that," Zoie interjected. "You're going to want to cover the smell but also blend in yourselves. It stands to reason that if you think they smell terrible that they feel the same way about you." Then she added, "Remember, Hugh, what I told you at the Vulcan? You smell like old books and tea, but I never told you what the third thing was? It's *warm dog* when it wakes up after sleeping close to your body."

Stevie sighed. "If she can smell it, they definitely can."

"Could we mask it with something?" Cayden asked.

Zoie pressed her lips together. "Before we decide what to mask it with, don't you think we should discuss who all would be there? If you all have this reaction, wouldn't other creatures have reactions to certain things, too?"

"My parents won't have anything in particular," Stevie said. "With Alvin and his minions being there, they will already smell wolf. But you should still be careful that they don't smell you in the halls that you don't belong in."

Zoie asked, "Are you going?"

She shook her head. "I'm staying behind to protect you. Plus, it's a risk that my parents would sense me or, worse, see me."

"Oh."

"The witches." Cayden pulled the conversation back to topic.

Hugh nodded. "Yes, The Shrews Three."

Zoie shot a disgusted look at Hugh. "You've mentioned them before. Why do you call them that?"

"They consider that title an honor, Zoie." Stevie continued her explanation. "Only women can hold the highest seats in the witches' realm. Warlocks aren't even allowed to ever take the seat."

"I don't know if that's progressive or if they find it archaic in the way that we find it archaic when only men hold a position." Zoie pondered.

"Because Warlocks cannot carry children, the witches' realm does not see it fit that men would make all the decisions over everyone else. The witches would want to have the best interest of everyone in mind because the magic within woman creates men, women, and any other gender." Stevie smiled. She then got back closer to the topic at hand. "Representing Sun magic is Ha of Vietnam. Earth is Jade of Spain, and Moon is Chandra of India."

Cayden tapped a fork on the edge of their nacho plate. "Can we get back to making the plan?"

—Zoie—

"So, Bran Castle?" Zoie opened her laptop and did a general search, hoping to maybe find blueprints, or even pictures of the inside to try and create a map. "This place is huuuuuge." She turned the laptop around to show her friends.

Cayden suggested, "Do you think that we maybe first should

figure out the endgame, here? How we're going to off him? That may change how we get in."

"Or maybe the way that you can get in changes how you off him?" Stevie countered.

Hugh started pacing again. "There's dismemberment, decapitation, poison, silver bullet, and killing him in human form."

"Wait," Zoie asked, "I thought you couldn't die in human form. That's how you became a wolf?"

"That's just the first violent death. Anything after that, in human form, we can die." Hugh ran his hand up and down Zoie's back. Then he looked over at Cayden, "I think silver bullet is out because we'd not be able to carry ourselves without potentially hurting ourselves."

"Agreed."

Stevie then suggested, "I think you need to consider a way to get him while he's in human form. There's going to be so many beings there protecting him that any real fight would result in your deaths."

"You also may want to make it look like an accident or maybe even natural," Zoie suggested. "Especially since you're planning to take his spot as the representative."

"What are you thinking, Zoie?" Cayden asked.

"Okay…" She took a deep breath. "I'm thinking that if you could get a heavy sedative in his drink, you could knock him out and sneak into his room and, I don't know, suffocate him with a pillow or maybe drip some poison like yellow jasmine into his mouth." She continued, "There wouldn't be any blood, and you may be able to do this without being traced. You just have to do it without getting caught in the act." She also suggested, "You could always use insulin and put the needles in between the webbings of

259

his toes and pump too much into him. He would die."

"Okay, there's some good ideas in there." Hugh asked, "Would they be able to detect the yellow jasmine?"

Zoie shrugged. "I think yes, you can detect yellow jasmine. But how much will kill him? Insulin wouldn't be able to be detected."

Cayden suggested, "I think we go with the insulin. Just do, I don't know, five times the needed amount to kill a human. It's natural in everyone's blood, and, like Zoie said, it can't be detected."

"Stevie, do you know how much would be needed?" Zoie asked.

Stevie shook her head. "I've not studied the anatomical and physiological makeup of any being." She asked, "Where do we get the sedatives? How do we ensure that he gets them?"

Cayden said, "For the sedatives and any potential poison, I *know a guy.*"

Stevie snapped her fingers. "Each afternoon, at about 3, tea is served to all the rooms. It's customary at the retreat. I remember it from when I was a little girl and my parents took me along. You could slip it into the tea." She looked at Cayden. "You're not well known. You could probably sneak in and pose as a kitchen worker. Maybe even the person that rolls the cart all the way to the door." She turned her attention to Hugh. "Then, you could sneak in the room and do whatever it is you need to do."

Zoie chewed on her lower lip a little. "You went when you were a kid? Do you think that anyone else will be in Alvin's room?"

Hugh shook his head. "His mate, Edie, is dead, obviously, and his son, Miles, lives on his own and is around 150 years old. I doubt he would be hanging out in his dad's room like a kid on a business trip with their parent."

Zoie tried to say something but couldn't get the words out. Hugh took her hand. "You okay, Zo?"

She tried again to speak but none of the words would come out. "Nevermind." She remembered the spell that the black hooded figure put on her. "I've lost it," she lied. "If I think about it again, I'll ask then."

—Hugh—

A quick trip to Canada to meet with the *guy that Cayden knew* and another quick pass through NightBrooke to Romania later, the four of them were holed up in Club Vila Bran. Hugh would be lying if he didn't acknowledge to at least himself that he was nervous. This wasn't just some regular kill. This wasn't following a rapist into a dark alley and ripping him to shreds. This was an assassination attempt. An assassination attempt on one of the highest-ranked figures in the supernatural realm.

Hugh knew that it was risky for him to even make an appearance near the location of the retreat. Any bounty hunter could be around the corner and could intercept the plan and take Hugh out of the picture before he even could get started. That would leave Zoie impossibly vulnerable.

It was nearly time for him to leave, so Hugh was going over the plan in his head, until Zoie stepped out of the shower. She walked out of the bathroom with the towel wrapped around her. His focus went to her, immediately. "Don't stand way over there in just that towel and tease me. Come here."

She blushed but did as told. He was sitting at the edge of the

263

bed, so she walked over to him and stood between his knees. "I need to tell you before…"

He put his index finger over to her lips. "Not right now. Not like this." He knew that she loved him without her ever saying it. He pulled her close, his clothes and her towel — not any air between them — being the only thing that separated them. Hugh kissed her — really kissed her — knowing that, if this plan went sideways, it could be the last time that he ever did.

Even after the kiss, his mouth lingered close to hers, and he kept his eyes closed. His spoke in just a whisper. "What are your plans today?"

He felt her fingers twist in his hair. "Sit by the pool and try to read." She kissed him gently.

He kissed her again. "What book?" He ran his hands on her back and then tried to pull her impossibly closer.

"Neverending Story." Her voice became shaky. She took her hands out of his hair, and Hugh felt her hands shake, even though she was trying to hide it by gliding them down the back of his neck to his shoulders.

He felt a tear travel down the side of her nose and hit his. He still kept his eyes closed and his mouth near hers. He didn't want her to have any inkling that he was nervous. "I'm going to be okay. This is going to work." Another quick kiss. "And then we're going to be together, and everything is going to be as it should be." He opened his eyes and finally put a little bit of space between them. "Look me in the eyes."

Her eyes opened, but she didn't look up. Tears were still escaping. She pressed her lips together and closed her eyes tightly once again, trying to stop the tears.

"Zoie." He touched her chin. "Zoie, look at me." He ran his

thumb on her cheeks, catching her tears. Once she looked at him, he told her again, "I will be back here with you in no time." He caught another stray tear. "Tell me that you believe that. Look me in the eyes and tell me that you believe that."

"I do." She twisted some of his hair in her fingers. "I need you to return to me." She started to cry, nearly uncontrollably. "I promised myself I would never need anyone ever, ever again. But I need you in my life."

He pulled her close and let her sob into his shoulder. "You will always have me, Zoie. You remember the vow I made to you?" He continued to hold her. "There is nothing that could keep me from you. Nothing."

There was a knock at the door. "You ready?" It was Cayden.

He finally let go of her and offered Cayden a quick response. "One sec." He stood up and changed his shirt, casting the previous one aside haphazardly, and then pulled his hair back. "Stevie will be here to protect you."

"I'm not worried about me."

He took her hand and locked their pinkies together. "Promise me that you won't spend the entire day worried about me. Pinky swear it."

"I can't."

He pulled her close, pinkies still locked. "Do something for five minutes that is just for you so that you can't worry about me. Pinky swear it."

"Pinky swear."

He placed his forehead to hers. "You can't break a pinky swear." Hugh kissed her forehead and then quickly walked over to the door, looking back as he turned the doorknob. "I'll be back in a few hours."

—Zoie—

She picked up the shirt that Hugh had just thrown on the chair and then sat on the bed and cried. She hadn't wanted to cry in front of Hugh before he left — of course, that was a failure. It wasn't that she didn't want him to know that she cared so deeply for him, it was simply that Zoie didn't want him to think that she had any doubt in his abilities or this plan. The truth was, even while she was helping them plan this all out, she thought that it was a shot in the dark that they actually would accomplish what they were setting out to do.

She then decided to put on some underwear and threw the shirt on. There was a faint knock at the door, and Stevie announced herself on the other side. Zoie approached the door, looked through the peephole just to be sure, and then slowly opened the door and let her in.

Stevie hugged her friend tightly. "I'm scared for them too."

She knew that Stevie's hug and declaration was meant to show empathy, but it didn't ease her mind whatsoever. The fact that her friend who understood and lived in the supernatural world had her doubts just meant that there was some merit in Zoie's fear. "I should have told him that I love him. I tried but he stopped me. I should have made sure that he knew."

"They both know how loved they are by us." She let go and put her hands on Zoie's shoulders. "Why don't we both get ourselves pool ready and meet poolside in about 30 minutes?"

Zoie nodded and, as soon as Stevie was out the door, she went back into the bathroom and washed her face, hoping to get the crusty tears off of her cheeks. She looked in the mirror and touched her lips gently, closing her eyes and making the memory of Hugh's kiss permanent in her mind — just in case.

Zoie quickly put on her bathing suit — this one was of her choosing: a black one piece with a little skirt — and, instead of her usual coverup, she put Hugh's shirt back on, not caring if it looked silly. She tucked her necklace under the collar of the shirt and then grabbed Hugh's book and headed out to the pool.

She had only taken 10 or 15 minutes to get ready, so Stevie wasn't out there yet. Zoie looked at the choices for seating and picked something on the far side of the pool. Because Zoie hadn't been living in Alabama long before all of the recent events started to transpire, the temperature was perfect to her — it was similar to what she would experience back in Pennsylvania during the summers. When she took her flip-flops off, the tile of the pool deck was still cool to the touch, so she walked barefoot over to her intended seating area.

She put her towel on a lounge chair next to the one she was taking to hold it for Stevie, even though no one else was out there. In fact, there actually weren't many people staying at the hotel at all, and those that were usually went out during the day to see the sites.

Zoie took a moment to appreciate that she was able to have this peacefulness. She silently thanked a few goddesses for this and centered herself with a few breaths in and out of her nose.

Once she felt a little more at ease — well, as at ease as she was going to get that day — she got comfortable and started reading her book. It wasn't long until she was interrupted by someone that called her name. "Zoie." But that someone was not Stevie.

—Hugh—

The run to Bran Castle was about 30 minutes. They had to take a long way to stay hidden, and they opted to not change into wolf form to save their energy for when they really needed it. Luckily there were plenty of trees and brush for them to hide in.

"There's the entrance," Cayden whispered.

"You go left, and I'll go right. When it's clear, I'll signal to you." Cayden nodded in acknowledgement and then they separated.

Hugh made his way to a tree just outside the grounds, and then found his way to the wall outside the castle. He signaled to Cayden and they both made their way into the backdoor of the kitchen. Quickly Cayden found their way into the uniform room — courtesy of memorizing the path via maps and pictures from the internet, grabbing one that fit and then heading for one of the carts for afternoon tea. Hugh went in next, praying there was a uniform large enough for him.

Cayden found the cart that was obviously for Alvin; the kettle, cups, and saucers all had wolves on them, just as Stevie had said they might, as she remembered the ones for her parents having fish on them. Looking around and listening for anyone nearby,

Cayden then lifted the lid to the kettle, pretending to make sure there was water in it, and they dropped the sedative in.

Hugh had attempted to move on ahead to find the wing of the castle where the wolves would be housed, but not before hearing that Cayden had gotten stopped by someone.

"Make sure that you don't forget the pastries," one of the cooks pointed out. "I see you have the little sandwiches, but you forgot the cakes." Cayden nodded and grabbed them. "And for God's sake, tuck in your shirt. Were you born in a barn? Have some decorum." Cayden fixed their shirt and adjusted their bowtie and headed towards the door. The cook then said, "In case you forgot, since you seem to have lost all sense, Master Irvings is staying in the west tower." He then rolled his eyes. "Amateurs."

As soon as they were through the door, Cayden signaled to Hugh where they were headed, and they got on their way. The pair of them were, at first, extra careful to not make the wooden floors creek under their weight. Then Cayden suggested that they proceed as normal. "These old castles have their quirks, and it would be expected that we make noise as we travel the halls." Hugh nodded in agreement, too worried that his boisterous voice would give them away at this point.

The distance between the kitchen and the west tower seemed to be miles upon miles. Hugh had often needed to duck into other rooms or hallways to hide from others, as he could have been more easily recognized than Cayden.

Just as they were approaching Alvin's suite, Hugh started to feel strange. It wasn't anxiety about the mission; as soon as they got out of the kitchen area, all of that had disappeared for him. This was different. His heart felt as if it was beating out of rhythm. He took a couple deep breaths and moved forward.

Then, just as they were one hallway and two doors away, Hugh felt his breath be sucked out from his lungs. He felt like his throat was closing, and his head started to pound. His back hit the wall, and he slid down to the floor.

Cayden stopped and came back to him. No one was in the hallway with Hugh. "Hugh, are you okay?" They whispered. "Which direction did they go?"

He shook his head. "No. There was no one." Hugh tried to catch his breath. "Zoie." He felt the connection to her fading in and out.

Cayden reached their hand out to Hugh to help him up. "What?"

Hugh's heart was now pounding. "We need to go. Zoie's in danger. I can feel it."

"Well, we need to be quick about it. You made a lot of noise."

Hugh pointed towards the suite door. "Leave the tea. Knock and run. Maybe there's enough sedative in it to do the job for us." He was still trying to catch his breath.

"Start down that way; I remember seeing an exit." They waited for Hugh to start making his way towards the door and then dropped the tea off and ran.

The pair of them found the exit and Hugh immediately shifted into wolf form and took off running for the hotel. He was faster than Cayden, even with the trouble he was having with his mating bond, but he knew that his friend would understand the urgency.

271

—Zoie—

"I told you that the very first moment when you were unprotected, I would come for you." The hooded figure was back — but this time, the voice was not augmented. She recognized the voice. Male. Southern. Lacked the characteristics of an older voice.

Thinking back to all the interactions that she had had since moving to Birmingham — because that was when all of this supernatural stuff began — she tried to locate the face to match the voice. She couldn't place it, so she decided to attempt to get him to have a longer conversation.

"I'm not unprotected. He'll be right back." Zoie stood up, dropping her book onto her chair. Determined to keep the distance between them, she didn't make a move and prayed that the pool between them would protect her while she thought of a way to get help. She prayed Stevie would show up quickly.

She reached over to the table where her phone was, but suddenly it was floating in the air near the center of the pool. "Don't start that shit again," the figure ordered. "Who were you going to call anyways?" The figure lifted his hand and pulled off his hood.

"Miles," she said under her breath. She realized that she had no

273

idea that supernatural beings integrated themselves so much into the human world. Zoie had always thought that Hugh, Cayden, and Stevie were in the minority, but this was making her wonder — just momentarily — how many witches, shifters, mermaids, or anything else that she encountered in her life without knowing.

Miles' voice brought her back to reality. He smirked. "So, you do remember me? Even though I wasn't good enough for one date?"

She shook her head. "That wasn't it. I actually was busy, Miles." Her voice came out as a plea, rather than a firm response.

"Not too busy for that foul dog you've been traveling the world with." He looked around and smirked again. "Where is he, again?" He pointed at the phone and then moved his finger down, sending the phone plunging into the pool.

"He's just stepped out," she lied. Confidently, she added, "He'll be back in a few moments."

Miles waved his hand and with a quick flick of his wrist, slammed Zoie's mouth shut. "Stop talking. You bore me." She couldn't open her mouth, no matter how hard she tried — her lips were fused together by magic. "Your beloved," he stated, his voice dripping with bitterness and hatred. "He will not return soon enough to save you." He glared at her. "I hope you are ready to suffer. To suffer like he made my family suffer for over a century."

Zoie watched Miles manipulate some of the water into an orb and float it towards her in the air. "I know I promised to send you to him, piece by piece, but I just… well, I just have something a little more fun planned."

Suddenly, that ball of water was surrounding her head. Frantic, Zoie attempted to push the water away with her hands, but it would not move. She couldn't swim out of it, and she couldn't part the

274

water. She tried pulling it off like the bubbles from their dive. She resolved that this was a different kind of water magic than Stevie's. She needed to come up with another solution. *Fuck's sake, Stevie. Get here. Help me.*

She felt her feet separate from the pool deck. Quickly, she was pulled to the edge of the pool closer to Miles.

At least I'm not within reach, she thought to herself, knowing that it wouldn't make much of a difference, either way, if she couldn't hold her breath long enough. *You held your breath through the Well. You can do this.*

With another quick motion, Miles pushed his arm forward in the air, the power of his magic knocking Zoie into the pool, and she felt her back hit the floor of the pool. Then her head — but luckily it didn't slam, due to the resistance of the water.

She tried to swim up towards the surface, but something kept pulling her back down. *Miles' powers*, Zoie reasoned, with her eyes tightly closed.

She tried to concentrate on turning back time so that she could change these events. *C'mon Zoie. If you could do it at age seven, without knowing you could do this, you should be able to do this now.* It was useless. She was too in her head. Even so, she wouldn't be able to go back far enough at this point.

Forcing her eyes open, accepting the burn of the overly chlorinated pool water, Zoie looked up through the distortion from the bubbles and motion of the water. Air continued to escape through Zoie's nose, despite her attempts to hold her breath as long as she could.

She locked eyes on Miles, willing herself to cast away any visible fear.

Suddenly, the bubbles stopped blocking Zoie's visual path to her attacker. She still attempted to fight to the surface, but it was no use. Everything went black.

The fear she was trying to suppress took over. She grabbed her throat. *Stop trying to breath. Stop trying to scream. Hold your breath. Ignore the pressure.*

Zoie stopped the fight. There was absolutely no use. Miles — and subsequently, Alvin — had won. And Zoie felt oddly calm about it.

Her throat burned.
Her sinuses burned.
Her lungs burned.
This was...
death.

—Hugh—

Hugh shifted back into human form in the parking lot but didn't bother to wait for the glass doors to open to get in the lobby. He ran straight through them.

Once he finally arrived poolside, Stevie was next to Zoie, as she was lying on the pool deck. Still running, he essentially slid on the wet tiles to get next to her, once he had tried to put on the brakes.

He saw her skin was a bluish-grey and knew that she wasn't breathing. "Pull the water out of her lungs! Your magic, Stevie! Do it! Do it now!"

"Hugh, I tried. I was too late."

He grabbed her arm and yanked her. "You're wrong. Save her!"

"I already did. Her lungs are clear."

He growled, "You had one job today. One job — to protect her! What happened to that?! I trusted you... *She* trusted you!"

"There was a warlock — Miles something. I think he was a bounty hunter..."

He ignored her. There was nothing that she could say that would be a good enough excuse. He went to start chest compressions and she pulled him back. "Stop! It won't do anything but break her ribs.

It's been thirty minutes."

"It can't be true." He sat her body up and held her in his arms, hugging her. "Zoie, no no no." He started to cry, holding her and rocking. "You're not gone." More rocking and more tears. "I'm not whole without you." The hole in his heart felt like it became larger. Large enough that it seemed that a cavity took the place of his heart behind his ribs.

As he held her lifeless body tight to his, he didn't even realize that the rest of the world disappeared. He couldn't hear the conversations that were happening around him because they didn't matter anymore. There was no need for him to see any of the people because the one that matter wasn't there anymore. The only thing that he could smell was chlorine, instead of her usual perfume — Prada Candy Sugar Pop.

"I'll do anything, just come back to me." He wanted to squeeze her tighter — squeeze the life back into her — but he didn't want to crush her either.

He barely even felt when Cayden put a hand on his arm. "We have to go, Hugh. The authorities are coming, and if you're at the scene, it won't be good. Especially since you ran through here still in wolf form." They added, "We've caused quite the stir. We have to go now."

Hugh got on his knees and then moved to cradle Zoie's body in his arms, but Cayden stopped him.

"You have to leave her, Hugh." They put their hand on his shoulder, trying to provide any small comfort. "Leave her here."

"No." He shook his head, never making eye contact with Cayden, just looking at Zoie.

Cayden knelt in front of him. "You need to leave her, and you need to go. Her body needs taken back to her family. The authorities will make sure that happens." They added, "If we stay, they are going to take you in, possibly blame you for this. Worse, they could turn you into a science experiment."

"Doesn't matter." He pushed her wet hair out of her face. He closed his eyes and placed a tearful kiss on her cold, blue-grey lips. Slowly, he laid her back on the pool deck and Cayden and Stevie peeled him away from her. He tried to go back to her.

"We have to go, Hugh." They guided him to their rental car and sped off, just as the police were pulling in.

Hugh stared out the window, not even registering that there was scenery on the other side. For over an hour, they rode in silence. Not even music. Just the sound of the engine as Cayden accelerated to go up hills.

Finally, Stevie said, "It was someone named Miles. Do you think he's the same Miles that is Alvin's son? Do you think we should start searching for him immediately? He's already got a two-plus hour head start."

"No." Hugh still stared off to the void.

Cayden looked in the rearview mirror. "Do you want to wait? Or do this alone?"

"Neither." He continued to stare. "He's taken everything from me already. There's no need to fight back."

"Hugh…"

"I took everything from him when he was a child," Hugh admitted, flatly. "I ripped his mother apart and threw pieces of her at him. Then his father couldn't even care for him — because… because he felt like this." He put his hand on his empty chest. Then he let out a long breath. "Oh yeah, and, in his senior year of undergrad, I gave him a C in a class, ruining his perfect GPA." He was annoyed with himself.

"None of that gives him the right…"

He slammed his hand on the door. "I have nothing to fight for." He had no tears left to cry, as they all were part of the pool water now. "I waited more than 190 years to find her, and she's gone." He tightened his jaw. "Just take me home."

"There's a portal nearby," Cayden announced.

Hugh was back to staring. "Fine."

———————

"Do you think that we should stay with him tonight?" Cayden asked Stevie as Hugh haphazardly threw his keys on the table next to the door.

He turned to the two of them, slowly. "I just want to be alone."

Stevie insisted, "Hugh, we can stay and watch movies."

"No." He waved his hand in protest. "Leave me alone." He reiterated, "I just want to be by myself right now." He walked over to the couch and lay down.

Cayden motioned for Stevie to go outside, and then they sat on the coffee table. "Hugh, brother, I can stay if you want."

Hugh's bottom lip started to shake. "No, I'm fine."

They put their hand on his arm. "No, you aren't, and that's okay."

He sat up and covered his face as he cried. "I loved her. I *love* her." He shook his head. "I just need to be alone with my thoughts right now. I need to figure out how to get through this."

"I can help you with that." Cayden paused for a moment. "I will support you any way that you need."

Hugh nodded and looked at Cayden. "Right now, I just really want to be alone. Will you check on me tomorrow?"

Cayden forced a smile and nodded. "I can do that."

After Cayden and Stevie left, Hugh laid on the couch for a period of time — he didn't know what time had passed because time didn't matter.

It was dark out, so he decided on a walk. He didn't know where he was going, until he got there.

Hugh approached the front door. He tried the doorknob, knowing that it wouldn't work. Reaching into the hanging plant, which was now mostly dead from Alabama heat combined with lack of water, he grabbed the spare key that was lying on top of the dirt.

He quietly entered, the scent of lemongrass still hanging on even though the tenant of the home hadn't been there in weeks. Hugh went directly to the bedroom. The bed was neatly made, and what he was looking for was sitting right in front of the pillows. "Judy." He hugged Zoie's stuffed maltese close to his chest.

Then Hugh began walking through her home and trying to see if there was anything of hers that he felt like he just had to have to keep her close. At one point, he considered taking her hairbrush, just so that he would have her red hair.

From the kitchen, he heard the wooden wind chimes that hung on the back patio hit each other from the light breeze there was that night. Knowing how Zoie had everything set up, Hugh only needed to open one cupboard in order to acquire her favorite mug and a couple of bags of her favorite tea. In her dining room, he stopped momentarily in front of her altar. He glared at it and growled, "A lot of good her protection spells did for her. This shit doesn't even work." He considered breaking her entire witchcraft collection, but he didn't want the place to look broken into.

Making his way to her bookshelf, he pulled a few books to take with him: all of the *Twilight* books; *Wicked Fox*; a rare edition of

Little Women; and *Clap When You Land*. He grabbed her favorite bookmark, which was made of wood, and then her journal, which she had kept on her bookshelf because that was *where anyone would naturally keep a book*. He started to make his way towards the door, when he saw a cardboard box with a black sharpie label that read MANUSCRIPTS. He put everything in that box, with Judy at the top of the mountain, and decided that was enough.

He slowly made his way back out the door and locked up. As soon as news made it back to her mother that Zoie had died, everything would be packed up or discarded, and someone else would move in, so he stood at the front door, with his hand on it for a few seconds.

He slowly made his way back to his place. He slumped down on the couch, wrapped himself in a blanket, pulled Judy close to his chest, and chose a manuscript to read. Having her handwriting and something written in her voice would have to fill that hole in his chest for a while.

He laid his head down on a pillow while he read — until his eyelids were too heavy to keep open.

———————

Buzz. Buzz. Buzz.

Hugh reached over for his phone and noticed that he had 37 missed text messages. He quickly opened the messenger app, hoping that he had just been in a terrible nightmare. He prayed to see Zoie's name.

There were 2 general messages from work about a suspicious package found on South Sixth Street, 7 from Stevie, and 28 from Cayden.

He sent a reply to both of them. *I'm awake :)*. He figured the smiley face maybe would keep them away. He just wanted to be alone.

He got in the shower and stood under the water for about 45 minutes. He really had believed that he could rinse the pain away, but the moment he thought about how she was never coming back, he sunk to the floor and cried until the water ran cold.

Hugh dried off and then went out to the kitchen and poured himself some cereal. Took two bites. Sat the bowl on the counter and walked back to the couch.

He wrapped himself in the blanket and held Judy again. He stared blankly out the window and thought about other people that he'd lost in the past and people he left behind when he became a wolf. How did he get through that? *You made it through all of those losses; you certainly can make it through this one.*

He wasn't sure how long he blanked out for, but suddenly it was dark outside and there were no lights on in the house. Hugh didn't really need them, though, because, while his heart was broken, his wolf senses were still going strong.

He bent over and rummaged through the box of manuscripts. He felt something that wasn't a spiral notebook. The pages felt glossy, and it was a little more than an inch thick. He pulled it out and sighed. Hugh glanced over at Judy. "A bridal magazine?"

Looking at the cover, he saw that it was a recent edition. Then he flipped through the pages and looked at the ones that were dog-eared. She had dresses she had loved. Locations. Place settings. Color schemes. She had circled things in black ink — he recognized the thickness of the lines as a Pilot G2-10, which was Zoie's favorite pen.

Love and marriage wasn't the central theme of any of Zoie's work; she didn't write romance. This magazine was bought because she was thinking about her future. A future that was stolen from her. A future that may have been with him.

Hugh threw the magazine across the room, knocking over a potted plant, shattering the pot and spilling dirt everywhere. He closed his eyes and rubbed his temples.

"Judy, how am I supposed to go on with my future when so much of it included her?" He clutched Judy to his chest and fell back onto the couch and fell asleep because he felt that it was the only thing he could bring himself to do.

———

A set of heavy knocks at the door woke Hugh from his — perhaps third or fourth — nap of the day. He groaned. "Nobody's home."

The screen door creaked and then the heavy front door swung open. "Then you should start locking your fucking door." Cayden took a few steps in and then stopped abruptly.

Stevie gagged. "Hugh? When was the last time you cleaned in here?"

"I took out the trash yesterday." He pulled the duvet tighter around his body.

Picking up what appeared to be an old banana peel — she wasn't sure — Stevie asked, "Did you consider taking out more than one bag?"

He shrugged.

Cayden frowned. "Are you okay? I've texted you every day for the last three weeks, and you've barely replied more than a word or two…" They stepped closer to the pile of blankets that was Hugh. "You've not been out for a drink or dinner in over a month." They added, "You're able to go back into Nightbrooke now…"

"Are you eating?" Stevie cut in because the only reason that Hugh was allowed back in Nightbrooke or anywhere in the Supernatural Realm was because Zoie was out of the picture, absolving him of a crime because the subject of said crime no longer existed. She grabbed a trash bag and started putting pretty much everything in sight in it. "I mean, besides junk food."

He shrugged. "I'm fine."

Cayden took a seat next to the lump of blankets. "What can we do to help you?"

He shook his head. "Bring her back."

Stevie tied a full bag and shook open another one. "We can't do that."

Hugh turned and the blanket fell off of his head, revealing unbrushed, dirty, matted hair and sunken eyes. "*You* could have."

Stevie stopped gathering trash. "I beg your pardon?"

Hugh squinted his eyes. "You were supposed to be watching her. Not to leave her side." Then he added coldly, "You have the power to manipulate water. You could have pulled it from her lungs." He growled a little and turned back to the TV, which was muted but playing an old Three Stooges episode.

Stevie dropped the bag and slammed her hand on the kitchen table. "You forget that I tried that?"

Hugh snapped back around. "You didn't try hard enough!"

"I tried everything!" She shook her head. "She was my friend too."

Hugh stood up. "She's the love of my life! My soul mate. You have no idea what this pain feels like." He clutched his shirt that covered where his heart used to be and fought back tears that he didn't even know that he had left. "No idea at all."

Cayden, trying to be reasonable, interjected, "I'm certain that if something happened to Stevie or…"

Hugh rolled his eyes. "You don't even love her."

Cayden's jaw dropped to the floor. "Are you fucking kidding me?"

"You don't. You've told me loads of times that you know she's not your true mate. That you'd be able to move on if something happened to her."

Cayden pressed their lips together and tightened their jaw. Letting out a deep breath, they replied, "Look, I know you've got this depression thing going on, but, like, fuck you."

Stevie had had enough of this. "Stop it, the both of you." She shook her head at Cayden and then turned her attention back to Hugh. "Hugh, you need to get out of this house and go for a walk. Get some sunshine. Exercise. Drink some water. Eat a salad."

He opened a curtain and sat on a chair next to the window. "Getting some vitamin D now, OK?"

She sat on the ottoman in front of the chair. "Look, why don't you get a shower? You smell like death, to be honest." She continued, "I'll clean up in here while you do that." She looked over at the pile of dirt on the floor and the dead plant that was shriveled up next to it. "I think you'll feel better."

He shook his head. "I don't want to feel better, Stevie."

She took his hand. "The best way to honor her is to live your life. She gave hers…"

"Because she thought I could get there in time to save her." He put his hands over his face and started to cry. "Because she trusted me to take care of her." He cried, "I made a vow to protect her, and I failed."

Stevie's face softened. "No, Hugh. I think she knew that if she kept Miles distracted, it would give you the time to complete the Alvin job." She looked around for some tissues — unused, preferably

— but then just pointed to the paper towel roll in the kitchen.

Cayden brought the roll over. Sitting down on the coffee table, they added, "What can we do, Hugh?"

"I don't know." It was an honest answer. He didn't know what he needed. He just needed. He needed someone to make sure that he did the basics. He needed someone to listen. Someone to hold him. He. Just. Needed.

Cayden asked, "Do you need help with lesson plans?"

Hugh shook his head. "I took a sabbatical." He added, "I'm lucky they didn't fire me. When they found out I needed a break because my partner — a student — died, they could have terminated me." He looked aimlessly out the window. "They still might."

They stood. "Let's get you in the shower. I'll go mow the lawn while you do that, and Stevie will do a clean sweep of the area for the trash."

"Sure, give me the hardest job," Stevie scoffed.

Hugh slowly nodded and got up and walked to the shower. He turned the water on and let it warm up. Looking into the bathroom mirror, he just stared for a few moments. The fog that formed was the picture of his brain for the last several weeks. He really didn't remember anything. He never knew how long he slept or even what day of the week it was. He had no idea how long he had been on that couch.

He got in and stood under the water, letting it drench his hair. He wanted to cry, but he convinced himself that it was pointless. No amount of tears would bring her back.

No amount of sulking would either. He knew that. He willed himself to wash his face and then his hair.

No amount of waiting was going to bring her back. He convinced himself to wash away as much pain as he could.

He considered never shifting again and allowing himself to age and die. But he knew that it wouldn't reunite them. He reached out to the sink and grabbed his toothbrush and toothpaste. He trimmed his beard and brushed his hair the best that he could. He knew he could have it cut later.

And he realized that nothing would ever bring Zoie back. But he figured out what would make him feel better.

He grabbed a particular pair of jeans that Zoie had always told him that she liked; she would put her thumb in one of the belt loops while they walked together. Hugh grabbed a belt and a belt buckle in the style of the Davidson clan crest. He grabbed one of his war tartan handkerchiefs and tied it around the belt loop that Zoie's hand used to occupy. Then he threw on a black V-neck T-shirt and shoved his wallet in his back pocket.

Hugh walked out to the newly trash-free living room. "I know what I need your help with — both of you." It smelled like Stevie had sprayed the entire house with Lysol. It definitely woke him up as it burned his sinuses.

Stevie and Cayden looked up at him. "Anything, Brother," Cayden replied.

Hugh smiled, with a little touch of evil revealing itself in his eyes. "Anything?"

Both nodded.

"Good." He pulled his hair back into a manbun and said with the most confidence that he had commanded in over a month, "I want revenge, and I'm going to need your help to get it."

Stevie asked, cautiously, "What do you mean?"

He matter-of-factly said, "I would feel better if those responsible for her death were eliminated."

"Hugh, I have to ask," Cayden took Stevie's hand in theirs. "You don't mean Stevie, do you?"

Hugh paused and looked directly at Stevie. After a moment, he replied, "No. Not Stevie. She didn't intentionally bring harm to Zoie."

Stevie and Cayden both let out a deep breath that they didn't know they were holding. Stevie, with as much empathy as she could muster, asked, "Hugh, I'm just getting back in my parents' good graces…"

He took in a deep breath through his nose and let out a low growl. "They are the ones that went over the top and put a hit out on her. We would have never been in Romania…"

She cut him off with a plea. "Hugh, I can't help you get revenge on my parents…"

Cayden interjected, "Hugh, we know — *you* know — that Miles is Alvin's kid. That is independent from the hit on Zoie. He was going after her anyways."

Hugh thought about it for a moment. He paced back and forth in the kitchen and then said, "I will go after Miles first, and then, if I decide that I want to pursue retaliation against your parents, I'll act alone."

Stevie closed her eyes. "Fine. I understand." Hugh knew she didn't understand; he didn't care.

"Do you have a plan?"

Hugh shook his head. "No." Then he asked, "Did Alvin survive?"

"Yes." Cayden frowned. "Someone tipped him off, so he never drank the tea."

Hugh growled. "Whatever. He'll suffer like have when I take away the last thing that he cares about." He said it without any care. "Then, I'll go for him." He poured himself a glass of water and said, as if he was reciting the alphabet, "And he will suffer. Slowly.

And, then when there's barely anything left, I will be merciful and cut his heart out of his chest with a dull knife while his eyes are forced open so he can watch through a mirror."

Cayden looked at Hugh with concern in their eyes. "Hugh, what I'm about to ask is because I love you to death." They waited for any reaction from Hugh, but it never came. "Are you sure that this is going to make you feel better?"

Hugh shrugged. "No, I'm not sure. But it definitely won't hurt."

He started off towards the door and Cayden intercepted him by putting a hand on his shoulder. "Have you *really* thought this through?"

Stevie added, "You haven't even thought it through enough, Hugh, to tell us what help you want from us."

He turned to them. His eyes appeared as if they could have shot daggers out of them. "I've thought about this every minute of every day since I saw her lying on the ground." He continued, "I just want you to back me up. Not necessarily in the fight, but just... be there for me. I want to mostly do this myself, but I may need some of your resources." He grabbed his keys. "I'm heading to Nightbrooke right now to see what I can find out about Miles's whereabouts."

Cayden and Stevie looked at each other and then followed. "Here we go..."

———

As they approached the Lunar Brewery, it was obvious that the place was hopping that evening; the roar of conversations spilled out into the street.

Closing his eyes and taking a deep breath, Hugh prepared to open the door. He wasn't sure if he was ready to go somewhere that he had been with Zoie. He wasn't sure if he would ever be ready.

So he opened his eyes, took another deep breath, and opened the door. The entire pub fell silent at the sight of him. Then, suddenly, someone dropped a glass, and the volume level increased instantly, as if someone had just muted the crowd momentarily.

Hugh, Stevie, and Cayden took a table in the corner. A waitress came over and handed them menus — as if the three of them didn't know every item on the menu. Stevie ordered a red wine, and Cayden asked for a Captain and Coke.

"And for you, handsome?" she asked Hugh.

He didn't look up from the menu. "Guinness."

She repeated the orders back to them and added, "I'll also bring over a pitcher of water and some glasses for each of you and come back for your orders in a couple minutes."

As soon as she left the table, Stevie nudged Hugh. "I think she was flirting with you."

"Don't care." He put the menu down and looked at Stevie. "She just wants a good tip, and it's obvious that you two are together."

Stevie giggled. "Hugh, she's looking at you from the bar."

He shook his head. "I'm not interested."

"She would want you to be happy, Hugh."

He picked the menu back up and pretended to read it. "Well, if she would want me to be happy, then we need to find Miles and eliminate him. That would make me happy."

Stevie sighed. "She would want you to be happy in *love*."

He rolled his eyes. "She's been gone a month. A month, Stevie. I'm not going to just move on from it like that." He snapped his fingers. Then Hugh tightened his jaw. "I will never love again."

"You will never love *like that* again. You will love again." She reinforced it. "You can love again, Hugh."

The waitress brought over their drinks. "Captain for you. Red wine for you, and Guinness for you, Love." She batted her eyelashes at him.

"Thanks." He was watching the door for some reason.

"Are you all ready to order?" she asked, and both Cayden and Stevie placed their orders, but it took Stevie elbowing Hugh to get him to speak.

"Fish and chips." He handed her the menu while still looking at the door.

Stevie waited for the waitress to be out of earshot, and she nudged Hugh again. "You're being extremely rude to the waitress."

He shrugged. "I don't want to give any impression that I am returning interest." Just then, the door opened, and Hugh growled. "That asshole... what are the odds?"

Stevie put her hand on Hugh's shoulder, and Cayden said, "You can't do it here."

"I'm not going to." He watched Miles take a seat at a table on the other side of the room. "I'll be right back."

He made his way across the room and sat down next to Miles, blocking him in against the wall.

Miles put as much space between them as possible. "What do you want?"

"I'm just here to warn you." He made eye contact with Miles, to make sure that he knew how serious he was. "You took everything from me. Do you know what that means?" Miles shook his head and rolled his eyes. "It means that you should be looking over your shoulder for the rest of your miserable life."

"Why's that?" Miles smirked. Hugh could feel the arrogance dripping off of those two words.

Hugh leaned in. "It means that I have nothing left to lose. So one day — I don't know when and I don't know how — but one day, I will avenge her by taking your life. No matter what it takes." He patted Miles on the shoulder. "See you soon." Then Hugh stood up and walked calmly over to his table.

He sat down, but kept his eyes on Miles, barely even looking away to eat or drink. Miles waited an appropriate amount of time to make it look as if he wasn't intimidated by Hugh and then got up and left.

A few minutes later, he came back in and walked directly over to where Hugh was sitting. Miles grabbed a chair and took a seat at the table. He looked directly at Hugh. "Why wait?"

"Hmm?"

"Why wait? Let's do this today. Tonight."

Hugh took a bite of one of the chips. "Why? Do you not want to live in fear for long? Or is it that you simply aren't interested in living?" He wiped his hands on his napkin.

Miles took in a deep breath. "No, it's because I feel sorry for you. I want to do you a kindness and reunite you with your beloved." He produced an overdramatic pout. "Don't you want to see her again, even if it is in death?"

Hugh chuckled. "Where do you want the setting of your death to be, little boy?"

Mile scoffed. "Do you know the City Federal Building in downtown Birmingham?" Hugh nodded, so he continued. "Meet me on the roof. 3 AM."

Hugh grinned. "I hope you're ready to meet whatever God you choose. My face is the last one you will ever see."

It was Miles's turn to pat Hugh on the shoulder. "See you soon." Then Miles made eye contact with Stevie, which Hugh thought was peculiar, but it could just be that she had been glaring at him

293

the entire time.

As soon as he exited, Hugh turned to Stevie and Cayden. "Well, that worked out." He was almost happy.

Stevie's jaw dropped, and Cayden asked, "Are you sure you are ready? You've been kinda out of commission for a month, and today is your first day actually getting off of the couch. Maybe you should eat some Wheaties or something."

Hugh nodded. "I'm good. I wish I didn't have to wait until tonight." He downed the rest of his Guinness in what seemed like one gulp. "You two are available tonight, right?"

"Of course." Both said simultaneously.

The waitress returned and asked if they needed anything else, and when they all declined, she handed them their bills. "Thank you all so much for dining here this evening." As she walked away, she turned back to look at Hugh.

Hugh rolled his eyes when he looked at his bill. "For fuck's sake..."

"What did she double charge you?" Stevie asked.

He chuckled. "No. She wrote her name and phone number with a smiley face on the bill." He shook his head.

"Are you going to call her?"

"Absolutely not." He reiterated, "I told you, I'm not interested, and I never will be interested."

When the three of them got out the door, the waitress came out after. "Sir, you left your wallet on the table."

Hugh groaned as he checked his pockets. "Damn it." Hugh turned to take it from her, and she lingered her hand on his for a few seconds. He looked her in the eyes, and gently said, "I'm really flattered by your advances, Charli, but I'm spoken for."

"She doesn't have to know." She flirtatiously batted her eyelashes.

He smiled. "I love and respect her and could never do that to her." He turned and walked away.

"Let me know if anything changes, Love."

Stevie called back to her. "His name is Hugh!" Charli thanked her and ran back into the pub.

Hugh glared at Stevie. "What the Hell are you doing?"

She smiled. "You're going to want to move on someday, and she was really cute, with all that long brown hair." She added, "and I secretly think you may have been interested. You have never forgotten your wallet anywhere." She nudged him. "You wanted her to come after you."

Hugh rolled his eyes. "I was in a hurry to get back to Birmingham."

"Time doesn't move out there when we are in here," she pointed out. "Try again, Loverboy."

Cayden took Stevie's hand. "I think you should stop pushing him. We just got him out of the house for the first time in a month."

She shrugged. "I'm just planting some seeds."

"Well, I won't be watering them." Hugh pressed his hand to the door to Birmingham, which, instead of leading them back through the fountain, it brought them out to the creepy alley that mortals stayed away from.

Hugh thought about the first time that he took Zoie through that fountain door into Nightbrooke and how he had looked forward to bringing her back through that door. She would have had a very brief moment of seeing the image of herself in the alleyway. After that, he had planned to walk her home and begin to win her heart the old-fashioned way.

Even after that plan was shot to shit because of Jack's big mouth, Hugh thought that he would have the time to win Zoie's heart in a way that was independent of the mating bond, so that she would feel like she had a choice. A real future.

As they walked out of the alleyway, Hugh turned to Cayden. "Miles robbed me of every single plan I had for the rest of my life. I'm going to take away all of his."

"Okay. What's the plan?"

"Let's talk about tactical advantages and disadvantages."

Cayden nodded. "Well, you've definitely got him in size and strength, but he has magic at his disposal, and he can fly."

"So throwing his ass off the building…"

"…pointless, yeah."

Stevie interjected, "I think you should play on his arrogance. He obviously thinks that he can kick your ass without issue basically right now."

"That's a good point. Let's think about that a little bit more…"

Cayden replied, "I will for sure. Stevie and I have a couple of things to do first; we hadn't planned on today going as it has." They suggested, "Get some rest."

————

Hugh, Stevie, and Cayden walked out of the elevator in the empty City Federal Building on the top floor and then headed to the roof access point.

Miles floated down from the sky, the wind whipping his jacket around. "I see you brought backup."

Hugh scoffed. "Them? They are just here to help me carry your dead body away."

His feet touched down on the roof, and he called out over the roar of a sudden burst of wind. "Oh no, that one — they are your backup. But her," he pointed to Stevie, "she's here to help me push

296

your body off the roof once I end you."

Cayden's head about snapped off their neck. "What does he mean, Stevie?"

Miles laughed. "She never told you, did she? Do tell Hugh now, Stevie, about your part in this whole thing."

Stevie was silent.

"Don't be shy, Stevie, your part was instrumental in all of this." Miles grinned.

Cayden grabbed Stevie by the forearm. "Speak."

She glared at them and attempted to yank her arm free. "Don't talk to me like that."

Miles rolled his eyes. "Let's get on with this. Just tell these dogs how you played them these past few months."

Stevie's chin started to shake. "I... I had to get back in the good graces of my family, Hugh. I'm sorry."

Hugh made eye contact with Cayden, and, as if they could read each other's minds, Cayden turned and put his hand on Stevie's throat, pinning her to the wall behind her. "I'll deal with you later."

Miles snickered. "Stevie, you really should tell them your excellent work. Like telling my father about the tea, sending the messages through your parents."

She shook her head and tried to speak, but Cayden pressed their hand harder on their throat. Cayden looked her in the eyes. "How could you do this? To him? To *us*?"

"Dog, I just want to make sure that I'm the one that you want to fight." He finally put his feet to rooftop. "I'm, yes, the person that held your sweet pet under the water, but, Stevie — what was it that you did?" He tapped his lips while he thought. "Oh, no, it's what you didn't do."

"Stop!" Stevie strained, but Cayden grabbed her throat and

297

pulled her close to them and then slammed her head back against the wall. She cried out in pain.

Miles paced back and forth. "I sat around nearby and watched you beg, Hugh. You begged Stevie to draw the water from her lungs. She swore that she already did, but…" He smirked. "She lied."

"Enough stalling." Hugh knew that he could deal with Stevie later. There was no water around for her to manipulate and Cayden had her under control. Miles was the current threat. Hugh let out a howl and wasted no more time to change into wolf form.

Miles used his powers to pull each of the four Ls from the City Federal signs on each side of the building and crashed them into Hugh. The glass from the red lightbulbs shattered and caused small cuts all over Hugh's arms.

Hugh snarled and threw one of the Ls at Miles, who floated out of the way. "Fly away like a little coward," he growled. "I knew you didn't have the courage to truly face me. You know you can't win."

Miles landed back on the roof but lost his footing when a gust of wind howled through. He caught himself on one of the metal bars, and, once he was stable, he yanked it off. He spun it like a sword. "I am going to pierce you with this, as if it was a skewer."

Hugh didn't fear death, and he definitely didn't fear being stabbed. Miles moved to stab him in the chest by Hugh simply put his hand around the bar and slammed Miles to the floor.

Miles groaned, and blood was coming out of the back of his head. "Is that all you got?"

Hugh grabbed Miles by the neck and picked him up. "You should have done some research on werewolves, little boy." He dug his nails into the sides of his neck. "There's no fucking silver bullet up here."

Miles gagged. "My father will not stop until you're dead."

Hugh pulled Miles so their faces were inches apart. "Let him come." He slammed him back on the roof and placed his foot on his chest. Grabbing Miles' right wrist, Hugh twisted and yanked, separating Miles' arm from his body.

Miles screamed in pain. With his remaining hand, he reached up and used what power he could pull from his spirit to latch onto something and hit Hugh with it. It just so happened to be the access door.

Losing his balance as the door connected with his back, Hugh fell down and rolled, never letting go of Miles' severed arm.

Miles rose slowly to his feet, but wobbled. Cayden moved to release Stevie and attack Miles, but Hugh yelled, "No!"

Miles looked directly at Hugh just in time to see the arm that used to be his connect with his face, knocking him back down — face first.

Hugh got back up, slammed his foot on Miles' back, causing a Miles-shaped indentation in the roof. Hugh leaned over, put a hand on either side of Miles' head and applied pressure.

Miles screamed out in pain, but Hugh just slowly applied more and more pressure until his skull shattered. For good measure, Hugh twisted Miles's neck and ripped his head off, tossing it towards the lonely arm lying haphazardly a few yards away. Then, to ensure that the job was complete, he tore off the remaining arm and both legs.

Then he turned to Stevie, who was still being held by Cayden. She was crying. "I'm sorry. I'm sorry. I had to get back into the good graces of my parents, Hugh. I had to. It was the only way I could."

Hugh shook his head and then glared at Stevie with his glowing, yellow eyes. "I trusted you with the thing most precious to me." If he didn't know better, Hugh could have sworn that he smelled her fear.

"Cayden, don't let him hurt me," she begged.

Cayden didn't answer her, but instead looked at Hugh and nodded. Hugh lifted his arm in preparation to scratch her with his long wolf nails.

"Please, please! We are friends." She shrieked.

Cayden shifted so that they were standing between the two of them but still facing and holding Stevie. "You put our lives in danger. You said you loved me, and you still put my life in danger. Then, you paraded as Zoie's best friend, and you let her die. You *helped* him kill her." They threw her at Hugh. "You were never our friend." They nodded at Hugh. "Do with her what you will."

Hugh slammed her at his feet and then scratched down her torso, knowing that any amount of time in water wouldn't reverse a scar from a wolf's claws. Then he sliced into one of her arms. And, to give Stevie a fate worse than death for her, he clawed down the left side of her face.

He grabbed one of the sharp metal bars and put the point right at her heart. "You made Zoie suffer. You let her drown. Slowly. I should kill you where you lie."

She was sobbing, and blood was pooling round her with pieces of skin floating in it. "Just do it."

He stood up and then hit her across the head with the bar, knocking her out. Letting out a breath he didn't know he had been holding, he looked over at Cayden. "Let's clean up." He shifted back into his human form. "Let's bag him and take them both down the elevator, though I really want to roll them down 27 flights of stairs."

Cayden was already pushing Miles back in the building. "Sloss Furnaces?" Hugh nodded.

"What of Stevie?"

Coldly, he replied, "We'll send her back to the Abyss as a warning." They stuffed Stevie and the bag of the body formerly known as Miles in the trunk.

It was basically a straight shot from the City Federal Building to Sloss Furnaces. A mere five-minute drive, so that's where they started.

The Sloss Furnaces were considered one of the most haunted places in Alabama, with good reason. When they were in operation, people were thrown into the furnaces and killed. The citizens of Birmingham often reported strange sightings and sounds coming from the furnaces. Maybe they really were haunted. Or maybe the strange phenomena were just those from the supernatural realm disposing of their dead.

Hugh and Cayden dumped Miles, lit him on fire, and stood waiting for the flames to die down.

Hugh turned to Cayden. "I'm sorry about Stevie."

They frowned, still watching the flames. "I'm oddly at peace with it." They looked at Hugh. "We've been friends for over a century. I hope you know that I would never betray you. I didn't know…"

Hugh put his hand up in protest. "The thought never crossed my mind, Cade."

They stood in silence until the fire died down, and then they got in the car and headed back to the portal to Nightbrooke. It was the middle of the night, so if anyone was at the fountain, they would be homeless, and no one would believe their account of what was going on.

After getting into Nightbrooke, Cayden and Hugh made their way directly to the entrance to the Abyss and sent Stevie's body through. She would eventually wake up, but Hugh would deal with the repercussions of that later.

Then the two of them went back to Hugh's place. Once inside, they sat at the dining room table in silence for about fifteen minutes, nursing the drinks they had poured for themselves.

Suddenly, Cayden asked, "Was it worth it? Did it help?"

Hugh shrugged. "For now, it was worth it. I know that Alvin will come for me." He shook his head. "I massacred his life. I took his entire family from him." He continued, "To answer if it helped: I don't know yet." He looked over at the box of manuscripts, with Judy sitting on top. "It didn't bring her back, but at least I feel like I was able to fight for her."

"What will you do now?"

He thought for a moment. "Well, I'm going to have to be vigilant. Alvin is still coming for me, but now the Abyss will, too." Then he added, "I have this next semester off, but I think I'm going to use the time to get back to a good place so that I can start teaching again in the spring." He stated, "I understand if you don't want to see me for a while."

Cayden swatted at their friend. "I already told you, I understand. And you were right, I didn't really love her." They explained, "I didn't feel what you felt. That loss. That inability to even breathe. I know Stevie isn't gone, but that betrayal…" They paused. "I kind of felt it coming."

Hugh admitted, "Part of me either doesn't believe Zoie's gone, or maybe a part just doesn't want to believe it. That's why I can't let go. When I look at photos of her in my phone, I still feel the mating bond."

"Do you think that will fade?"

He shook his head. "I couldn't even begin to guess. It hasn't faded yet." Hugh quietly added, "I hope it doesn't."

Cayden looked confused. "You want to stay in a state of depression for the rest of your immortal life?"

"I don't remember my parents, any of my childhood friends, you know? I don't remember anyone from my human life. I don't even really remember the faces of the men that killed me. I don't remember people from fifty years ago. The memories fade." He continued, "I don't want to forget her."

"I don't think you will."

Lightning Source UK Ltd.
Milton Keynes UK
UKHW010657051022
409964UK00006B/532